Blunt Instrument

ALSO BY AMY BLOOM

I'll Be Right Here

In Love

White Houses

Lucky Us

Away

Where the God Of Love Hangs Out

A Blind Man Can See How Much I Love You

Normal

Come to Me

CHILDRENS BOOKS

Flower Girl

Little Sweet Potato

Blunt Instrument

Amy Bloom

THE MYSTERIOUS PRESS
NEW YORK

BLUNT INSTRUMENT

Mysterious Press
An Imprint of Penzler Publishers
58 Warren Street
New York, N.Y. 10007

First edition

Interior design by Maria Fernandez

Library of Congress Control Number: 2025949835

ISBN: 978-1-61316-760-1
eBook: 978-1-61316-761-8

10 9 8 7 6 5 4 3 2 1

Printed in the United States of America
Distributed by Simon & Schuster

For W.A.M.

Tuesday, August 6

The summer was going. He rolled his chair back and stood at the big window, looking down on the campus. The lawn was dull, matted brown in places; there wasn't enough money to keep it all green until September, when the students, the "customers," came back. One of the men from Physical Plant, a man he saw every morning, moving bushes and filling planters, was now mending a patch of sidewalk.

It was a pleasure to look down and see people marching, or limping, or dragging along in the heat. They looked like ants.

He put a finger up on the glass. Crush this little ant. Expunge that little ant.

He poured himself a glass of wine and stole a look at the clock. It was too early, but who would know or see? It's five o'clock somewhere, some colleague used to say at every gathering, right before he went face down. It was five o'clock somewhere. And today, at five o'clock in Centerville, he'd pull up into the driveway of the only person who actually knew him, who saw him clear and cared for him, anyway.

He felt, rather than heard, a knock on the door. Then he did hear it.

He tucked his wineglass behind a stack of reference books. *Hypocrisy is the tribute vice pays to virtue*, he thought, and if the visitor did notice the wineglass, which was not deeply hidden, he might say that.

He would have.

Since I Met You, Baby

Tuesday, August 20

I had been lying on my office floor, minding my own goddamn business and avoiding the heat, listening to Sam Cooke and thinking about sex and death (Did that girl set him up? Or was it his wife and that no-good bartender at Martoni's Bar? I have questions) when my phone rang.

Paganini's *Caprice*. My father.

"You're going to get a call, Dell," he said, shouting into his cell phone in the manner of people in their eighties. "Pay attention. Cromwell University. Dead professor, English Department, not exactly a luminary but . . ."

"Pop," I said.

"Anyway, the police have done nothing about this murder and when I saw Liz Cutty today at this Yale funfest on Keynes—

she was a student of mine—I told her this was your area of expertise."

"Murder?"

Since I was sixteen, I'd run my uncle's office (Martinez and Associates, Private Investigations) every summer and five days a week after school. (We were not sporty or clubby people.) Uncle Lou, my mother's brother, taught me to drive a stick, to hot-wire, to shoplift, to eavesdrop, to forge like an artist, to walk quietly. I introduced Uncle Lou to computers, then to laptops, to Facebook and the World Wide Web and beyond (Tinder, Silver Singles, Latinamericancupid.com), and he died loving TikTok. In these last three years, we'd gotten to the point that a solid day of Googling, creating fake business cards, and impersonating public officials or salespeople from security and cable companies (I owned four polyester button-downs with short sleeves: gray, brown, blue, and beige) could almost always tell us what we needed to know. Martinez and Associates was finally breaking even but a year ago, single once more and facing a rough uptick in his Parkinson's, Uncle Lou told me he had no plans to retire and no plans at all for a riper old age.

His death was no less awful for his having done everything he could to bring it about and I spent a year dashing from liquor store to steakhouse to his condo, like a grim, obedient hamster. I paid for a good-looking hospice nurse, as requested and not that hard to find. I took only easy and local cases and played gin with Lou for as long as we could. He left me everything: ancient laptop (password: JLoTush), six months' rent paid in advance on the office, his coded Rolodex, and his old service revolver, with precise instructions on how to get a gun permit in the State of Connecticut. I studied the manual, went to the shooting range every day, being the only woman I ever saw and the only Democrat, as the bumper stickers revealed. I got my license with less trouble and supervision than when I got my driver's license. I am, marginally, a better shot than a driver. Lou would be pleased.

Armed private investigator was better than the definitively-not-renewed, frankly unemployable assistant professor I had been before Lou and his kindness. Four years ago, my mother was dying for nine terrible months and then dead. That year I did everything you're not supposed to do, and I did it often: yelled at my students, made insulting remarks about everyone's favorite graphic novels, failed to grade (read) papers, came to class drunk, and cried for most of the ninety minutes. I did not have sex with undergraduates, only because depression made it unappealing and Prozac made it unlikely to be rewarding. My father pretended not to know what had happened. I became unemployable in my chosen field of English literature (a friendly colleague, of which I had very few at the end, did say, "You'd have to win a Pulitzer to get hired at the worst school in the country") and I did not have the skillset to be an assistant manager of anything.

Uncle Lou had made room for me immediately.

He said, "You're tall. You're not a pussy, sorry, I mean, you're tough. PhD, that looks good. Whatever we clear, you get forty percent."

We did custody investigations, custody snatches, occasional corporate investigations, cheating spouses (Dear Cheaters: Do not text. Do not), missing spouses, missing teens, old people bamboozled by new friends, old people gone missing (and not always happy to be found by their concerned children), quiet inquiries to get the money or the Basquiat painting or the person back and not involve the police, social media searches to determine if white, hetero, able-bodied and studly executive Bill Smith/John Jones/Dave Brown was the catch his photos and texts made him out to be. (You guess.) I knew exactly as much about murder as every other person who watches *Law & Order*, in its many forms.

My father kept shouting at me. "I told Elizabeth Cutty for $500 a day, you'd find the murderer."

"How could you say that?"

"How else do you expect to make a living? Do you have a job I don't know about?"

"I appreciate your—"

I heard my father say, "Never mind."

And then static. Then nothing.

We're not a great combination. But my dead mother makes sure that I have a meal with my father every three weeks, rain, shine, or lack of enthusiasm so—not as bad as it seems. We still had two weeks to go before our next eggs-and-toast dinner, and I opened a can of zero-alcohol mango margarita which, like the other thing I just mentioned, is not as bad as it seems.

Elizabeth Cutty called me twenty minutes later.

Oh, boarding school. Without loosening her jaw or raising her voice, she told me that a professor died on her campus almost two weeks ago. She said that it seems not to have been a fatal accident, *helas.* (She said *Helas.*) but a murder. She said the killer has not yet been found, leading to a general hue and cry about the police's ineffectuality on the one hand and lots of side-eye for the elitist, unappealing goings-on at Cromwell on the other. She had a board of trustees meeting coming up in about two weeks and this carelessness could not continue. She said that my father (that is, the actual Professor Chandler) had told her that his daughter was a former academic and a private investigator, licensed by the State of Connecticut. I said that this was true.

Because of my anger management issues, my impulse control issues, and my apparently unresolvable issues with authority, I said, "Is the job to find the killer or to help with Cromwell's PR problem?"

She cleared her throat, which is the Darien, Connecticut, way of telling you to fuck yourself, and that was good enough for me. She asked if I could meet her the next day and I said I could and then, like my father, she hung up on me. I packed my bag, just in case she hired me and just in case I stayed on, maybe at some charming inn: nice sleeveless black silk-polyester dress and black patent leather heels, in case there's "an occasion" (my mother on loudspeaker), an all-purpose gigantic black, white, and navy scarf, navy pants and a matching jacket, Kamala Harris–style, with two white jersey T-shirts to go underneath, for meeting the president and whoever, and my jeans and a ratty college T-shirt ("Smith College: Den of Satanic Communism") for the rest. I threw in all the underwear I owned that's not sex related, running shorts, and my sneakers. I took the gun I don't want to have. I put the bullets inside a pair of socks.

I didn't have anyone special to say good-bye to. I was current with my office rent, now known as my rent, after I lost my condo, formerly Lou's condo, in a series of what a compassionate person would call unfortunate events. My father knew how to get hold of me.

And still, not as bad as it seems. I saw familiar faces in the Glorious Pan-Asian Market and in Buster's Cast Iron BBQ, and Buster and I have had some nice chats about barbecue in other countries and the pointlessness of soccer. I ate an occasional appetizer at the semi-fancy tapas place where I was still liked by the chatty owner, her son, the waiter, and her niece, the busperson. Every month, on the street or at the tapas place, I'd run into a few old hookups, all now married, or living with a nice woman, or comfortably out of the closet and living with a nice man. My mother's death left me lonely, my father surviving her enraged me so deeply, I could barely speak to him or most living adults, and Uncle Lou's death-by-porterhouse-steak finished me off. Some people might say I watch a little too much TV, especially crime investigation, especially *Law & Order*, old and new, but that show has been to me what blow jobs are to men: not always great, but never bad.

I got myself to bed early, wanting to be gone already.

I dreamt that I was running, sweaty and tearful, down a school corridor, late for my French final. There were no seats available in the classroom. Students were writing. The clock ticked loudly and my eighth grade French teacher, Mme Aspinard, was humming to herself, also loudly. "I'm not ready," I sobbed.

Wild Is the Wind

Wednesday, August 21

I got on the road, listening to Miss Nina Simone, one of my mother's favorites. (She raised me with a wall of music from the '60s and '70s and the smell of oil paint and that music still sets the world right for me.) It's a perfect hour's drive up to Cromwell, not too much construction on the highway, flat, ready-to-rain sky. I did want to get there but I'd have been happy to just drive.

The houses changed from the dumps, with three dismantled Chevys in the yard, to planned housing "communities" with a serpentine main road and four barely different kinds of Capes and ranch houses. Off the highway and all that gives way to fast food, dry cleaners, We Buy Your Gold, Gas & Go, and all the useful, ugly debris of small city life. Cromwell University loomed up ahead on my right, an actual and huge wrought iron gate permanently swung open over the pea-gravel drive, leading to the small brownstone castle, complete with turrets and dozens of leaded windowpanes, which was the president's house. I parked and looked at four marble benches, two fountains, and a handful of bronze plaques.

I chickened out. I drove on, to my godfather's house. It was quiet. The lawn seemed a little darker than the others on the street. There was a burgundy Volvo in his driveway, Connecticut plates. Unless things had really changed in the last six months, Theo Gurwitz was still blind and still not driving.

Visiting student? Colleague come by for a sherry? I walked up the flagstone path and paused at the door. I heard muffled sounds inside and I knocked, sharply. No footsteps came. I rang the doorbell and nothing at all. The doorbell had been broken my whole life. The sounds of a struggle grew louder. I couldn't make out any words. The door was unlocked, and I stepped in quickly, scanning the living room and the dining room. Someone groaned, painfully, and I ran to the bedroom.

I threw open a door and almost burned out my eyeballs. A naked woman faced me, back arched, breasts lifted, hands gripping the brass headboard behind her, eyes tightly closed as sweat poured down her ecstatic face. She opened her eyes and, naturally, screamed for real. I shouted over her screams, not wanting Uncle Theo to die of a heart attack right then and there: "It's me! It's Dell! I'm sorry!"

The woman slid down, like she'd been shot. The huge lump under the sheet didn't move but it did speak.

"We're all very sorry, Della. Now, close the door and come back later."

I was shocked. And envious. And out of time.

At the president's house, Cutty's assistant—pearly, white, and blonde—sat behind her desk and watched me walk in like I was a dangerous refugee. She told me there was a room available for me at the guesthouse and that I could meet with President Cutty right now and check in right after or meet with President Cutty now and check in whenever I liked (or, she indicated: never, if it comes to that).

"I guess I'll meet with President Cutty," I said, and Pearly led me into Elizabeth Cutty's office.

If the assistant was a stockbroker, Elizabeth Cutty was clearly the chairman of the board. She had a rosewood desk the size of a dining room table and bookshelves like small condominiums; even their solid dimensions didn't dwarf the room. She wasn't taken in by some less-is-more bullshit; she did not climb up that ladder just to abandon hierarchy. When you were in this president's office, by God, you knew where you were. I peeked around to my left and saw that, yes, there was a rose garden.

The ceilings were about eleven feet high, with plaster moldings all the way around and ivory garlands in each corner. Sort-of Sargents mixed with portraits of old men who I assumed were donors of yore, when a mere million could get your name chiseled over the lab or the squash courts. There was a large photo on canvas of a middle-aged man in a polo shirt, over the mantel. I thought he'd probably be President Cutty's late, or conveniently absent, husband, dispelling the cloud of lesbianism while exploring the butterflies of Chile or Peru.

Elizabeth Cutty stood up behind the huge desk and came towards me, over the vast rose oriental rug, past the rose-and-ivory striped couch and around the two rose velvet wing armchairs. Not my taste but very impressive. The spruceness and the pink made me think that this was all new, just for their first female university president after almost two hundred years. We assessed each other. She was used to having her measure taken; it didn't bother her a bit.

Sharp and sixtyish and didn't care who knew it. There was no professional mileage in being a sweet young thing and she wasn't built for seduction. Short silver hair, with little spurs on each side of her handsome cheekbones. No earrings and hardly any earlobes, which if I were a nineteenth-century phrenologist, would have been a big clue. (Insomnia? Necrophilia? Kleptomania?) Her blue eyes slanted up. Her long nose pointed down. She put out her long, thin hand with its short unpolished nails and her one enormous sapphire ring and I thought if she were a dog, she'd be a Russian wolfhound, with a powerful set of jaws. She wore a white button-down shirt, a long gray skirt, and beautiful gray suede pumps with scalloped edges, a glimpse of fuchsia lining, and a tall, thick heel. If I could have had a relationship with the shoes, not the woman, things would have gone better.

"Dr. Chandler, I appreciate your coming so quickly."

She pressed the edge of her ring into my palm. She might not have been conscious of her wish to impress me with the size of her sapphire but I was impressed. It was as nice, in its way, as the shoes.

"Well, these things go stale pretty quickly."

That's what Ice-T says: With murder, every minute counts.

"Not stale enough," she said dryly, and gestured for me to sit. I sank into a pool of rose velvet and made myself straighten up. Dr. Cutty sat very lightly in the other armchair, rubbing her long fingers against the nap. I stared at the bridge of her nose, which creates the illusion of eye contact but is much less tiring. I waited.

She broke the silence and smiled, to show it didn't really matter who spoke first.

"Professor Bullfinch was killed in his office on Tuesday, August 6, in the English Department building on Cheshire Street. The outer edge of a bloody footprint—a fraction of the outer edge—was found outside his office. He was hit with a blunt instrument, possibly his bronze bust of Hawthorne, if you like irony. It was wiped clean. The police have begun to examine, to interview possible suspects. The way they do this offends people. Their failure to do this would also offend people. And that's the least of it. Professor Bullfinch's death has opened the door to irresponsible articles, well, reels and podcasts about Cromwell's faculty and its general intellectual and inbred awfulness. You remember how worked up people got over some course we offered on pornography? They are absolutely salivating now about our high salaries and base behavior and the dangerous atmosphere, simultaneously coercively conservative and godlessly liberal. It's nonsense but it's fun to read and people lap it up. It needs to stop. The police are slow. I'd like you to be quick."

She didn't even glance at her notes.

"There you have it. We have been getting a lot of unpleasant publicity. In our business, it is not the case that all publicity is good publicity."

My father would have been beside himself, hearing academia referred to as a business.

"Professor Bullfinch's body was found by one of the cleaning people, Mrs. Binh, when she was making her rounds. She reported to her supervisor, Mrs. Jones, who called campus security immediately, and our guard, Dan Flatley, came to the English Department building, saw the body, touched nothing, and then called the police from there. No one was observed entering or leaving Professor Bullfinch's office for the entire afternoon. He met briefly with Dan Fiske at 11:00 A.M. and was seen at the campus deli, having lunch alone from 11:45 to 12:30. Professor Bullfinch told the woman at the cash register that he planned to go to the gym and then go back to work. Mrs. Groth, the English Department secretary, gave him his messages at 1:45 and he went upstairs to his office on the third floor. She rang him at 2:15 to remind him that there was a department meeting the following morning. No one saw or spoke with him after that phone call. Professor Bullfinch was a widower and he had no children. I should say, he has no children that anyone knows of. I don't want to speak carelessly. There may be suspects at this time but I don't know who they are, the faculty will not speak openly with the police, and no one, least of all myself, believes that Mrs. Binh, who is this high"—she raised her hand to an unlikely three feet—"murdered Professor Bullfinch and then ran to her supervisor to inform him that she'd found the body. We need to find the murderer or find that there is none, that he bludgeoned himself to death, which would be ideal."

"Yes, you do. As my father told you, I charge $500 a day, which includes all expenses."

"Don't most private investigators keep an itemized account of their expenses, which they then present to their clients?"

"I don't know what other private investigators do, Dr. Cutty. I charge a flat fee and we don't have to quibble about how much my gas costs or why I drove to Bridgewater Chocolate. I don't enjoy bookkeeping."

She smiled.

"They do make very good toffee. Five hundred a day. You are now in my employ."

"Not that of Cromwell University?"

She hesitated for a minute, pressing her fingertips together in a long, tense arc.

"Yes. Well, no. You are being hired by the university, and you will, in fact, get a paycheck from the university in due time but I'll be your conduit to the university. I'll pay you a . . . a stipend for that, as well."

"Why?"

"So that I can decide what should be done with the information you come up with and so that you will come directly to me with whatever you find and will not feel obliged to share it with the academic vice president, the dean of the college, or anyone else."

Or any other inconvenient, intrusive dim bulb.

I arced my fingers like hers, to show how simpatico we were, and visions of my rent, my loans, my car repair, and Liz Cutty's beautiful shoes flooded me.

"As long as you understand I won't conceal knowledge about a homicide from the police, a mistake I can't afford—even if it makes one of your Cromwell family look bad."

"You will come to me first?"

I heard the little growl at the back of her throat, like when you try to take the bone away before the dog's done chewing.

"So," I said. "Who do you think it might have been?"

"I cannot imagine anyone from Cromwell doing this."

"Oh, yeah, you can. Family first is the rule and since there's no biological family that we know of, as of yet, that leaves the Cromwell 'family.' It doesn't seem likely that a stranger walked in, crushed his skull, and walked out without so much as his wallet."

"I don't know that his skull was *crushed*. And, the wallet was taken. I forgot to mention that. The police found it, empty, lying at the edge of Miller's Pond. That's near our athletic center."

"That's a credible motive?"

"No? You're very sure of yourself," Dr. Cutty said.

"Do *you* think he was killed for his wallet?" I said. "In broad daylight? I'm a mugger, even a crazed junkie, and I schlep over to the English Department building, looking for a big heist?

Rolexes? Fancy technology? Bags of coke? I'd be better off in the dorms, even with summer school, if I'm looking that way. Also, what about a will? No will?"

"None that anyone has been able to find. If he has one, it wasn't drafted by anyone local, I'm sure of that."

"Why?"

"The police contacted all the local attorneys. No one had had him for a client."

"How do you know all this?" I said, finally. "How do you know so much?"

"Chief DiCenzo is a friend. Both of his children have gone to Cromwell. He has let me know a few things."

"Good friend to have. Bullfinch must have had some money. Years of raises, pension fund."

She sat.

"Dr. Cutty, give me a break. He had some money, right?"

She sighed. "Point taken. I could make you go through HR but . . . he had almost one million dollars in his portfolio through Cromwell. He was a frugal man. He had some fine qualities. He was respected but not well liked, I believe. I can't imagine someone murdering him because of his little quirks of personality. I can give you a list of his colleagues and their addresses. You'll probably want to start there. There's a gathering at my house tonight at eight-thirty. Some faculty, spouses, administrators."

"What's the occasion?"

"We're honoring some of the faculty who are getting special attention this year: notable grants, prizes, publications. Something intimate, just before school starts."

If by "intimate," you mean vulgar and distressingly public, then intimate is the word.

"How nice. Could you get a list of the honored guests for me? And a map of the campus? And information about Bullfinch's family, if you happen to have it, in some files? And the layout of the building his office is in, if you have it? Maybe an old architectural drawing, pipes and pathways?"

I got this from *Law & Order*, too. Obscure maps and plans could lead to the killer, often in about forty-five minutes.

"How thorough. Let me call in Jennifer, my assistant."

Pearly walked in, maroon leather notepad in hand, Mark Cross pen, ready to roll. I love a notepad instead of an iPhone. No password. Dr. Cutty told Jennifer I'd be helping the police find out what happened to Professor Bullfinch and to give me whatever assistance I require. She ticked off all the items I asked for and told Pearly to have the information hand-delivered to me at the guesthouse by 8:00 this evening. Jennifer blinked and opened the leather notebook, which held her phone after all, and began to type notes. She'd see to it, she said. I hope I live to hire someone like that. I expected her to back out, bowing, but she marched out and Dr. Cutty stood up, so I stood up, too. I'm taller.

"I did call the chief and tell him you'd be coming by today to see whatever material they were willing to share with you."

"You were pretty sure I'd say yes."

"People don't usually drive an hour plus to say no. Let me give you a week's pay in advance. Your father suggested that."

I didn't hate either of them, right then.

"Of course, if I takes you less time than that, you can keep the rest, as a bonus, as a token of my deep appreciation."

It seemed unlikely, although not impossible, that Dr. Cutty was the murderer. And if she was, I already had $3,500 more than I did before. Bribe or incentive? Tomato, *to-mah-to*.

"Let's meet Wednesday morning, at 8:00 A.M."

Another power move. I was supposed to roll my eyes at the early hour. I didn't give a damn, I get up at 6:00 most mornings, because I have the sleep patterns of a lab rat.

"Okay. Bye."

I put out my hand, ready for the giant sapphire.

She grabbed my hand and looked more wolfish than ever. "Come to me immediately when you find out. I expect you to come to me immediately."

She forced herself to relax and dropped my hand.

"Please send my regards to your father; I have counted on his advice many times over the years. I look forward to seeing you tonight."

She walked me to the door and handed me over to Jennifer, who walked me down the hall. I tried to drum up a little gossip.

"Dr. Cutty is a very impressive—"

"Yes, she is. Here we are. I'll get started on that list right away."

You've got to be under thirty to move that fast in three-inch heels.

I opened the door and looked at Cromwell's campus, delectable even in late summer, dappled with sunlight and the soft green shadows of the maple trees.

⟜

Efficient Jennifer had forgotten my suitcase. It was there, in her office, happily tucked beside her empty chair. And, lucky me, there was her phone and a nice old-fashioned notebook of a calendar, also bound in burgundy leather, begging to be seen and probably mostly for show. Reverence for the past when things were done properly, etc.

Dr. Cutty's door was shut. I heard a hum of well-bred voices. Solid wood doors make eavesdropping much harder. In my building, you can not only hear your neighbors' discussion, but you can offer color commentary and enjoy some real give-and-take.

Dr. Cutty's schedule for the day was front and center with meetings almost every forty-five minutes from 8:00 A.M. to 6:00 P.M. I memorized the names. I synced our phones. *Meet with Det. Hadley and Funeral: 2:00. Reception (?) to follow.* I flipped back a little further, setting my posture so that I looked as though I was reaching over the desk for my bag in case the door opened suddenly. In the midst of this woman's busy day, there was a three-hour block of time unaccounted for, on a Wednesday afternoon. And during the preceding week, another two-hour gap, this time on a Monday afternoon. In my life, that would be *Real Housewives* or sex.

I got my bag and walked down the hall, boot heels clicking, so people would hear me. A few minions watched me and nodded their heads. I nodded back, in what I hoped was a memorable fashion. Outside, I leaned against a column, contemplating what

I'd said yes to and giving a passing thought to why. Bills to pay. Also, rescuing or at least investigating a university instead of being crushed by it. Like that.

The guesthouse was a badly proportioned colonial, its small front porch sagging between two peeling columns. A bored, ear-budded milky-skinned girl with barbell piercings in her helix, eyebrow, and cheek sat by the register in the threadbare front hall and watched me park in the gravel driveway.

"Can't park there," she said.

"Where should I park?"

She shrugged and then glanced towards the side of the building. I went out, moved the car, and came back in.

"Hey," she said.

"Hey."

She didn't take off her earbuds but she did watch me write my name in the register. She watched some more, while I hauled my bag up the stairs to my room. I leaned over the landing and called down for a key. She didn't look up. I yelled, "HEY," and then she did look up. She had a key for me, she said, and I said I was glad to hear it and would look forward to her bringing it to me. She dragged herself up the stairs, like an injured veteran, and handed me the key. She didn't seem to expect a tip.

My first phone call was to the man I had intruded upon earlier, Theodor Gurwitz, my godfather—if Jews had godfathers, which we don't—and one of my mother's closest friends.

He was seventy-five and blind and supposed to be retired but was still teaching one class at Cromwell, to keep his hand in. Unlike Oliver Bullfinch, he was not swimming and bicep curling into old age. His seminar met in his living room and young people went in and out of his kitchen, bringing him mugs of tea and plates of cookies. When he needed extra cash, he gave lectures at other schools, often in places like Provence or Orvieto, accompanied by at least two adoring art history students, to help with the luggage and uncorking the wine. Another career I'd like to have.

The phone rang a few times and before I could hang up, I was amazed to hear his voice telling me to leave a message. He did not say he was sorry he couldn't come to the phone and he did not say that he would get back to me as soon as possible.

At the sound of the beep, I said, "Theo, it's Dell. It's 10:00 A.M. I'll be at your house in a half hour and if you're not at home, you can call me on my cell."

I unpacked quickly, stuck a hair where the top of the door meets the frame, a classic, and drove to the Centerville Police station, which looked like a 1970s beige brick elementary school, low, flat, styleless. I asked to see Chief DiCenzo and offered Elizabeth Cutty's name. The desk sergeant was just what TV had taught me to expect: sleepy, hostile, indifferent.

Joseph DiCenzo was not what TV had taught me to expect. He was a gorgeous, aging lion in a pinstripe Brooks Brothers suit, a disturbingly white smile, and a salt-and-pepper mane. He brought me into an ugly office with plaques and trophies and photos of him with three American presidents, two university presidents, and a lot of players from the US Open. He was friendly and pleasant. He made great eye contact. He held my hand in his two, like a pol working the line. I asked to see transcripts or videos of interviews with suspects and he chuckled, warmly. He said that he wanted to do everything he could for his good friend Elizabeth Cutty, and that meant extending the courtesy of a conversation like this, in fact, *this*, to me, as her employee.

"I'm all for cooperation, leveraging resources, and information sharing in certain circumstances. For example, you, with your background, might provide a better understanding of university politics than we have here. On the other hand, my wife teaches at Yale Law, so we might not need you for that. Or, maybe there's some surveillance technique you picked up working for your uncle, may he rest in peace, that you can share with us. On the other hand, your Uncle Luis—who I knew—was pretty much a ham-and-egger, the kind of guy who'd sit in a car overnight with a bottle of rye and a camera, hoping to catch some poor *gavone* in the act. Or, maybe you can bring some special insight into Cromwell because your dear friend Ted Gurwitz still teaches here. On the other hand, he's almost eighty and blind and not really in the thick of things."

He shrugged, open-handed. A very Italian, benign gesture of what-can-you-do?

"You reach out to Detectives Morse and Hadley. And if they have something you can help them with, I've instructed them to ask for your help. If you have something to offer, I've instructed them to be responsive. I'll tell Liz, President Cutty, you came by and we had this chat. We will get this wrapped up and we're grateful for any assistance which you can offer, without, of course, interfering with an ongoing police investigation."

I said of course. I asked if by any chance Detectives Morse and Hadley were in. Chief DiCenzo held up one hand and tapped out a number on his phone with the other. We could both hear the voicemail message. He shrugged, pleasantly. I handed him my business card and thanked him, twice. What a handsome dead end.

I went for a walk, down to Washington Drive, where the dead man had lived. Another dark house but at least no naked lady was going to be waving her tits at me. Professor Bullfinch had lived in a Dutch colonial. Raggedy strips of yellow Police Business tape flapped off the front porch and the police were long gone. No one cared. The old lady across the street watched me watching the house. I couldn't outwait her; Neighborhood Watch could be her full-time occupation and even from across the street, I could see her mean, interfering mouth. I'd be halfway through the window, my ass hanging out, and she'd be calling the cops. I decided to be upwardly mobile and go from breaking and entering to impersonating an officer.

I showed her my Jr. Lawman gold badge, which was the best three dollars I ever spent online, and I dropped every university name I knew.

"Glad to help," she said, pursing her lips. "Myrna Wallace. And anyway, aren't we all in danger now? A murder? Of one of our own neighbors? Not that he was normal."

I agreed. I asked her if she had any other observation that she'd like to share. Nope, she said. I liked the looks of his friend she said, with a little nudge, nudge, wink, wink. Really, I said, packing in as much salacious innuendo as I could. Beautiful? I said. A real looker? She had me talking like a Dashiell Hammett paperback. The old lady narrowed her eyes.

"Not beautiful. Handsome. What do I care if some woman is beautiful? This guy was something. Like a movie star."

I asked about his car. He walked, she said. I asked about what he wore. Clothes. She didn't just sit by the damn window all day, she said. I asked about his coloring and she was on it. Tall, blond, and handsome. He only visited once, which was a shame in her opinion, but with gay people, it was like that, wasn't it? Mating like fruit flies. I said, Sure, and I went across the street. She watched me for a minute and then called out, projecting beautifully, right across the street, "Oh Miss, I mean, Officer, the other police officers used the rear door, maybe that's easier. Not such a climb."

I thanked her and hoped she couldn't see me blush.

The back door was easier to jimmy than a high school locker. I eased my way into the kitchen, which was post-murder, post-investigation, post-cleaning service tidy. I walked through the house, tossing all the drawers, full of neatly folded underwear, rolled socks, and five frayed polo shirts, all gray. Life had stopped. There was a picture of a pale young man, in Navy dress whites, with a name, Wilson Bullfinch, and the date of his death, 1966, on the back of the picture. There was one photo of the senior Bullfinches, back in the day. Mrs. Bullfinch was in a cocktail dress, with her arm through Mr. Bullfinch's, in a dinner jacket. There were candles stuck in a pair of Chianti bottles on the linen-covered table near them and a tuxedoed waiter at the edge of the photo. I couldn't imagine that the restaurant was still open. On the back, a woman had written *20th anniversary.* The Bullfinches looked middle-aged and stoically straight. I put the picture in my bag.

There seemed to have been no one left behind to empty the house, to send the spatulas and sneakers and overcoats off to the Goodwill, to give away the canned goods, to empty the medicine cabinets (Pepto-Bismol, Imodium, cortisone cream, Band-Aids, aspirin, drops for dry eye, for dry ear, and for dry mouth and—Hello, sunshine!—a prescription bottle of Viagra, with no scrip on the outside of the bottle). I did recognize the famous little blue pills. I am almost forty. Viagra didn't necessarily mean Professor Bullfinch was a live wire; some men keep Viagra the way some women keep their four-inch heels—just to show that no matter how it seems, you shouldn't count them out.

There were hundreds and hundreds of books, half of them shelved alphabetically. The other half crept around the edges of the living room, up the stairs, down the hallway, and into a room with nothing but piles of books. I ran my finger around everything, the backs of pictures, the insides of cushions, the outsides of valences. Dust had finally gathered and there was one piece of paper, crumpled at the back of a desk drawer. It was a photo reprinted from a camera or cell phone. A lovely woman, mid-thirties, round and sexy in jeans and a T-shirt, her light hair piled in a messy, stylish bun. There was no writing on the back. She was barefoot and smiling and she was not Mrs. Bullfinch, a thin, sad brunette. She might be Ms. Viagra. I took it with me and headed down the hall for another pass at Bullfinch's study, and the possibility of a whole photo album, although I couldn't blame either Bullfinch for not wanting leather-bound recollections of their marriage.

I heard the faint click of the back door, a sound that delights me when I'm the one making it. The house was arranged shotgun-style: a straight line from the front hall to the living room, beyond which, the kitchen and the back door. No way I could get out the front door without meeting my visitor. I did want to meet whoever it was, just not unarmed. Having a gun and being able to hit a paper target with some accuracy had not translated into carry at all times. I made a mental note but I couldn't imagine going back to my old shrink and complaining, not about the usual (I miss my mother, have fucked my life, and can't commit) but about my reluctance to carry a firearm, even though I had a license to do so. Maybe he'd have found it a refreshing change.

The cautious visitor was moving slowly, aware of my presence. I stayed at the edge of the study and heard the footsteps stop in the middle of the living room, about twenty feet from me. I could sashay in, accusing the interloper of interloping, and hope that it was an embarrassed relative or snoopy neighbor. I could wait until the interloper found me and hope for the best. I could call out "Yoo-hoo" or whatever they say around here and again, hope for the best. I noticed the other person was also not calling out yoo-hoo and I thought: intruder, like me.

A woman said, "Come out with your hands up. I am a police officer and you are trespassing. Put down your weapon and come out."

"I'm not armed," I said, walking out with my hands stretched high above my head. I wiggled my fingers for emphasis.

The huge gun was aimed at my chest. The police officer was at least my height, plus twenty more pounds of muscle, a good-looking blonde in jeans and a white T-shirt and cross-body white bag. Her strong hands were rock steady. The standard issue cop sunglasses made her look cold and mean and her lips were compressed in that state trooper tight line.

"ID?" she demanded.

"In my back pocket. I can get it out if I can lower my hands or you can make me lie on the floor and take it out of my pocket yourself. Do you have any ID?"

I was trying not to mouth off because even though I'm white I think bravado with the police is stupid and because I needed to have a civil relationship with the Centerville cops. I was pretty sure this woman was not going to kill me and I was pretty sure that she, unlike me, was the real thing.

Keeping her sunglasses fixed in my direction, she grabbed the chain around her neck and flipped it towards me. A small brown case fell open and I saw the gleam of her not-gold-plastic shield.

"Of course, I can't really make it out from here, but thank you. Do you want me to show you my ID now? I'm

Dell Chandler; I'm a private investigator. I've been hired by Cromwell University to assist in the investigation of Oliver Bullfinch's death. That's why I'm here."

"Keep your hands up and turn around once, slowly. Right hand above your head and reach into your back pocket with your left hand. When you get your ID, drop it gently to the floor and kick it towards me. If you move suddenly, I'll shoot the part of you that's closest to me."

I followed her directions as carefully as she'd given them. She took her time with my wallet. She found the slip of paper with a quote from Longfellow: "Give what you have. To someone, it may be better than you dare to think." My mother had done it up in calligraphy and decorated it with minute lilies and irises for my twenty-first birthday. The cop stared at the slip of paper and I stood there silently, imagining my mother, watching this scene, shaking her head. She used to say to me, many times: *El pez muere por la boca*, which means "the fish dies because he opens his mouth." She was a Mexican Jew; she was a painter. She's been dead four years and she manages to keep popping into my head daily with proverbs and eye rolling.

"Sit," the cop said. I sat. She tucked her gun into her purse (Oh, I thought, that's why a purse) and sat down across from me. Finally, she took off her sunglasses. Round marine blue eyes with fair, invisible lashes. Not angry, curious.

"I didn't catch your name," I said.

"No, I guess you didn't. I'm Sgt. Blanchfleur with the Centerville Police Department. Michelle Blanchfleur." She didn't put out her hand.

"Was Bullfinch your case, too?"

"No, Hadley and Morse are doing most of it but we pitch in. We're a five-person bureau, we help each other. I was just passing by when Mrs. Wallace across the street flagged me. She was very pleased that our department is continuing its investigation, still."

"Obviously, she misunderstood. And the investigation, not entirely successful, right? The case is still open."

She didn't look insulted. "Not successful at all, which is why Elizabeth Cutty hired you. I guess. To keep Cromwell University looking good. It seems to have been a murder. That's what we've got. I hear there were hairs and prints and footprints from everyone in his office and several on his person. The place was like Grand Central station. The uncertainty is upsetting to people. Hence, you. Police were not real pleased."

"I didn't come to show anybody up or to step on your toes. The President is concerned about the university looking bad, she needs to show that she's making extraordinary efforts. I'm the extraordinary effort, you all are the effort that everyone figures they're entitled to."

She nodded her head, a country grin; slightly crooked, white teeth and a big dimple in her left cheek.

"I've met with your chief. I didn't get the feeling there would be lots of information sharing," I said.

She didn't hesitate. "Nope. Hadley and Morse are very by the book, the pair of them, and that doesn't include sharing information with, um, with, you know, PIs, and they're marginally competent assholes, which is why this investigation is stalled out. Also, what's in it for them? Also, I never said this."

"Didn't hear a thing," I said. "Sorry about the disgustingness of being a PI."

"Not a problem," she said and pushed herself up. "Time to clear out."

"It would be a problem, if I stayed behind?"

She shook her head. "Yes, it would. It would be trespassing. Out."

We walked out together and she offered me a lift to the guesthouse. I said that I preferred to walk. I do like to walk. I wasn't stupid enough to go back into the house right then and there. I started walking very slowly and she rolled up right alongside me, looking over the top of her cop glasses.

"Do not go back into that house. I will arrest you and you will not have gotten off to a good start with the police, which is just never smart."

She waved to me from her car. I waved back, wondering if she was on my side, wondering what it would take to get her on my side. She seemed nice. I was not unaware that I was a little lonely.

Theodor kissed me on both cheeks when I showed up for the second time, ready for early lunch. He was dressed, upright, and unembarrassed. He had his sunglasses firmly situated. He led me into the dining room. Mrs. Martinelli, his gorgon of a housekeeper, had gone all out for us and left a beautiful stuffed capon and cold green beans in vinaigrette and, on the sideboard, a cold, open bottle of Mâcon-Lugny.

"Holy shit," I said. "Sorry about today—"

"Let's eat."

I served us both, poured some wine to get him started, poured me a quarter-inch, and told him where everything was located on the table.

We tucked in and ate before we began our serious conversation. Theo rarely talked while he ate.

"You heard? I'm investigating Professor Bullfinch's death."

Theo nodded.

"Did my father tell you?"

Theo shook his head and ate and then spoke.

"Well, he did leave a message. He said 'Dell is coming.' You know how he is."

"Why would someone want to kill Oliver Bullfinch? For sex? For money? For a secret in someone's lurid past? Did he have a past? I mean, I know he must have."

"For any of those things, I suppose," Theo said. "Sex is a powerful motive but . . . he was old. Probably not for sex. It's delightful when you're old, but it's not a motivating force. Alas."

Theo took a sip of wine and I was glad that he was blind, so that he couldn't see how distressed I was by this part of the conversation.

"Stay calm, Dell. Let's get some cognac and go sit down. These little chairs really won't do for a thorough postmortem."

He shifted slowly but steadily out of the chair and into the living room, where he eased into his great leather Chesterfield sofa. I poured.

"I found a photograph of a woman," I said.

I described the barefoot, smiling woman.

"Doesn't sound like his wife, Miranda Bullfinch," he said. "The smiling. She didn't sound like a smiler."

"I know. Does that sound like anyone you've ever . . ."

There was no point to this conversation. Theo turned his face away.

"You make the woman sound like your mother. Oliver never mentioned a daughter or another wife. Or a mistress. I think you might want to show a photo around to people who aren't blind."

"Good idea. Did you know what . . . Did you ever see my mother?"

"My eyesight was almost gone when we met. It was completely gone by the time she married your father. Her hair was red. I got to see that. And her green eyes. When I meet women I like, even now, I visualize their hair as silky and red. Your mother's hair was silky."

"I know."

Theo cleared his throat and played with the stem of his wineglass.

"Was Bullfinch unhappy after his wife died? Starting fights, holding a grudge?" I asked.

"He was an academic, Dell. Of course, he was capable of holding a grudge. Look at your father. Jesus, look at me. Anyway, he was probably happier after her death. She was a harpy. She hated intellectual conversations, she preferred reality TV to Shakespeare and she said so all the time. She drank a bit. She made loud, unpleasant remarks about other people's marriages and their children. She served stale Triscuits before dinner, without so much as a slice of cheese, so we wouldn't spoil our appetites. Appalling woman. And her voice. Like a cat with its tail caught in the door. One could hardly blame him for carrying on with the girls."

I didn't bother explaining that a screechy wife was no excuse for sexually harassing your students.

"So, I know why someone, even you, might have killed Mrs. Bullfinch. But they didn't, or if they did, bully for them, they got away with it. Why Mr. Bullfinch? Maybe he was mixed up with one of those girls he carried on with and her father or her lover or her protective mother found out and killed him."

"You're not listening. He wasn't perceived as a sexual threat. He was a nuisance. He was pathetic. He fondled the girls' necklaces and scarves and made gauche remarks. It was nothing."

"It wasn't nothing," I sighed.

"He was a decent man. He cared about his subject, he was honest and thoughtful in his writing, he was fair and rigorous with his students, and he was a supportive colleague. We used to have a beer together on occasional Friday afternoons. He called me on a Sunday, the week he was killed, and said that he had some interesting news. He sounded unusually animated. We agreed to meet over here, for our Friday beer. Someone killed him on Tuesday. And that someone killed him—not to avenge their sexual harassment, believe you me, and not for money, because he was a professor after all. I have to think he knew something he shouldn't, or had something that didn't belong to him, and someone capable of violence didn't like that."

Nothing wrong with that summary. I would have rather we'd gone on gossiping and speculating and maybe even had some snappy back-and-forth about sexual harassment and how men's views on it were as reliable as foxes reporting on chickens but Theo missed his friend and someone had killed him. Chances were good that it was someone at Cromwell and that I'd be chatting with him or her tonight. I have felt concern and sometimes pity and sometimes disdain for the people who needed my services, and for the people in their lives, but so far, I hadn't been afraid.

Theo took my hand and I leaned back, away from him. He must have guessed what was happening; he touched my face and ran a forefinger around my eyes. They were not completely dry. He held my hand as he'd been doing since I was fifteen and pregnant, since I was thirty and unable to cry at my mother's funeral, since I was thirty-one and making so many bad choices, I had to straighten out or die.

"What's the worst thing that can happen," he said.

"There *is* a killer and I don't find him. Or her. My failure is public. Again."

Theo patted my hand.

"That does sound bad," he said.

"Thank you. I'm gonna go get ready for this big bash," I said.

"Why don't you wear something pink and knock their eyes out? You still have the red hair? Your mother said all your baby clothes were Schiaparelli pink."

I felt encouraged and kissed him good-bye, locking his door as I left. I didn't think that the Hot Tamale from this afternoon would be zipping over for after-dinner delight. She probably had a key, anyway.

I got back to my room, with air-conditioning I couldn't turn off, and crawled into my twin bed, with my scarf and sweater on, to read the files about the English Department faculty until I had only fifteen minutes to get out the door.

Mary Clark, 69, Spelman BA, Harvard PhD. All about Jean Toomer, with a sideline in Jessie Redmon Fauset. No spouse mentioned. Allison Shein, 33, Women Writers of the Eighteenth Century, no spouse mentioned. Dan Fiske, 40, studied astrobiology as an undergraduate at Penn State, now teaching the relationship between literary form and social history, which I hoped he'd explain to me. Divorced, no kids. Harry Markham, 32, Hemingway and Paris and, I hoped, Gertrude Stein and the sexy poem about buttons, which is all I remembered about Gertrude Stein. No spouse mentioned. Albert Freedman, 84 years old, apparently immortal, and still teaching seminars on Hart Crane and Walt Whitman with a hand wave to Willa Cather. Married to Lois Freedman. I had a sheaf of other files but one guy was just retired and in a wheelchair and the other likelies were all on sabbatical and far away. If one of them had snuck back from Oslo, Banff, or Prague to kill Bullfinch, I would have to let them get away with it.

I put on my burgundy suit and my pink top and hung my mother's garnet earrings (like big, red quarters) on my ears and wound her garnet ropes around my neck. I'm built fairly big and very solid. I look best in smooth, tailored clothes or in jeans. I look my very best stark naked. In ruffles and florals, I look like a pale side of beef with ribbons around it.

I fluffed out my hair and looked closely in the mirror. I smoothed a little Rosebud Salve on my eyebrows, eyelids, and mouth and slapped some blush on my two pale cheeks. I have classic redhead skin, which tends to make me look like a dead person in winter and like a cooked lobster in summer. On a good day, though, I am striking. *You're striking*, I thought. *Five hundred dollars a day*, I thought.

Smiling Faces

Back to the president's house, to another huge room with fifteen-foot-high ceilings, scattered Persian rugs, faded settees in various shades of blue, and blue porcelain urns, filled with irises and white tulips. I hadn't known until then that blue and white were Cromwell's colors.

There was no trace of the Russian wolfhound in Liz Cutty now. There was no trace of anything. She wasn't chic, she wasn't dowdy. She was just college president, celebrating her stewardship. If there had been light in her eyes or mischief in her mouth, she would have been a handsome woman. As it was, when she shook my hand, I could almost feel the wiring under her cool skin. I was already sweating, in that stuffy hall, filled with strangers, one of whom might be of interest.

"So glad you could come tonight, Dr. Chandler. I wanted to introduce you to Professor Clark, Professor Markham, and a few others."

She backed away, giving me a push towards a woman around five feet tall. Her brown face was strong with broad planes, very short white hair, and a slash of red lipstick. She was, like me, in a Kamala Harris suit, with well-worn Chucks. Unlike me, she wore a sparkling brooch on her lapel, which seemed to be Lady Liberty with a machete.

"Professor Clark? I'm Dell Chandler."

I stuck out my hand, because it's the fastest way I know to find out something about a person. Even if what you find out is that they're assholes with great handshakes, there you are. She put out a small, arthritic hand and shook mine, gingerly.

"The detective. My pleasure." Only her handshake was tentative. "What would you like to drink?"

And she turned her head towards the bar, which was doing a booming business.

"Club soda with some lime. Thank you. I'll get it."

"No, no. I'll get it. You're our guest."

She walked behind the bar, stared down the young barman, and came back in less than a minute with my club soda. She took a sip of her large dark brown Scotch, in which floated two of the world's smallest ice cubes.

"Cheers," she said. "About Bullfinch. I liked him. We were both old-fashioned scholars and rather old-fashioned people."

That's not what I'd say about her. She looked at me with clear topaz eyes. It was like being looked at by beach glass.

I said, "You must miss him."

She gave the smallest sigh and looked into her glass. "Well, it's just a rolling list, now, isn't it? Oliver wasn't exciting or funny or even very charming. But he was a good man. He was a little bitter and that's not an attractive quality. A little harsh in his judgments. Surprisingly, not a racist."

We stood for a moment, sipping, watching the other people. I wondered how to ask who she thought killed him. Mary Clark spoke.

"Well, it could be any one of us, couldn't it? The students are gone, although someone could have come back long enough to kill him. I don't know why one would. He was a hard grader, once upon a time, but he'd eased up, now that they're our 'customers.'"

She put up the air quotes and looked nauseated

"I can't imagine why someone on the staff would kill him. Is it gossip if I praise him? He could have just slipped and brought the bust down upon himself, but no one, not even the Centerville police, an excellent argument for defunding the police, seem to think that's what happened. Well, look here," she said grimly, as a tall, radiantly blond man came towards us.

"Mary, what a pleasure!" he said, kissing her on the cheek. (Kissing Mary Clark! Of course, all his life, women, young and old, had enjoyed his attentions—why not Mary Clark?) She stood still as a stone and when he'd finished embracing her, she turned to me as though it hadn't happened. She introduced him the way the biology teachers show you the first slide.

"This is Harry Markham, also in my department. Here, celebrating having gotten tenure. Harry, this is Dell Chandler, she's investigating Oliver's death."

One beat, two beats. The radiance dimmed just a bit, for a second.

“Harry and Oliver did not get along,” she said, pleasantly.

“That’s not true, Mary. We had our differences. We all do.” He bared his teeth. “It’s great to meet you. The administration did the right thing in calling you in, I think. Terrible loss to the community. So, you’re a private eye. Wow. Great.”

I put out my hand and he ignored it. He brought one big, golden hand up, almost touching my cheek to make sure that I was looking straight at him, at his lively, blue-green eyes, with the dark-blue iris. I flinched but I didn’t really mind.

“If I can be helpful, please let me know. We’re a tough crowd, aren’t we, Mary?”

Clever enough and he must have known, after thirty years of experience, that women were inclined to overlook certain minor flaws (like selfishness, insincerity, and heartlessness, to name the first three that occurred to me) for those lovely eyes and those big hands and the very thick, wavy blond hair falling softly onto his thick, tanned neck, with its prominent pulse. Mary Clark looked across the room.

I told tenured Harry Markham I’d be calling on him in the next day or so and he said that that would be . . . great. He walked away with the belly-forward gait of an athlete, like a penis on feet, which is not unappealing. The nosy neighbor had said the visitor looked like a movie star.

Mary Clark had started on Scotch number two and asked me if I wanted to meet Allison Shein. Her red lips almost curled. She nodded towards a slim, olive-skinned woman in her thirties with dark circles under her eyes, a face with all the fun and exuberance of a Talmudic scholar.

We moved towards her, but not fast enough. Liz Cutty put a knife to her glass and made a toast. She singled out a few people, including Harry Markham for his promotion and a short black man with big eyes and big ears whose book on something about the planets was causing a stir internationally and a tall white woman in a purple jumpsuit and white-people dreads who had just gotten a MacArthur grant for something to do with pianos and now had to put up with people cheering and yelling "Genius!," which probably didn't suck.

I saw Harry Markham lift his glass a little higher towards Liz Cutty and she nodded, smiling. Allison Shein didn't give a shit for the toast or the applause. She frowned and pulled hard enough on Harry Markham's linen sleeve to almost knock him over. They didn't strike me as a likely pair. Her pale yellowish face began to redden at the tip of her nose and at her dark eyelids. He put his arm around her, as though comforting her, and dragged her out of the reception room. I thought that was interesting and turned to Mary Clark, who was watching intently.

"My, my. A year ago, Harry published an article on Hemingway. Actually, he published the same one twice, in slightly different form, scholarly and popular. It was a great success in *The New York Review of Books*," she said. "Back then, Harry was very nice to Allison. It's his habit to be nice, to be likable, but he doesn't usually put himself out for women like Allison. You're more his type, I'd say. But she may have hidden depths, bless her heart. You'll want to talk to Dan Fiske, too. He's not here. He's not the handsomest horse in the stable but he's not a fool. And Albert Freedman, too. Poor thing. But he does know things. Well, least said, soonest mended. I'll say good night now."

She offered me her rough hand, again, warily. I held her hand gently and looked into her troubled, topaz eyes. That was a lot of information from a quiet woman.

"Thank you for taking the time to talk to me tonight, Dr. Clark."

"I didn't mind," she said, quietly. "Call me Mary."

"Thank you. I'd like to have a drink or a cup of tea with you in the next few days, if you can find the time."

"Of course I can. I don't know who these terribly busy professors are. One teaches, one writes, there's still time to have dinner and sit on the porch. You come to my place. Any morning." She smiled for the first time and I was smitten. "I'm on Washington Drive, with all the other old folk. Any morning, after eight, before eleven."

And off she plowed, scattering the bright lights of various departments before her.

I looked into the coatroom and saw Harry Markham cradling Allison Shein, a linen napkin draped over the shoulder she nestled on. A couple of elderly professors slept on matching blue silk settees. A tall, bearded man dropped a small silver dish into his pocket and the young bartender slipped out through the French doors to hand a bottle to a waiting friend. I circled the rooms a few times, tossing my hair, letting everyone get a good look at me. I said the word *murder* to every guest and waiter I encountered. I told everyone I was staying at the guesthouse, on the second floor. Room 209, I said. I did everything but draw a map and put out three bowls of porridge.

We're Having a Party

Thursday, August 22

In my dream, I was spying on Harry Markham and Allison Shein as they walked hand in hand, in a forest of black leather trees and bushes covered in big berries of black leather. Mary Clark landed behind them in a golden bubble, like Glinda the Good Witch, and, lifting her glass of Scotch in my direction, told me to turn back. My late mother sat on a flower-covered bench, brushing her hair and saying, as she often had, "Big fish are caught with little hooks." Fine, I thought. Thank you, subconscious.

I made it through my morning routine, sweating like a pig, running a lot, walking a little, and then I went back to the guesthouse, where there was now no air-conditioning at all, and almost passed out from the pleasure of plentiful, painfully hot water and a previous guest's very expensive, rosemary-scented shampoo. The towels were the size and texture of ancient hankies and I'd gone from room to room until I had a dozen and then I used them all, feeling Egyptian.

I was ready to go meet people, deceive them, analyze them, pull apart their alibis, rifle their Dropboxes, open folders, and eavesdrop on highly personal conversations. My father was safe at home. I was surrounded by strangers. I felt good.

The English Department was in a three-story brick building, like a small-town high school, with the familiar peeling pillars and chipped marble trim. Inside, the department office was cluttered without being cozy. The lack of coziness was due, in part, to the pale green linoleum, the olive-green molded plastic chairs, the blank smudged white walls and mostly due to Mrs. Groth, secretary.

Mrs. Groth was Lord Voldemort, or Moby-Dick, or Mrs. Danvers (whom she resembled), or whoever your most memorable literary baddie might be. Angular and elderly, pale as parchment, she slammed drawers, broke pencil points, tore stapled reports apart, opened mail up with a talon-like forefinger, brushed dust off her keyboard in a rage, while her cell phone buzzed like a bee. I tried not to jump to conclusions, to consider that this was just a bad and busy day. She looked at me and turned away.

"Mrs. Groth? I'm Dell Chandler, the private investigator called in by President Cutty to investigate Professor Bullfinch's death."

She had the look of someone impressed by titles; I kicked myself for not having referred to myself as "Doctor."

"The police have already asked me hundreds of questions. Perhaps you could get the notes from them."

She turned her back to me. Above her pinched, Germanic face, she wore a startling black wig, cut in a Louise Brooks bob. Someone had given Mrs. Groth bad advice after chemotherapy.

My voice softened. "Mrs. Groth, I see how busy you are and I know that the last thing you want on a busy morning is someone bothering you. I don't want to be in your way, I just want the key to Professor Bullfinch's office and to take a look around. That's the only thing I have to trouble you for. I would also like to talk to you for a few minutes because you knew the deceased and because you've been with the department for twenty-five years, so really, there's nothing you don't know."

Mrs. Groth squinted at me and adjusted her wig, slightly. My mother's elegant, bald head flickered in front of me for a second.

"I was here before any of them, except Professor Bullfinch. Now he's gone. He was a decent man, reliable. He never missed a class and I mean never, except for that one week, about a year ago. Didn't miss a class when Mrs. Bullfinch died, the year before. Dedicated. Gave up driving. Walked to work after that and still never missed a class, is my point. I wouldn't give you one thin dime for the rest of them, except Mary Clark. Well, Albert Freedman is not a bad man. The rest of them, God help us."

What happened to all those adoring and fiercely protective guardians of the ivory tower? Gone the way of dedicated butlers, devoted housekeepers, and brilliant executive secretaries, I guess. The unintended consequence of social mobility and feminism.

"Why do you stay?"

"Are you joking," she snapped and threw me a key with a red rubber band around the base. "You think I'd do well at Walmart?"

"I know. Presidents come and go, your old friends leave or die, new people come in and they're not nearly as interesting or nice as the old ones. And you just keep on with what you're doing, keeping the department going."

She sorted through a huge pile of folders.

"Aren't you clever. I am old. I am, in fact, dying and I do feel totally unappreciated. I type eighty-five words per minute, no errors. Do you know how valuable a skill that is when everyone has tablets? I take shorthand. Do you think anyone cares? Facts and beliefs are now the same thing and if you feel, deeply and with conviction, that the sun shines out of your ass or mine, how dare I suggest otherwise. I used to dine with Professor and Mrs. Bullfinch several times a year. She was a very nice woman and they had all the staff over for dinner. A lovely gesture. There's something that's disappeared: the lovely gesture. The faculty held a tea for all of us in the office, every spring. Do you know how we organize our Christmas party—excuse me, we have to call it a holiday party now—these days? These days, the two most junior—and I mean most junior—text me about who's coming and they offer to bring paper plates and cups and they drop them off in my office. That Christmas party was a high point for us; all the girls in the offices baked something special and the chairman made fish house punch. The president came by and we had a Santa pass out gifts and it was just . . . Now, we have cakes from the supermarket and a bottle of piss and we don't even have a Santa. They toss the gifts for the children on the table. And most years, there aren't even any children. Maybe someone has an autistic stepson. Never mind. You can look through their files: Clark, Shein, Markham, Bullfinch, Freedman, Fiske, Adler, Schwartz, and Hunsecker. You need the key to his office, third floor, two doors down from the stairs. His file is over there, top right, under *B*, of course, and the filing is chronological. His personal correspondence is in his office. This is for the building."

She threw another key at me and turned away.

"Thanks for your help, I'll keep the keys for a couple of days, if I may. Also, have you seen this woman?"

I showed her Barefoot and Lovely.

"Never. Looks like round heels to me."

I slid the photo and the papers into my satchel and said good-bye.

"If you want my opinion, ask Allison Shein," she said, not turning around. "I know Harry Markham looks too good to be true and is and Miss Shein looks like a Jewish wet hen but I think she's trouble."

Just then a student came in and Mrs. Groth gave the poor kid what for. I hoped Mrs. Groth had a couple more weeks.

I went up to Bullfinch's office, noting its proximity to Shein, Markham, and Fiske's. Freedman, like Mary Clark and the three on sabbatical, were at the other end of the building. I hoped the police had the budget to check out transatlantic hit man contracts. I didn't. It was possible that Mary Clark lied about liking Bullfinch and had killed him, but I couldn't imagine why and I didn't know how she'd lift that bust of Hawthorne. I unlocked the office and it was as scraped clean as his house. Hadley and Morse might not be cooperative, or even bright, but they were certainly tidy. (I kept reminding myself to drop by and visit Hadley and Morse and I kept forgetting, by which I mean, I didn't. Chief DiCenzo had outlined the circumstances under which the police would be helping me. I did leave them each a friendly voice message every day, expressing all kinds of high hopes.)

The corner of the desk, on which Bullfinch had hit his head, must have been covered in blood and hair and skin that day as the sun was setting. Now, it was just a smooth, gray metal corner. And sharp. I pressed my thumb against the very tip and the metal sank into my skin, like a steak knife. The bronze head of Nathaniel Hawthorne that someone had clubbed him with, just to be on the safe side, was in police custody. I could picture it. My father had a similar bust of Adam Smith. You would not have got up in a hurry if someone had hit you with it.

I stood in front of the big window, watching people go about their business. All the drawers were completely emptied, not even a paper clip. Nothing on the desk, nothing behind the desk, taped to the bottom of it, or tucked into the fluorescent lights. No computer. That left the hard copy files and I had to skim through eight drafts of *Light and Air: Nathaniel Hawthorne's*

God and four more of *The Power of Blackness: Hawthorne and Melville.* Apparently, these books were enough of a hit that his CV showed a promotion to full professor one year early and Bullfinch left Michigan State to come to Cromwell as the Edna P. DuPont Chair of American Literature, the post he'd held for twenty years. The rest of the files held personal correspondence, from the old days, and hard copies of recent email, mostly of the "I'll cite your article, if you'll cite mine" variety, and a few genuinely sympathetic notes following the death of his wife. They all began "Although I never had the pleasure of meeting Mrs. Bullfinch . . ." I stuffed the personal mail into my satchel and scoured the file cabinets. Not a photo, not a card. No nudie shots of Barefoot and Lovely. A stack of receipts from Bill's Texaco Station, stuffed into an envelope. I took that, too.

The air was musty, with a faint tang of chalk and sweat, books, stale coffee, a little red wine, and under that, the rusty smell of spilled blood. Aside from the blood, the smell was my father's office and it made me think of him more kindly than I usually did. I got down on my knees and ran my hands over the linoleum, checking for a loose tile, for a secret stash, for a hair or coat button. I found a triangle of paper, a scrap. The typed words *to be a*. Not a slam dunk. I put it in my bag.

I heard footsteps coming towards me, slowing as they reached the door. I sat back on my heels. The footsteps stopped for at least ten seconds, and started again, in the other direction. Sneakers and a small person. I cracked the door and saw Allison Shein's skinny butt going around the corner. I taped a note to the top of Bullfinch's dry-cleaned desk: *If you've gone to the trouble of breaking into this office, call Dell Chandler.* I left my number. Maybe that would draw the hounds. I locked the door behind me. I strolled down the hall in a here-I-am fashion. No one stopped to chat with me as I left. I Googled and called the dean of faculty at Michigan State as I walked. Her secretary put me through when I said I worked for Liz Cutty.

Dean Abubakar told me that Oliver Bullfinch was before her time. She said admiring things about him and about Elizabeth Cutty and she gave me the name of the university's lawyer. I emphasized that all I wanted was Bullfinch's old personnel files and financial records. I emphasized *only*, to make it sound reasonable. I also said that President Cutty appreciated the cooperation. The dean said, again, that Elizabeth Cutty was a fine person, that I probably was, too, and that I should feel free to call the university lawyer.

Liz Cutty texted me that we were due for a meeting at 8:00 A.M. I texted back emojis of a big bicep and a cup of coffee. It felt blithe, just a good-humored insult, and I knew, even as I sent it, that I'd be sorry. I left another cover-my-ass voice message for the police and one for my father, reminding him where I was and why I wasn't coming to dinner anytime soon.

I Can't Help Myself

I napped. My phone vibrated.

"Dell Chandler," a warm, gravelly man's voice said. "We're the Freedmans, old friends of your father's. Do come to dinner tonight. Professor Shein has kindly offered to give you a ride. Seven? It'll be great to catch up."

No mention of Bullfinch, but it couldn't be coincidence. And it was dinner, made and served by other people. I washed my face. In ten minutes, there was an irritable honk below my window and I saw Allison Shein's dark hair inside a sparkling gold Prius whose front right fender and headlight had been recently demolished. I wondered if she consciously chose the most unbecoming colors. I got dressed and ran down carrying my lipstick and shoes.

Allison nodded curtly and then lost her nerve. She was brought up to be polite, at least to people's faces.

"Hi. I'm Allison." She put the car in gear with a painful crunch and we jerked forward and stalled. A bottle of cheap white wine rolled out under my feet. "That's for the Freedmans."

"Hi. Dell. I hope this isn't too much out of your way."

I didn't want to make her more tense. She gripped the wheel so tightly, her knuckles shone white.

Allison started the car again and we made our way down the driveway. She was an unusual and terrifying driver: very slow and very anxious. At twenty-five miles per hour, we rolled through stop signs, brushed against the sidewalks, and straddled the double yellow line all the way to the Freedmans' house. She drove cautiously through a red light and the pedestrian banged his hand on the hood. "Watch where you're going, you fucking blind bat."

She pulled over to gather herself.

Allison Shein looked the way she did last night, maybe a little worse. She might be an insomniac: purplish-brown circles under the eyes, premature creases on her eyelids, a little eczema in front of her ear. She wore a dark brown dress, with little gray and yellow flowers, which was too big for her, as well as being fugly. The neckline kept slipping, revealing her very sensible white bra straps and her skinny yellow shoulders. She looked waifish and pathetic and irritating. How could anyone stand to go through life with all their loneliness and vulnerability hanging out, for all the world to see and step on?

I resisted the urge to fix her dress. She went back to driving.

"So, is their house far?"

"We're almost . . ."

The effort of answering distracted her and she swerved towards a parked car. Without thinking, I put my hand on the wheel and whirled it in the other direction.

"I'm sorry," I said. "That was presumptuous. It was just a reflex."

"It's okay. I'm sorry I'm not a very confident driver. Harry taught me to drive last fall. I grew up in Manhattan."

Her driving steadied a little bit and I took my hand off the oh-shit strap. Maybe everything would work out, maybe we'd get to and from the dinner party intact, maybe I'd find the murderer, maybe things would work out for Allison and Harry. Maybe.

Allison took a deep breath. "Freedman's a Shakespearean. He got tenure as a wunderkind a thousand years ago and hasn't published much since. He's always talking about his 'new' project. He's going to do a 'valorium' edition of *The Merry Wives of Windsor*. The man's nearly eighty. He said that he's just an old-fashioned scholar, which means he thinks everything after 1780 is just trendy garbage. And he calls women 'wenches.' And he drinks too much. But, you know, eighty."

All righty then.

"Is there a Mrs. Freedman?"

"Oh yeah. Lois." So much for sisterhood. "I guess she's a lot younger. I think she was his student. She helps out in the alumni office. She's, uh, very nice. Well, I mean, classic faculty wife."

Huh.

"He's not so bad, really. It's surprising that he's interested in Gertrude Stein."

For Allison, old age had defused Freedman and he'd been clever enough to stroke her ego. For all her criticism, if there were a departmental conflict, she'd be in Freedman's camp.

"I'm leaving in two weeks to go to Paris, to work on a new project. I got a grant from the Omni Foundation—it's on Gertrude Stein, her theater projects. The radical inconsistencies are fabulous."

"Sure. Omni Foundation, that must be a big deal. Can I ask who wrote your recommendation letters?" Who likes you, is what I meant. Who's your squad?

She clenched the steering wheel. I could ask but she did not have to answer.

I swung again.

"Does your work tie in much with Harry's, then? That's his thing, the moveable feasties? Hemingway and Stein in Paris . . ."

"We're here." The temperature had dropped very quickly. She slammed on the brake.

"So we are. We can go over some of these questions tomorrow," I said. "Will you be in your office?"

She nodded.

"I'll come by, midday. Okay?"

She shrugged, meaning *Not if I see you first.*

I asked her if she wanted the car locked and she shrugged again. I left it unlocked as invitingly as possible and she walked a hundred feet ahead of me.

The house was standard Connecticut, circa 1953: slightly warped white clapboards with black shutters and a chipped slate walkway leading to a tiny front porch, with exactly enough room for two guests and a weathered macramé planter with one hopeful pink geranium in it. The general dreariness was overcome by mountains of peonies in full bloom, white, cherry red, pink, and lavender. I rang the doorbell and smiled reassuringly at Allison, who was holding on to her neckline.

"You look fine," I lied.

What's Goin' On?

A leprechaun opened the door.

Professor Freedman was as bald and red as an apple, just about five six and wearing the classic hairy Harris tweed jacket, in a novel shade of avocado. His baggy brown corduroys drooped under his round belly and his tie was emerald green with brown and beige diamonds. I expected his socks to be green argyle and the toes of his wee boots to curl upwards and I was right about the socks. There was something irresistible about his sense of himself as a snappy dresser at his age. He twinkled.

He ducked his head in a professorial half bow, to make eye contact with my breasts.

"Artemis . . ." he murmured into my chest.

A lot of people find this kind of thing annoying and worse, but I don't mind it so much, nearing middle age, although I don't say I encourage it.

"Professor Freedman," I responded. "We brought wine!"

A faded pink wraith appeared next to my host. Mr. Freedman had used up their collective allotment of vitality and color. A little taller than he and ash blonde, she looked like a gladiolus at the end of the season. She tottered towards me on scuffed pink silk sandals and clutched her husband's shoulder. My God, I thought, she must have muscular dystrophy or something. Then I looked into her face and saw those wet, bluish-red eyes and knew she must have been downing vodka since lunch, if she'd had lunch. Mrs. Freedman stared at me, damply, for a long minute; we all stood very still while she tried to get into gear.

"Come in, come in," she barked. "Don't just gawk, Albert. Make them drinks." She wasn't able to do the hostess routine very well, anymore, but she knew the basics and did what she absolutely had to do.

"Dumb as a bucket of worms," she mumbled, kicking their fat gray cat out of her path. I didn't ask who.

The living room was cheerful, in its way. There was a shabby beige velvet couch (covered with gray cat hairs) and four matching armchairs, their nap rubbed off at all the corners. And, everywhere, there were bits of Ireland. Shillelaghs on the walls, four-leaf clovers in amber cubes, ceramic mugs with John Kennedy's face and Leo Varadkar's, sepia prints of lasses and laddies kissing in the back streets of fair Dublin. It was a shrine to Irish kitsch and you knew that Albert Freedman had lovingly collected and arranged every bit of it. (*Freedman*, I thought. *Irish?*)

I sat down and jumped again. Underneath me was a horsehair cushion with a painting of the saint with the snakes, embroidered, 3D-style. I settled back in, with the white wine Freedman handed me. I would have gone for a real drink or three, but then I would have gotten friendly, and then I would have gotten nasty, and if I've learned nothing else in my thirties, I've learned that if I do drink, I have to do it the way Allison Shein drives, slow and worried. Allison, that party animal, had apple juice. Mrs. Freedman continued to sip from a tall full glass, with not so much as an ice cube or lemon slice for camouflage. Freedman (who was starting to seem like "poor old Albert") drank Laphroaig whiskey and discoursed about its pedigree as he gulped. There was no food on the table, except a small bowl of fuzzy cashews. I sniffed for a reassuring food smell, but I couldn't pick anything up. My stomach growled.

The doorbell rang and Harry Markham burst through the door, the Sun God in white jeans, white cotton shirt, and blue blazer. No socks. No little tiny wings on his ankles. He hugged Mrs. Freedman, who actually smiled, and he pounded poor old Albert on the back. Harry focused a dazzling smile on me and gave the tail end of it to Allison, who started to perk up, remembered her injury, and wilted back into her chair.

"Great to be here. Laphroaig? Great whiskey, Al. How about on the rocks, with just a splash. Great."

Just as Harry was settling into one of the armchairs, the doorbell rang again, and our last guest arrived. Mrs. Freedman yelled, "It's open," and a dull mouse of a man came in.

"Hey, Danny boy," Harry said.

Poor man, thinning brown hair, worn long and floppy, a pronounced overbite, pink little mouth, small, sharp nose, and an unfortunate tendency to wear gray. But his eyes were not unfortunate. They were shiny brown and bottomless, seeing everything and thinking, clicking on all cylinders, about all he saw. At the moment, they fastened on Allison, whose gaze was locked onto Harry's perfect profile. And people think nothing ever happens in Centerville.

Mrs. Freedman made the introductions.

"Dan, this is . . . Jesus, who are you? Dell Chandler. Marvin Chandler, you know, *God and Money*, right? She's his kid. Liz Cutty thinks Oliver's murder makes Cromwell look bad, so she hired . . . this one. She investigates. This is Dan Fiske; he's been visiting this year. Rising star. Don't get attached. He'll be gone in a day or two."

At least, she didn't make you squirm with her desperate efforts to please.

We sat around, passing the inedible cashews back and forth, and they talked about the kind of things academics talk about: Albert's latest bird-watching venture, the faulty transmission in Harry's old Honda, Dan's love of all things Apple. Mrs. Freedman's eyes closed, Allison seemed lovesick, and I was bored out of my mind, imagining that at any moment, someone could leap up with another bloodstained bronze bust and head for the Library, Colonel Mustard in tow. I needed to focus. Suddenly, Mrs. Freedman lurched out of her seat and headed towards the kitchen. She emerged, shouting "Dinner!" I still didn't smell anything.

We shuffled along to the dining room and stared at the table. The Freedmans didn't give us any indications of where to sit and, in any case, we were all mesmerized by the table laid with a huge platter of cold sliced corned beef, garnished with clumps of potato salad, each clump topped with a big bush of parsley (that was Mrs. Freedman, asserting something), another platter covered with slices of bologna, laid out like a mosaic, a trifle bowl of macaroni salad, a bigger crystal bowl of coleslaw, and a tarnished silver platter covered with sliced white bread. All in dusty Waterford glasses and Belleek plates.

"What lovely crystal," I said and maneuvered to sit next to Mrs. Freedman, who seemed a likely informant, if I could get to her before the next six ounces of vodka. "Where do you get corned beef around here? Or do you make your own?"

I wasn't sure how far gone she was. Mrs. Freedman stared at me flatly and smiled, a slow, shaky, genuinely amused smile.

"Hilarious," she said drily. "I don't make my own anything, anymore. Beef Wellington with two screaming babies. Salmon *en papillote* until it was coming out of my fucking ears. I did baklava from scratch, while carpooling my brats to violin and swimming lessons, so they could become fucking swimming violinists, for Chrissake. Now, I don't cook a goddamn thing."

I smiled pleasantly. "That's why God made takeout. So what do you do now that you're no longer chained to the stove?"

"I drink, detective girl. My chains are right here."

She waved her glass around, not spilling a drop. At the other end, Albert looked at me questioningly, I smiled back. He turned to Allison.

"Albert drinks a little too much and he paws the girls and he pretends he's Irish. Harmless, harmless, harmless. On the other . . ." Mrs. Freedman stared at her glass.

"On the other hand . . ." I prompted.

She paused, the way they do, as though they're gathering their thoughts when all they're really doing is trying not to drool or spill the drink. If I could knock over the glass, maybe we could get somewhere. If I could have met her before whatever it was that had shriveled her, maybe we could have got somewhere. Mrs. Freedman took a big gulp of her drink and glared at Allison, who felt it and turned towards our end. Mrs. Freedman opened her mouth, shut her eyes, and slumped back in the chair. Her night was over. Allison seemed delighted. For the first time that night, she smiled. We all ignored Mrs. Freedman's little faux pas.

Albert got up to make coffee and since the dinner partner on my right was no longer available, I turned to Dan Fiske. I have manners.

"So how do you find Cromwell, after a year?"

The bright-penny eyes took me in, with appreciation but without the passion he had been casting at Allison. Takes all kinds.

"I find it interesting. I'll miss it when I go to Iowa. I'll miss the people here, some new friends, some of my colleagues. And you, how do you find it, from your novel perspective?"

"Well, it's certainly interesting. I wish I had known Professor Bullfinch before his death. His habits, his likes and dislikes, his congeniality or lack thereof. I'm sure he was a complex person and, honestly, it would help to reconstruct the events leading to his . . ."

"Murder," Dan said.

"What was your impression of him, just from faculty meetings and things like that? I don't know if you hung out."

Fiske snorted. I'd asked the right question. He told me about Bullfinch going all out to see that Allison was denied tenure, about this vicious, doddering old man, vain about his reputation and indifferent to those of his junior colleagues. Fiske spoke about Allison as though she was Shirley Temple in *The Little Princess*; terribly hard done by and plucky, brave and pure despite her shameful treatment. I looked at Allison, leaning wistfully towards Harry, who never took his beautiful eyes off Dan and me.

Fiske went on about poor Allison and Harry's great good fortune in getting tenure.

"Dan, forgive me, but I have to start somewhere. Where were you Tuesday, August 6, that afternoon?"

He smiled. "The police won't even share our alibis with you? They're really making you reinvent the wheel. I was at the Apple Store in New Haven until about six. It was a nightmare—but a great alibi. Afterwards, I had dinner at Geronimo's. I treated myself. My waitperson was Moxie, who's waited on me before, I don't know her last name, long purple braids, and I left there about eight."

Without comment, Fiske and I managed to swivel in our chairs so Harry couldn't follow our conversation.

I directed the conversation back to Harry and Fiske said, after the usual disclaimers ("I'm not saying he doesn't deserve it . . ."), that Harry was the administration's golden boy but not "so well thought of" in academic circles. He said "administration" the way my father said *Internet*, with a sort of envious loathing.

Harry and Allison were talking softly across the big mahogany table and Allison was agitated. I tried to listen to them and "uh-huh" appropriately to Fiske. For a few seconds, Harry and Allison both looked at me with the same, worried look.

Allison turned back to Harry.

"You promised." Allison's awful whine; even if you were on her side, you wished she'd shut up. "Can't you . . ."

Harry put his hand on her shoulder, tucking away her bra strap. She froze, like a mouse tickled by a snake.

"Of course, I will . . ." Harry's honey flowed around Allison. "Not a problem, Allie."

That did it. Whatever point Allison had hoped to make, she'd given up between the hand on the shoulder and *Allie*. Tranquilized.

I couldn't stand it. I went into the kitchen to see if there was any dessert. There was a Sara Lee pound cake on the counter and a carton of good vanilla ice cream in the freezer. I went back into the dining room.

"Dessert in five minutes, everyone," I sang out, like Ina Garten.

Everyone brightened up a little, as if this was a normal dinner party. Then one of the murder suspects came in to help the detective dish out ice cream, while the hostess snored and the host brought his personal bottle of Jameson to the table. Who would pretend to be Irish, and why?

I started slicing pound cake with a dull knife and putting the slices on little crystal plates. The plates were old and fragile, like dragonfly wings, probably given by someone's grandmother to the young and hopeful Freedmans. I think Mrs. Freedman must have had great charm, and her life with that perfectly adorable man just sucked it right out of her. Harry found the ice cream scoop and for a few minutes, we sliced and scooped in a comfortable silence. It was the nicest moment I'd ever had with him.

Everyone gobbled their dessert. No one wanted to prolong the evening. Fiske and Allison cleared as Albert poured himself another drink, leaving his cake untouched. He lifted his wife's head, and slipped a napkin under her cheek, tenderly.

Harry turned to me and said, "Let me give you a ride home. Please."

Please. I was curious about what would come next.

"You're very kind." I jumped up, thanked Albert, apologized silently to Mrs. Freedman, and went into the kitchen to say good night to Fiske and Allison and tell them I had a ride with Harry.

Fiske was thrilled. Allison dropped one of the pretty goblets and as we left, Dan Fiske helped her pick up the tiny pieces.

Danger and Heartbreak Dead Ahead

Harry held my arm lightly as we walked out of the house. We both sighed, standing for a moment in the warm night air, breathing in the honeysuckle and the cut grass.

"This is mine," he said, pointing to a little blue MG. "I finally got rid of that old Honda I was telling everyone about."

The car was dashing and silly. It could only be driven by some English twit or a seventy-year-old geezer with a checked touring cap perched on his bald head. I would have thought a man like Harry would drive a mud-splashed Jeep or a safari-battered Land Rover. Even a Ford truck would get more points in the manliness sweepstakes.

"Doesn't look like you," I said. "It's adorable. It's just not what I would have envisioned for you."

"Nice that you envisioned me and my car. I know what you mean. I wouldn't have picked it out myself, but, it's what I got and I can't complain."

"Good attitude."

I opened the door on my side and plopped in; it would have been as easy to toss myself over the low side. I wondered if he'd take me straight to the guesthouse, or suggest a drive down the river. If the world was run properly, all men who looked like Harry would be wonderful human beings and all the good-for-nothings would look like Dan Fiske, or worse, and women would be able to focus all their energy on their children, their careers, and world peace.

"Dell, I want to be open with you."

Clang, first punch.

"Yes. Good."

"There's something, well, in my past that most people don't know about. I don't want people to know. But I wanted to tell you about it, so you didn't hear it from someone else. Because I like you and . . . well, that's it really, I just like you."

The way a frog likes flies, baby.

"Harry, if there's something you want to tell me, I want to hear it. If it doesn't have any relevance to this case, it won't go any further."

How do I know there's no God? Because I was not turned into a sizzling pile of ash, right then.

He looked indignant. "It doesn't have anything to do with the case at all, Dell. It just doesn't reflect very well on me."

"Okay, fine. Let's forget about the case, then. We'll just talk, like regular people." Sizzle.

"I saw you looking over the piles of CVs in the department office, with Mrs. Groth. Not a fan, by the way. I was walking past, to get my mail. When you look at mine, you'll notice that it took me six years to graduate from Amherst, not four."

"I noticed but I didn't think anything of it." That was the worrisome truth.

"If you poke around, you'll find that I was suspended for a year and a half."

I nodded encouragingly, hoping that he'd tell me that during that year he'd discovered he was Oliver Bullfinch's bastard son, waited awhile, and then killed him with that bronze bust.

Harry glanced and turned left, away from town, away from the lights. I admired his beautiful forehead, with one furrow creasing it, the thick golden-red brows, smooth fox fur above the strong, Scandinavian nose, down to the movie-star jaw, and the constellation of dimples from cheek to chin. Ridiculous. Butterscotch in human form.

"I just need to ask you a question."

I was trying to keep my detective brain working while my downtown party district was figuring how we could take a little break from all this tedious good behavior.

"Sure. We'll just drive. It's easier to cruise and talk."

"Where were you that afternoon Bullfinch was killed? Tuesday, August 6? I really do have to ask."

He frowned and put his foot down. The little blue toy took off like a kid had hurled it across the room.

"I was with Allison from two until about four. Then I went for a swim. You can check with her and with the kid at the desk at the Y. Lots of people saw me. I'm in the clear. Obviously, so's she. Plus, I had no reason. I got tenure."

He shifted and patted my knee. It seemed premature to object. And I didn't want to object. I didn't want to die, but he didn't look like he was planning to kill me. Crush me, maybe, in his arms. Squeeze me where a woman wants to be squeezed. Please let him not kill me before we have foreplay, or, as women call it, sex.

"I'm not like you. Your professor father. Your artist mother. You have a PhD of your own, is what Allison told me. You're just slumming with this investigation. I grew up in Rice, Minnesota, population 1,500. The nearest big town was St. Cloud. My father drove a truck for the Prairie Potato Company and my mother worked at Katie Ann's Country Pie. They are still there and I don't visit the way I should. I got to Amherst because Katie Ann's older brothers went there on hockey scholarships and Katie Ann got Amherst to take an interest. The MG was her brother Don's, he died last May. If it wasn't for Katie Ann and Don, I'd be the manager of Country Pie right now. When I got to Amherst, I had three pairs of pants, three shirts, one sweater, and my dad's parka. No guitar. No bike. No car, no checkbook, and no ticket home."

I felt his anger and loneliness, still hot after fifteen years of practiced charm and simulated ease.

"I didn't know what a salad fork was, you know? That was okay because at that time everybody who did know pretended they didn't. But we all knew the difference between people who thought salad forks were bourgeois bullshit and people who just didn't know what the hell those little forks were for. Anyway, my roommates were three very cool guys from Grosse Pointe and Hyde Park and Long Island. They called me 'Harold' to be funny, sometimes they called me 'Junior' because the one time Katie Ann called, to see how I was getting on, she asked for Harold Junior. They were up and coming, and they made a consortium, started a business. Of course, I had no capital, so I was the legs. We sold dope and for the first time in my life, I had money. I bought CDs. I bought a bicycle, I bought a box spring. I was as happy as a pig in shit."

"And you got caught."

I cut him off because the streetlights were far behind and I felt too sorry for him.

"Yup, I got caught. They couldn't expel the brains of the group since his father had just bought them a laboratory, so they just suspended the three of them for a year. It was longer for me, because I lost my scholarship. I waited tables. I hustled." He shook his head and chewed on a thumbnail. "When we got back to school, a year later, the other guys moved into an apartment off campus. I couldn't afford it. I took classes part-time."

He pulled off to the side of the road, and turned off the lights and the engine in two quick, smooth passes.

"Doesn't make a very good impression, I know. Drug dealer. I want you to like me, because I like you."

He put his hand on my neck and began massaging it lightly. It was unpleasant. I pulled forward, away from his hand, and in the moonlight, I saw him watching me, unsmiling.

"It doesn't make a bad impression," I said. "It's who you were a long time ago. Everybody has a past with something not so nice in it."

"Whatever. Now, I'm doing okay. Still paying off loans and the lawyer but . . . Well, that's my dirty secret. What's yours?"

"I do have a PhD. I used to teach English and I fucked up."

"People do," he said. "How did you fuck up?"

I didn't say anything. Even in the service of this investigation, I wouldn't give it to him.

"Everyone makes mistakes. Slept with a . . . student?"

I snorted. "Slept with a nineteen-year-old? Why, for my sins?"

He smiled. He began stroking my leg, massaging it as he had my neck, round and round in delicate, tender whorls. Unpleasant.

"You don't like that, do you?"

"I don't."

I moved my leg. He held on to my hand and pressed it to his lips.

"I inherited a PI agency from my uncle. Now it's what I do."

"I'm very attracted to you, Dell. You know I am."

He kissed me, warm, soft, firm, and I kissed him back.

"You're very special," he said. "You are. You know you are."

The words undid the kiss. I didn't know if he'd done this too often and was just fed up with the whole trope of romantic banter or if he liked to demean women he was attracted to. If you want a man who likes women as women *and* as people *and* likes to have sex with them, I'm on your side but don't get your hopes up. Whatever Harry was, the hairs on my neck were as stiff as quills and I began to think, more urgently, about getting out of there.

"I'd like to lie in bed with you a few times, before we make love. Just lie with each other, get to know each other's bodies, enjoy each other, without sex, without pressure." He murmured in my ear. "I want to appreciate you, watch you, I want you to teach me all about your body and I'll teach you about mine. And then, when we're ready, we'll make love."

Oh, that should have sounded good but it sounded bad. I'd have rather babysat Mrs. Freedman. I'd have rather watched *Riverdance* with Mr. Freedman.

I spoke very softly, concentrating on not yelling. "Oh, wow, Harry. Gee, I'm a little overwhelmed. Could you take me back to my place, please? I can't think straight."

He laughed and started the car, snaking one hand under my shirt, stroking my stomach. I certainly had him on the ropes. My adrenaline was pumping along as visions of myself mutilated alternated with visions of Harry's golden head between my legs. The man had his wires crossed and it was catching.

Harry drove me back in silence, patting my hand, reassuringly. I don't think he knew he scared me. Or maybe that's why he was smiling.

I stumbled getting out of the car. Harry was right there to catch me. In the yellow, industrial light of the guesthouse porch, I felt safe again and let him put his arms around me. Another excellent kiss. It's in his kiss, Betty Everett said. I wished the answer was in his kiss. I was pretty sure it wasn't. We locked eyes and then he looked away.

"You're making me work for it," he said. "We've got a date, for sometime soon, right? Please, don't forget about me, 'cause I won't forget about you."

He drove off in the silly car and I thought, *What was* that?

The Lonesome Road

Friday, August 23

I slept badly, having the kind of dreams that men like Harry inspire. I woke up sweaty, damp in patches, and hearing my own groans. I showered and changed into my jeans and a T-shirt and put my hair up. It was 7:00 A.M. and I was ready to face the unpleasant music of more people who didn't want to talk to me. I was going to confront people and buy doughnuts. My plan was to ply everyone with fresh doughnuts. I hadn't seen this done on *Law & Order* but I was doing it, anyway. I got into my car and headed for town.

Two rabbits lit across the road. I rode into the swerve, the way Uncle Lou taught me, and eased down on the brakes. Nothing happened, so I pumped them. More nothing. And then, very slowly, a great deal seemed to happen. The bushes came towards my car and I heard glass splintering and felt the steering wheel leave the dash and the airbag explode into my chest and chin. My neck was pressed against the steering wheel and my face felt like a hard-boiled egg kicked over at a picnic. The airbag and the steering wheel, however, felt quite firm, even unyielding. Wherever I was, it was very dark. I could barely see daylight through the branches and they were strictly decorative.

I don't know how long I sat there, afraid of broken glass enmeshing me, wondering why my arms were numb. I was panting and there was a terrible, lurching pain in my neck and shoulders. I shut my eyes tight and began to brush things off my face and hair. Since my fingers didn't have much feeling, I sometimes poked rather than brushed but, eventually, I felt safe enough to open my eyes and begin to look around.

I had driven into a copse of oak trees, mostly saplings, or else I'd have been dead. The front of the car now extended about thirty inches past my feet and there was only a wide, lacy glass pattern where the solid windshield used to be. One large branch had knocked out most of the window on the passenger side and was resting right where my head would have been, if it hadn't been neatly tucked up over the steering wheel. My arms tingled, painfully, and I pulled my hands into my sleeves to dust myself off, hoping nothing had cut me any place that mattered. My face, for vanity, my hands, for dexterity. My legs ached and my hips were stiff but things seemed to be moving okay except for my left knee, which must have banged into the door and was pulsing like a heartbeat. I pushed open the door and dragged myself out, falling into a huge mountain laurel shrub. Leaves and branches crushed and crunched under me. Showers of glass came down with every move of my hands and arms. I could feel the tiny, biting sprinkles of it falling from my hair to my neck and under my shirt. I rolled out of the mountain laurel and fell onto the dirt. The path to the guesthouse seemed miles away. I got to my knees, gave myself a mental kick in the ass and either passed out and then threw up or the other way around.

My face felt like the bottom of a dumpster, rusting on damp grass. The sky was bright blue. I cleared my throat cautiously and rough, froggy sounds came out. I drew a few shallow breaths, got cocky, and took a deep one. I bit my lip to keep from shouting out. The pain was deep in my back and chest and like a wheel of knives, turning through me, coming back for another spin every time I moved. My spongy cheek felt not quite connected to the bone underneath. I couldn't wait to look in the mirror. I don't know how long it took me to limp to my beautiful room. I wasn't ready to call Theo and worry him and there was no point in calling my father. That girl was not by the desk and I could crawl up the stairs without her watching. By the time I got to the landing, sweat was pouring off me.

I lay down for a few minutes and crawled down the hall. I climbed from the floor to my bed and very slowly shed my stiff jeans, now covered in dirt, grass stains, vomit, and splotches of blood. My right arm hurt too much for me lift it past my rib cage, which also hurt like hell. I wrestled off my bra and my bloody T-shirt and heard the glass tinkle to the floor as my shirt pulled the slivers along my skin. There wasn't as much damage as I expected. I had looked worse when I got in Boom-Boom

Wolinsky's way at our championship rugby game. I turned on the shower and found that I couldn't raise my right arm to wash my hair and that I didn't really know how to do anything with my left. I poured shampoo all over my bruising body, coming up all colors, and mooshed it around with my left hand and a washcloth. Then I sat down in the shower until the hot water ran out. The drying off was worse than the shower. My phone rang as I was drying my hair. Hang up, you sonofabitch, I thought, and brushed my hair with my fingers.

Paganini rang and rang, filling the room.

"Pop?"

"Dell, I can't find my keys."

I sat down, so I wouldn't fall down, and saw that there was a trickle of blood coming from somewhere below my ear, slowly scrolling down my body.

"Okay, Pop. Where are you going?"

"I was going to go to the store."

"Pop," I said. "You don't drive anymore. You don't need the keys. Bev comes by, after breakfast"—I didn't know what time it was and I couldn't focus on the numbers on my phone. "Bev'll take you if you want."

"I like Bev," my father said, sounding like someone I had never met.

"Yeah, you do. Me, too."

"So, what time will Bev be here?"

"Oh, she gets there . . . after breakfast. You have breakfast, Pop. Eat a slice of bread with butter and honey. Go outside and get *The Times*. By the time you've seen what's what and who is ravaging our country, Bev'll be there."

"Fine," my father said. "Where the hell is your mother?"

I had to say what I hated to say but I couldn't bring myself to do what the doctor said: Deflect and redirect. "She's dead, Pop. Mama died five years ago."

"I know," he said. "I know that. Good talking to you."

Good days and bad days is what the doctor'd said. No lie.

The phone rang again.

Caller unknown. I couldn't decide if it was better to let someone know they failed to kill me or to play possum for a little while. I think a real detective would have known.

"Yes?"

No answer. Just someone making sure that I wasn't okay and I wasn't. I took four aspirin and would have taken four codeine or four oxy, if I'd had any. I lay down in bed, favoring my torso's left side and my face's right. I felt like a mother with screaming twins. I pulled up the blankets, making the most of their college-laundry smell and threadbare smoothness, reminding me of my goofy, golden college days when, despite all the idiotic things I did, I walked out with my BA and no real harm done.

My phone rang again. Goddammit to hell, Unknown Caller.

"Hello?"

No answer. Had I managed to pick up two enemies with homicidal tendencies in three days? I got up and put on sweats and sneakers, like an eighty-year-old getting ready for laps at the mall. If I was going to the medical center, I had to be decent but I couldn't manage a bra. The adrenaline had seeped out of my body and I lay down again. Glass slivers, pounding face, and throbbing knee got me up.

The girl at the desk was still MIA. A fifteen-minute walk to the Centerville Urgent Care was impossible. I rang the Centerville Taxi Company and got a recording. I rang them twice and then two Uber drivers ghosted me and then I couldn't do more. I walked for a miserable half hour to Centerville Urgent Care. I threw the receptionist my Mastercard, went through the swinging doors, past two boys in soccer uniforms with matching black eyes, and lay down in the first empty room. The receptionist or nurse wore tight, pastel scrubs, like she was starring in *Hot Babes of Urgent Care.* She followed me, my credit card in her beautifully manicured little fist.

I've always hated hospitals, nursing homes, places like that. The smell makes me sick. When my mother was in and out, that last year, I'd step off the elevator, head towards her hospital room, and have to stop in at stall number three in the ladies' room, every time.

A different nurse shook me gently. I didn't think I'd even closed my eyes.

"Hey, there, Ms. Chandler. Dell. Did you hit your head in your . . . fall?"

She loomed over me, a nice dark face with shiny, gold-flecked eyes, a pound of mascara, and a few acne scars showing through her foundation. Her braids swung down to her ass.

"I may have."

I felt wobbly and tearful and weird. I'd also forgotten how I'd gotten there.

"I guess I can go home now."

I stood up and felt her short, thick arms around my waist and under my shoulders.

"No, you can't. You can have a friend or family member pick you up, after your exam."

I started to cry.

"Or, we'll call you a Lyft. Dr. Weiss'll be in in a minute. She's good."

I blotted my face.

Dr. Weiss was good, thank God. And quick, with a light, sure touch, which was especially welcome since our time together was spent with her picking glass out of my legs and scalp, from my fall into the windshield-laden mountain laurel. She told me that I was the luckiest person she'd met all week. She was short and square with a long, solid pale face, too much nose, too many teeth, and intelligent hazel eyes almost hidden by her Coke bottle lenses.

When she'd put the last sliver in a large kidney-shaped bowl and covered me with antibiotic gel and checked my pupils for the fourth time, she put her hands on her wide hips and said, "So, who put you through a window face first?"

She looked smart and capable, easy with her competence and skill. She knew she could fix it, if I let her. I thought of explaining about the accident (I think someone tried to kill me) and thought she'd encourage me to go to the police and then I'd have to explain my mishap to the dread Hadley and Morse or worse, be told to leave the investigating to the experts. Worse, I might have to return the check.

I thanked Dr. Weiss for her kindness and climbed off the table, slowly.

"You're going to be black and blue for a while. Also, sore. If you get increased redness or swelling where I took out the glass, come back. Also, if you spike a fever, call me. Don't forget—Dr. Weiss. If this happens again, call 911, then call me."

I shook her hand and she looked at me closely.

She said, "You're not going to win any beauty contests this week. Buy some Dermablend, if you have to go anywhere. The right side of your face is pretty swollen, like your right arm. Your rotator cuff took a beating. Ice everything up and sleep on two pillows. You're very lucky."

"I can tell," I said.

There was an Uber waiting for me outside the big automatic entry doors. I told the guy where to take me and stretched out in the back seat.

You Send Me

I woke up feeling old, stiff, and worried. I now looked as bad as I felt. I studied me in the little mirror above the bureau. Half my face looked red and rug burned, the other half looked like an ad for a battered women's shelter. My right eye was a slit, surrounded by dappled dark blue and a green puff above and below. My right cheek was swollen purple and shiny, like a baby eggplant, and the right side of my jaw was a mottled yellow-blue up to my swollen ear. I'd thought vanity wasn't one of my sins (pride and smart-assery, is what I thought) and now I knew better. I didn't mind not being gorgeous but I wasn't prepared to be grotesque. I didn't think grotesque would elicit confession. I felt small, weak, and stupid. I decided that I would just fucking lie and cheat my way through the day, if necessary, with Dermablend, to protect my tiny, shell-less self, and I'd rent a car so that I wouldn't arrive for every meeting bathed in sweat.

My phone dinged with a voicemail from Detective Hadley; he said he was going on vacation but that should there be any reason to be in touch, Detective Morse would handle that. I called the police station and left a charming, even winsome, message for Morse. I apologized for my existence. I acknowledged that they were the experts. I repeated my line about my being the extra effort that Liz Cutty wished to show the world, and I made it clear that I knew my place. I expressed a fond hope that we'd be sharing information soon.

I showered, shouting and cursing through the agony of drying off. I Googled car repair in Centerville and went with the first place that had a good review in the last year.

I told Danny Gallitto of the ABC Garage where my car was.

"You're this morning's wreck on Sycamore?" he said.

I said, yes, that was me.

"Buy a lottery ticket, lady. That car is over. Finito."

"What do I do," I said, and I heard the tears coming up, and so did he.

"I'll tow it and sell it for scraps and what I'm gonna get will cover the cost of the tow and that's about that."

"Could you also check the brakes, please? I'd like a full report on the brakes."

"What am I checking for?" he asked.

"Please check and see if someone tampered with the brakes. I know that sounds ridiculous—"

"Nope. I've been divorced three times. I'll check. My cousin Steve owns a Rent-a-Wreck. You want the number? Or I can just . . . Stevie! Line two."

Steve Gallitto picked me up and rented me a filthy, smoke-spewing Honda from Gallitto's Garage in less than twenty minutes. He gave me ten dollars of free gas and made me an excellent espresso from his machine in the back. He did not flinch when he looked at me. He introduced me to the third Gallitto, Robbie, built like a brick shithouse, a soft-spoken bank teller at Cromwell Savings and an utter sweetheart. Robbie pulled out a folding chair and handed me a doughnut. I saw that I had completely misunderstood my own needs. I would make a good life in Centerville, answering the phones for and sleeping with the Gallitto cousins, and I'd let people say what they would.

I stopped at a pharmacy, where a cheerful gay man, as tall, slim, beige, and bald as RuPaul, wordlessly handed me the right shade of Dermablend as soon as I paused in front of him. I ducked into the restroom to smear it on and emerged squinty and misshapen but a uniform pale porcelain in color. I parked as close as I could to Callahan's Café in the north end of town and wished I hadn't left my stolen handicapped marker at the office. I didn't want to move. I wanted to read my phone, and wait for my face to heal, and maybe after a while some new leads would sashay up to me. This was not a plan. I didn't know what kind of plan to make for not being murdered.

Callahan's is the classic town-gown hybrid. The students from "up the hill" think that the steamed cheeseburgers and shitty coffee will put them in touch with the real world. Grown-ups come for the small self-indulgence, like buying Marlboros instead of generic cigarettes or going to the salon instead of having your sister's kid trim your ends. The two groups coexist. Mr. Callahan gives students the booth nearest the swinging kitchen door. I was about to plant my rear on a torn red vinyl stool when I saw Michelle Blanchfleur. She smiled and waved for me to come over to her booth. I was pleased. Maybe she liked me as much as I liked her. Maybe she'd contemplated my usefulness, as I'd contemplated hers. As one does.

"Hey, Dell. You want to eat with us? Mary, Mother of God, what happened to you?"

A man came out of the john and slid into the booth, next to me.

"This is my partner, Sgt. Nat Baker. This is Dell Chandler. She's the PI working for Cromwell on Bullfinch's death. Dell, sit down, for God's sake, before you fall over."

"Nice to meet you, Dell."

I couldn't tell if his not commenting on my face was good manners or indifference. I wasn't his partner, I wasn't breakfast, I wasn't important.

He was my height and broad through the shoulder and chest. His neck looked like a short, smooth tree trunk. He was very dark-skinned, more African midnight blue than American brown. His hair was cut short, almost eliminating the curl, and emphasizing his large, almond-shaped eyes with their tight, curly lashes. His ears were set neatly and very close to his skull. I had a great view of his profile, if I wanted. Small purple scar on the cheekbone near me. Clean-shaven, wide jaw, round chin. Nose like a hawk, sharp tip pointed towards the slightly compressed mouth, and arched, winglike nostrils. Tan windbreaker, to conceal his holster, tan and white polo shirt and khaki slacks not concealing sprinter's thighs. There was about an inch between us. His hands were longer than mine and very wide with rounded fingertips. His palms were pale pink, ashes of roses.

He cleared his throat. I may have been staring. I wanted to touch his neck, feel his Adam's apple move. My stomach hurt. I was acutely aware of my appearance.

"Bacon and eggs and rye toast," he said.

A pleasant tenor. He glanced out the window. I could hardly blame him. A man who was excited by my appearance today would be someone to stay away from.

"I don't know what to have, my jaw is a little tender, as you noticed. I had a car accident. But, I didn't hit the rabbit. What about you, Michelle?"

I decided to focus on my new friend, and on developing a new, bouncy personality.

"Lucky you didn't get hurt worse. I gotta watch my weight. I don't know. Just yogurt and coffee, I guess."

She sounded so wistful, like someone was taking her nice breakfast right out of her mouth.

"Bullshit." Oh, warm *and* forceful. "You do not need to lose weight and you can't go all day on scraps. You gotta eat right, girl."

And he looked at her affectionately. He wasn't a stone wall, he was a nice man. It was just me.

"Well, you know . . ." Her voice trailed off a bit and she slid a look at me.

Whatever the real issue was, it was obviously not going to be discussed in my presence. She ordered a fruit salad. Nothing more was said.

I had to order something.

"Poached eggs and a cup of tea."

Like a sullen child, hoping to be coaxed into the game. He was too short, anyway.

"Dell's here investigating Bullfinch's murder," she said again.

Nat Baker drank his coffee.

"Huh. Hadley and Morse?" They both laughed and I smiled as much as I could.

"I did leave messages for them. Multiple. I said I'd like to meet. I did meet with your chief."

"Hadley's fly-fishing in Canada. DiCo's put you on ice. They'll never see you," Nat Baker said. "You're white, which is a plus but, you're a woman and an outsider and snotty, with the PhD and all. They'll tell your boss that they tried, but they'd put your ass in jail before they'd help you."

Michelle nodded and shrugged.

"I'm not snotty," I said.

"Just saying what I've heard."

"Have you heard anything useful?" I said.

Nat Baker munched his toast. Michelle sipped her tea. They both looked at me, from a high, long way away.

Michelle pulled the blanket up over me and sat at the foot of my bed in the guesthouse.

"You're a mess," she said. "We had to bring you home. That accident did you in. Stop pushing."

And she was gone.

Dream a Little Dream

My sleep was so thick and deep, even phones ringing and the voices downstairs were just dream material. Nat Baker showed up in several. My message light was shining and my phone was still buzzing when I came back to life at noon. Harry's voice message asked me to meet him for lunch, at 1:30, if I could, at the Peking Gardens. He explained that he couldn't do it earlier because of his triathlon training. I lay in bed for a few minutes, patted my face to reassure me and it, and walked slowly down the stairs. Lunch with Harry might tell me something about something.

As I drove to Peking Gardens, I thought of my friend Junie, who graduated from Wisconsin, with a PhD in English, just when Harry did. If they were there at the same time, she'd have noticed him. Handsome, weird guy, I'd tell Junie. The kind of guy who might have tampered with my brakes before he got to the Freedmans' dinner party, twenty minutes late. The kind of guy who could have instructed Allison Shein, while he was kissing her, to fool with my brakes. Maybe. Probably not. Also, don't be a sexist bitch, Dell. Maybe she didn't need instructing. Or maybe she told him.

I strolled, if you can stroll with a limp, into the restaurant to meet Harry, who wanted to kill me, fool me, or have sex with me, or all three, or none of the above. I saw him before he saw me. He was a little less glorious. Blue shadows under his eyes and the twinkle on low. He looked almost real. He spotted me and the big, white grin spread over his pretty face, climbing into his eyes, like morning glory. We made pleasant remarks and I explained about my face and he made sympathetic noises about the accident and grabbed a table for two.

"That was some accident," I said. "Hoo boy."

I was laying breadcrumbs as thickly as I could.

Harry looked at me more closely.

"I see that," he said. "You should be more careful. Dell, excuse me, I'll just be a minute." He went in the direction of the men's room, waving to a few other faculty types, which did not seem, in itself, like a confession. I looked for a waiter. Michelle Blanchfleur sat by herself at a table for two. I smiled and waved. She hopped up and came over. Round and powerful, a Maillol in motion.

"Long time, no see. You're a hard woman to stop. Harry Markham? You like him for the . . ." She mimed bashing someone's head in and grinned.

"Could be. We could get together and talk sometime, over a beer."

"Sounds okay," she said, still hesitating. "You can meet Leah, the woman I live with."

I was stumbling in the dark. She seemed out, I seemed like someone who was fine with that. What was the problem with Leah?

"I'd like to," I said. "Maybe tomorrow night? Around 8:00? Text me your details. And, for the love of Jesus, if you see a waiter, send him this way, okay?"

Michelle set off for her table, still half frowning. She didn't agree to a get-together and something was wrong with her or Leah or her and Leah. Knowing that wasn't knowing much.

Harry came back to the table and we ordered. He wanted the vegetarian special with brown rice. I had egg drop soup, a plate of mei fun, and one steamed red bean paste bun because I couldn't quite chew.

Harry looked around and then grabbed my hand. "I just felt that last night, our conversation, and after . . . Maybe we're destined to be just friends. I didn't want you to hold it against me."

"Oh no," I said. "What's that country-western song, 'If I show you how much I love you, will you hold it against me?'"

He blushed, which was unnerving.

"It's okay," I said. "All of this murder and investigating and mistrust is getting to everyone I'm sure. I appreciate your confiding in me about what happened to you in college. At Amherst, right? Then, Wisconsin for your PhD, right?"

"Yup, you must have really studied my CV, Amherst and Wisconsin. You know, you're right, this murder is really eating some people up. I don't want to cast aspersions, I shouldn't say anything but I know how discreet you are, how professional."

Harry was even better at bold-faced bullshit than I was.

"Dan Fiske has seemed very odd, lately. Very tense whenever I see him. I know he likes Allison, of course, which is awkward, but, that's not all of it."

He'd noticed Dan's feelings for Allison; underestimating Harry was a stupid thing to do. Harry and Dan Fiske were two of the best observers of the department. Fiske, because he found the world interesting, Harry, because of his commitment to himself and his career.

"So, you and Allison—"

Michelle and another woman brushed past. Michelle and I smiled and the other woman stopped at our table. Her face was the opposite of Michelle's, no softness, no meadow prettiness. Just bone-deep willful beauty and too much getting her own way. A pair of dark arched eyebrows, two beautiful dark, dark eyes, and high, fierce cheekbones, under poreless chamois skin. Her teeth were as white as a toothpaste ad but Crest wouldn't advertise that sharp, feral mouth. Leah was shorter than the three of us, narrow shoulders and round hips, with breasts that almost overwhelmed her frame. She was wearing a beige tank top, soft brown yoga pants, and brown ballet slippers. Her glossy black hair was shoulder-length and thick, no wave. She was like a knife carved out of ivory, you couldn't resist running your finger along the blade, even as the cut opened up. She held her smile and stood there, breathing deeply, endangering the peace of mind of the men in her vicinity. Some of the women, too.

Michelle and I made introductions and Harry fastened his gaze on Leah Fields.

"It's great to meet you. Hey, do you guys want to go for ice cream with us? We're done, aren't we, Dell? We could go down to Bucky's."

He carefully counted out the exact bill and I added a couple of bucks. Not a generous man, I thought, or else very, very broke.

Bucky's ice cream has so much butterfat, you have to hold the cone with two hands. If I wanted to sell someone on Centerville, Bucky's ice cream would be where I'd start. When I lived with the Gallitto cousins, we would bring home Bucky's pints all the time. Leah smiled and held Michelle's hand for a moment. Harry's eyes blazed at that and then he composed a look of friendly interest.

Leah kept her eyes on Michelle's face and said, "Okay, Michi? Let's go."

No one was fooling anyone and the four of us trotted over to the ice cream shop. Harry made me his walking partner, to indicate that those tropical looks between him and Leah were nothing, really, just the way any two strangers might look at each other in a Chinese restaurant, on the way to really good ice cream.

His whole body leaned backwards, yearning towards Leah. It's hard for me to dislike the love struck. Even the lust struck. What he did with me last night was some kind of Kabuki of desire, painted to mislead, meaning something entirely different, but this wasn't that. His eyes burned when he looked at Leah. We settled into the shop, at one of the tippy, little Formica-topped tables, with the equally tippy wrought iron chairs. Leah looked like a Mayan princess, and the three of us looked like friendly giants from the North. I was about to comment on our sizes when I was struck by how alike Harry and Michelle looked: blond, thick hair, clear blue eyes, with thick lashes, flushed, pink complexions, and strong jaws. Harry's face was filled with desire and drive and Michelle's was already anticipating loss and loneliness. I couldn't think of anything to say that would make things better.

The waiter came with our cones and dishes and Harry tried to pay for everyone's. For one brief moment, the three women united in taking out our wallets. Harry grinned, sheepishly, and went back to staring at Leah.

I turned to Michelle.

"Did you grow up around here?"

"Do I dress that badly? I grew up in Boston, then we moved to Hartford when I was twelve. My father died when I was sixteen, my mother died the year after, and we moved down here to live with my aunt and cousins. We, meaning me and my little sister. I've been here—off and on—for twenty years. Too long."

She looked perturbed; the ones who always move question their capacity to commit; the ones who never move question their capacity to grow.

I told a couple of stories about my wild days, driving a truck across Alaska. Leah said she grew up in Montana, driving fast, at fourteen.

"Lead foot," Michelle said, fondly.

Leah shrugged.

Harry told the story of his little car and Leah said she had a Tesla.

"So good for the environment. And so quiet," she said. "They never hear you coming."

She licked her ice cream cone like a soft-core queen, pointy tongue swirling in and out of the ice cream, eyes lowered then suddenly, radiantly lifted. Harry licked his fingers, which didn't help. They were chaste and calm, waiting for their intergalactic, meteor-exploding rendezvous.

Michelle cleared her throat, wiped her hands, and threw the napkins down. She pushed back her chair. Leah made another pass at being present.

"So, Dell. A private investigator. So interesting. Fun."

She shook her head, gracefully tossing her black wave behind her. Harry was charmed. Michelle was, God bless her, embarrassed.

"We're out," Michelle said. "Nice meeting you."

She gathered up Leah, and napkins, and they left, with Leah giving Harry a perfectly calibrated quarter of a glance.

"See you," she said.

Harry stared after them with such naked longing, I wanted to throw a blanket over him.

"Well, what a treat," I said.

"Do you know Leah well? Flett, right?"

"Fields. I only just met her, through Michelle. They live together."

"What do you mean, live together? Like girlfriends? Leah's gay?"

"I think they're both gay, which is good, because they've been together a couple of years."

"Leah's not gay," he said, confidently.

Let me not assault a suspect, please.

"Oh, sure, it could be a huge misunderstanding that's been going on for a couple of years. Gosh, imagine their surprise."

"One swallow does not make a summer."

"Harry," I said, "why are we meeting? Why did we have lunch?"

I couldn't bring myself to say, *Why'd you change your mind?* It might have been the right question for a detective to ask but I couldn't ask a man why he'd lost interest in me, while my face looked like a farmer's market at the end of the day.

"No reason. You're interesting, like Leah said. Take care of those bruises."

I walked to my car groaning softly like an old person, which was now my habit, and smacked into a middle-aged blonde I thought I recognized.

"Excuse me, I wasn't looking where I was going."

"That's all right."

It was the screamer from Theo's bedroom. But, now her mouth was closed and she was dressed. Not really dressed, but floating in layers of ivory cashmere knotted at her neck and waist, her hands and sandals hidden somewhere in the creamy depths.

"Aren't you Dell Chandler? We have a mutual friend, Theodor Gurwitz."

How come everybody I met had more information and better manners than I did?

"Yes, I'm Dell." I wanted to scream: *I've seen your breasts! He's an old man!* "Theo's my godfather."

"Ah. I'm Daisy Lowell. Perhaps you'd like to stop by this evening? We'll be at home."

We'll be at home? They were living together and Theo hadn't told me. I needed a little time to process all the unsettling relationships flashing before me.

"Oh, busy tonight. I'm sorry. I'll call Theo tomorrow."

I did have Bullfinch files to read through.

"Of course. Anytime you can come, Theo would be delighted to see you."

The gentlest of reproaches, or maybe just my guilty conscience. My phone dinged with a text from one of my future romantic partners, Stevie Gallitto: *Brakes cut.* He added an emoji of a scissor and a black cat.

I called Junie Brown (now Junelle Brown-Mainor, PhD) at her home in Berkeley and finally got someone to tell me something useful. Junie remembered Harry clearly: uncircumcised, hygiene fanatic, and entirely capable of blackmail, in her opinion, but not murder. She said some dark rumors had circulated around his thesis and offered to call me back after she did a little research.

"He wasn't that smart, is what I'm saying. Weak upstairs, strong downstairs."

The research shouldn't be too hard, she said. She'd slept with the chair of the English Department when she was a grad student, flitting among the seminars, and he still sent her a very affectionate Christmas card and a dozen birds-of-paradise on her birthday.

"Damn right he does," we said, simultaneously.

Strange Things Happening Every Day

I piled on the Dermablend in my rearview mirror, and drove over to Mary Clark's house, my Honda announcing my arrival. I was going to solve this murder, get paid, buy a new car, and go the fuck home. Maybe Mary Clark, if she was inclined, was the person to help me. She lived in a small, navy blue house, almost a cottage, with long grass and wildflowers coming up to the windows. The shades were still drawn. I banged on the front and back doors and only the memory of Theo and Daisy kept me from barging in.

Mary Clark, now my favorite Cromwell professor, came to the door slowly and looked almost as bad as I did. Swollen eyes, red nose, and little red pimples on her cheeks.

"We had talked about having coffee together."

She stared at me.

"I'm Dell Chandler, I had hoped to talk with you a little about Professor Bullfinch."

"Ah. Yes. Not today. I'm too sick, I'm sorry. I got this dreadful summer cold—" She sneezed violently and pulled her red plaid robe tightly around her. "Call me in a day or two, I do want to talk to you, but I'm just too sick." She sneezed again and her eyes watered. "Two days. Good-bye. Be careful. More careful."

She shut the door in my face, and I stood on her doorstep, feeling deprived and injured. Two days? I banged on the door again. I was not going to be found dead because my manners were good.

"I'm sorry, I can't wait until you're feeling better. You get into bed; I'll make you a cup of tea or whatever and we'll talk."

I bustled her into her kitchen, taking advantage of her weakened state. I bullied her into lying down. I found some Earl Grey, made a pot, and threw in a jigger of gin, my own home remedy for colds. With her blankets pulled up, propped up on two big pillows, sipping tea, she didn't look so sick and maybe I wasn't such a bad person.

She sipped her tea.

"Something happened between Harry Markham and Oliver," she said. "I don't know what but he, Oliver, was furious and threatened to undo Harry's tenure, which was ridiculous. Oliver couldn't stand Allison, either, but her tenure decision was already made and she wasn't getting it. It was over, for her."

"Why?"

"Wonderful record of publications. Not a popular teacher. Not a very good teacher, either. Terrible colleague. Didn't do her share, ducked out of committees, and was disrespectful of conversations people thought were confidential. One time she called a job candidate who was a friend of hers and told him that we weren't going to offer him the job. She called him two days before the chair did and suggested he sue us! When we—Oliver and I—were designated to talk to her about it, she defended herself with some tragic bullshit about being brave enough to put her friend before her employer."

"Very E. M. Forster."

"No doubt. She was dishonest and disagreeable and although I'm aware that we are a motley assortment of oddballs and petty tyrants, we do follow certain rules of decorum. She didn't. Anyway, something got Oliver very upset this past spring. We had a departmental meeting after which I saw Oliver speaking to Harry in private, and then Oliver left, very upset, yelling his head off. Oliver took his name off his door and no one saw him for a week."

She coughed and slid down her pillows.

"Bullfinch took his name off the door?"

She looked embarrassed.

"It's what some people do when they want to show that they are . . . not participating."

I loved the image of professors, sulking in their offices for days, nameplates clutched in their hands.

"All right. His nameplate is *off.* Hellzapoppin'. Then what? Did you ask him what was up—when his nameplate was back up?"

"I did not. Right after he spoke to Harry, he was yelling down the hall at him, about common human decency and principles. Yelling all the way down the hall."

"Do you know how it was resolved?"

"No idea. I finished classes and went to see my daughter and my daughter-in-law in Savannah for two weeks. I got back the day before that reception you came to. I didn't come back for Ollie's funeral, I'm sorry to say. Well, not terribly sorry, I hate funerals."

"Me, too."

Her eyes closed.

"I'm sorry," I said. "Just two more questions.

"You knew Oliver Bullfinch and . . . Mrs. Bullfinch." I couldn't remember her name for money. "Mrs. Bullfinch's been dead for three years. Was there anyone else in his life? Did he love anyone?"

She cracked one eye open.

"We never spoke of love."

"What was Mrs. Bullfinch like?"

"Harsh. Not unpleasant—to me."

"One more. Could someone confirm that you were visiting your daughter in Savannah on Tuesday, August 6?"

Now I was embarrassed. She laughed and coughed.

"Sorry. Go to sleep," I said. "We'll talk some more later. It's okay. Rest."

I pulled up her blankets, washed the spoon and washed out the teacup, and locked the door on my way out.

I Said I Was Sorry

I slept for two hours and woke up knowing I'd forgotten something. Several things. I called Liz Cutty's cell phone and said I knew I was about eight hours late but I could be over in a few minutes, if she wanted to discuss things in person. I changed my shirt and reapplied the Dermablend.

She looked cool, even frozen, in pale blue silk everything. She poured two glasses of wine.

"What happened to this morning? Then, we would have had coffee."

I told her everything, such as it was. She looked mildly concerned about the accident, slightly more so when I said it wasn't an accident. She asked me whom I'd been pressuring and I told her the truth.

"I've been pestering everyone I can. The word *relentless* has been used. That Harry Markham, he's something."

"How do you mean?"

She sat on the edge of her desk, swinging one foot, in a weirdly girlish way.

"Well, he seems like a real lady-killer, you should pardon the expression."

She chuckled.

"Gossip like that tends not to reach my ears." She sipped her wine. "The downside of no longer being a faculty member."

"Is there anything that *has* reached your ears that might help here? I'm not making great headway. Dan Fiske is smart and ambitious, Harry is creepy and ambitious, Allison is sad and ambitious, and I'm pretty sure that neither of the Freedmans or Mary Clark killed Bullfinch. There's a woman in a photo I can't identify. Also, I saw Mary a few hours ago and she has a really bad cold."

Liz Cutty actually looked sad. "You're behind. She doesn't have a cold. She has pneumonia and the ambulance brought her to the hospital two hours ago. Her cleaning lady came by and found her unconscious, in bed."

"Shit. I like her."

I shouldn't have left. I could have sat by Mary Clark's bed and read from Toomer and kept an eye on her.

"Me, too."

I couldn't say a word. I showed Cutty the photo of Barefoot and Lovely. She shook her head.

"I have another appointment," she said. "Don't give up."

I knew the murderer was out there. Everyone in Centerville knew that. When I stopped by for my espresso, the Gallitto cousins offered me their futon in the back room, for safety. I didn't know if the murderer was also the Brake Cutter, or if that person was just a good friend of the murderer or someone whom I had pissed off for a different reason entirely. Maybe Allison Shein was capable of trying to kill me because Harry seemed, briefly, interested in me? Why was that interest so brief and so showy? Was he trying to provoke Allison, to call my attention to what she was really capable of? Did Harry cozy up just so he could turn my attention to Dan Fiske? So far, the people with motive had good alibis. And even people with no motive had some kind of alibi. Someone was lying, probably several people, maybe all of them. I decided to take myself back to the Gallittos and then onto Bullfinch's. Maybe I'd do better with the dead; the living were running circles around me and I seemed to have lost my only advantage—a cheerful doggedness.

Stevie waved me onto their floral sofa. Danny fired up another espresso and Robbie ("My day off") brought forth a plate of biscotti.

"'Sup," Danny said. "Ya look beat."

I sighed. We all ate Mrs. Gallitto's biscotti, which were, as I knew they would be, amazing. Lemon, with actual zest.

I said that I had a few suspects and really shouldn't talk about it.

The cousins nodded.

Danny, as the gracious host, led with subjects of mutual interest. He said that he'd heard, over the police transmitter, always on in his office, that there'd been a terrible hit-and-run late last night.

"Poor stunad. Walking his dog, side of the road. Bam."

We asked the usual questions: Did they catch the guy who did it (no), was there lots of blood (probably), did the stunad have kids (no idea) and we finished the biscotti. I kissed each of them good-bye, which was delightful, and went back to work.

I stood in front of Bullfinch's house and waved to Mrs. Wallace's kitchen window. My good luck, one window screen was loose and one window was not locked. Bullfinch's garage looked like my father's: tidy stacks of paperbacks on steel bookshelves, prewar filing cabinets, a neat row of six boxes, obviously filled with something, sitting on another set of steel shelving. And below all that, chaos. An old, dented Audi, under a very dusty, undisturbed tarp. Broken lawnmower, heaps of twine, rusted gardening shears, split garden hoses. Bullfinch took care of what he cared about and managed to ignore the rest. The paperbacks and boxes were dusty; the filing cabinets, tucked in the corner, were surrounded by a ruffle of crumpled newspapers, and they were not dusty. The key to them was hung on the back of the cabinet, with a tag marked "Files."

I blessed his orderly, obsessive, belt-and-suspenders heart. Recent emails were printed up and in the top file, and the very most recent in the front of that top file. The very top file was filled with insurance forms, bills, and payments from the last year. SOUTHERN CONNECTICUT ONCOLOGY and COMPLETE BLOOD COUNT, LIVER FUNCTION TEST, and SERUM BILIRUBIN were on almost every form. I recognized the test from my mother's pancreatic cancer. Unlike my mother, who tried every form of chemo and radiation they'd give her, Bullfinch was having nothing. He was just dying, maybe from spring to summer to fall or even past that. Someone had speeded it up for him. I wondered if he was grateful when he understood what was happening. I think my mother would have paid good money, that last month, to have someone walk into her bedroom and brain her with a bronze bust.

There were no photos. There were five red folders, marked "Bank," containing bank statements for what looked like the last ten years. Four blue, "Taxes." And three pink, "Inheritance," which were empty except for a stack of blank stationery from the Michigan law offices of Morton Schneiderman. The other folder titles were unfortunately, entirely, and remarkably creative. His emails from Allison Shein were in a folder marked "Succubae." I did like that, but then I read the emails. They made me feel sorry for her, on the fatiguing grounds of sisterhood. Each email (and some were emails then printed up on his stationery and placed in his file for some kind of emphatic officiousness) was a screed of condescension, arrogance, and evasion. The gist of her early emails was "I'm doing a good job, I'm getting to be a better teacher and I'm a brilliant scholar. I understand that you do not feel I have done my share of committee work. I will do better. Please, vote to give me tenure." The gist of his was "I've been assigned to work with you on your case, and so I must. I didn't vote to bring you here in the first place and your performance has confirmed my good judgment. You may be smart but you're rude. You have strange and unpleasant ideas and you have no respect for your elders. Do not expect the department to put you forward for tenure, if I have anything to say about it."

Her emails got increasingly bitter, his got shorter, and then they stopped, in May. I combed through all the folders, noting the names and dates. There was a last folder, brighter ivory than the others, the words on one tab: "Act IV."

A car door slammed and I slipped all the folders into my bag.

I Really Don't Want to Know

The front steps creaked. I flattened myself behind the door leading to the house and waited, trying not to breathe. I smelled him before I saw him. Nat Baker smelled like vanilla beans.

I said, slowly and calmly—in case he was trigger-happy—"Nat, this is Dell Chandler. I'm behind the door and I'd like to come out now."

He closed the door to look at me. He blinked twice, which I took to mean that he was surprised to see me.

"Hey, Dell." Charmer. "Mrs. Wallace was worried about you."

"Huh," I said.

"What'd you find?"

He looked over my shoulder, out the garage window and into the yard.

"Not much," I lied and managed not to hug my bag to my side.

If I put some pieces together, I'd tell Michelle to let him know. Maybe.

"Oh. Your face looks a little better."

"Yeah. So, I'll see you, Nat."

I've always been attracted to the unapproachable, but these last couple of years, I have made an effort. Nat Baker had a Do Not Touch sign as broad as his back and I was trying hard to remember that Do Not Touch means "Do Not Touch." It does not mean, "I look forward to your sensitivity and tenderness melting the barriers between us." I showed off my mental health for the Universe: I turned away and headed right out, leaving him to close the garage door.

It started to rain. I mean, it started to fucking pour. I'd never seen Nat smile before. His smile looked as reluctant as mine felt.

He followed me out.

"You want a ride, wherever you're going?"

"No, thanks. I like to walk."

"I like your walk."

I rolled my eyes.

Nat pushed me towards his navy blue Camry and I got out of the rain. After two miles, heading away from town, Nat asked me, "You want to come to my place for some coffee?"

He sounded like someone was strangling him.

"Coffee? Sure," said Bright-Eyed Susie.

We rode in silence all the way to his small red and white clapboard house, off a dirt road and right in the middle of a small forest.

We parked and I admired the view, putting off getting wet and whatever followed. I dashed between the Norfolk and white pines and through the remnants of an old stone wall. His front porch looked comfortable for one person, with an old red canvas director's chair and an embroidered red leather hassock. Nothing else. I hesitated at the front door. He turned and reached back for me. His hands shook.

We stood in his small, clean kitchen.

"Coffee?"

I felt like screaming, "Coffee? Are you out of your tiny mind? Did you bring me here for coffee?"

"No, thanks," I said.

"It's all right," he said and I thought, I certainly hope so.

He reached out his hand for me again and I took it. His hand was wet and hot, like a sick baby. He held my face and kissed me for a second, running the tip of his tongue over my lips, outlining my mouth. We went upstairs to his bedroom. I stood still, feeling foolish, watching him. With two angry pulls, Nat yanked the heavy gray curtains closed and the room became dusky. Suddenly, it was twilight and his face was impenetrable. I unbuttoned my shirt and he sat on the low, wide bed, watching me. He put his gun in the night table drawer and lay his holster on the floor, by the side of the bed. As I slipped off my jeans, he abruptly pulled his shirt up over his head and threw it on the floor. He stood up and pulled off his jeans, briefs, and socks, in one practiced move. I wanted to see him but he had closed the curtains so emphatically, I didn't have the chance. Not a good sign, for either of us.

I was cold and tired and realized I had nothing else to take off. He pulled me to the bed. I leaned towards him and he saw the big pansy of a bruise on my shoulder. Oh, he said. Maybe not?

I stretched out on top of him. He whispered sad little sounds into my ear and buried his face in my neck and disappeared into me. He held on to my shoulders as though someone was trying to tear us apart and he flipped me under him, bucking and rocking above me, drops of sweat falling from his chest onto mine, making us slide against each other, losing our grip. For a minute, before he came, he looked into my eyes and I saw such strain and evasion that I looked away. I lay still and limp, lacing my hands behind his thick, wet neck, waiting for him to stop. He groaned painfully, as if he'd been punched and fell off me, into a dead sleep. Or the imitation of sleep.

Well.

I pulled his sticky arm off my hair. I studied the veins in his wrist. I counted to a hundred and got up, feeling greasy and abstracted, the way you feel after a six-day hike and all you want is a hot shower and a decent meal. I gathered my clothes and my sneakers and went quietly downstairs. Most of me did not want him to wake up. I dried myself off with some paper towels in the kitchen, threw them in the garbage bag, and put on my clothes.

I started to run home and my knees and ribs stopped me at the corner. I got to walk home, in the lashing rain, through the puddles, without an umbrella, while cars passed me.

Perfect.

Can't Nobody Love You

Text from Allison: *In lounge, 3rd floor. Sorry.* No cute emojis, no *LOL*, no *hahahaha*, no *LMAO*, no *Sorry 4 ducking u, boo.*

She was alone, a small, angry marmoset with a laptop and a cup of tea. I was the enemy. Harry had driven me home from the Freedmans'. We had been seen eating egg drop soup together.

"Things have just been crazy," she said. "You can't imagine."

I could imagine. Killing Bullfinch, cutting my brakes, blowing Harry whenever he texted, trying to get your book published and your grant secured, and finding another job, when your last one ended with no tenure, and avoiding arrest. Crazy busy. Jeez, plus packing for Paris.

"Look, Dell. These are the facts. Bullfinch was a bully. He was also a sexual predator," Allison said primly.

"Really. Is there a record of complaints filed against him? Liz Cutty didn't mention that."

She shrugged. "No kidding. What girl's going to complain that her thesis advisor raped her, and still expect to graduate summa cum laude. He *was* the Honors Committee."

"He raped a student? At his age?"

"It's common knowledge. Ask around. Age has nothing to do with it. My God," she said, meaning, you self-loathing anti-feminist troglodyte.

"I sure will. Do you have a name of this student?"

"I'm not going to reveal the name of the victim without her permission."

Meaning, no idea. Possibly meaning, there is no such girl.

"Well, that'll make it hard for me to interview her," I said. "I can check with the university but they're not going to give me her name. How about Harry?"

She froze. She understood my question correctly.

"Harry is not a sexual predator. There are no charges against him, ever. I'm sure."

"Good," I said. "I mean, I gather he's quite a hit with the ladies but, everyone's willing and not an undergraduate, is my guess. Why not?"

She looked disgusted.

"I'm just asking. And didn't Harry have trouble with Bullfinch, too? Did the two of you compare notes, talk about how to handle him?"

"You don't understand. Harry and I have been working on some joint projects for two years. Bullfinch was opposed to everything either one of us did." She smiled, uncertainly. "Harry did everything he could to get me tenure, but . . ."

"It seems to me, frankly, it seems to everyone around here, from what they tell me, that you were the brains of the partnership."

Allison smiled and I thought, she's not ugly.

"Look, Harry and Bullfinch had problems. Bullfinch and I had problems. But, in the end, Harry got tenure. I didn't. Things . . . broke his way. They usually do."

I could see the story she was telling herself: partner not victim. But.

"When in the history of the world have things not generally broken the man's way? Rosalind Franklin. Katherine Johnson. Vera Rubin. You do the work, he gets the credit. Am I wrong?"

"Who's Vera Rubin?"

"Astronomer. Dark matter. Screwed out of advancement and fame. You know. When was the last time you saw Bullfinch?"

She sighed. "Didn't you read our statements? I saw him on the way up to my office. I was meeting Harry, we met every Tuesday to talk about our work. My office or his. I think it was about 1:45 because Harry and I always met at 2:00."

"Still doing that?" I said.

"We'll start again soon. I do need to go over some things with—"

Harry stuck his beautiful head in the door.

"Two of my favorite ladies! What's the scoop?"

Allison radiated warmth. Me, not so much.

"You can join us," I said. "We're just talking about the last time either one of you saw Bullfinch."

"You're a pit bull—1:50," he said. "Allison and I were meeting at 2:00 to talk about our various projects. I stopped in my office—where I happened to get a phone call about my book's publishing date and I ran into Bullfinch and told him the good news and then I ran to Allie's office and told her the same thing."

Allison looked less happy. She looked annoyed.

"Is that any different from your memory?" I said.

"No," she said. "That's my memory, too. Harry was very excited about his book coming out. We spent a lot of time talking about his book that afternoon."

"Harry," I said, "Allison said that you intimidated Bullfinch. I wonder—"

"Gotta go. I've got a call coming." Harry turned to leave.

Allison grabbed her sad little chartreuse sweater and her big backpack and put her arm through his.

"I'll walk you out, Harry," she said. "We need to catch up."

Who's the snake, who's the mongoose?

Just Out of Reach

I didn't take the grimy green elevator (*Mark sucks*, *Phi Delt blows*, *Take Back the Night*) down. Instead, I walked down the dark hallway, just the blurry light from one long fluorescent rod reflecting off the gray floor. What a tomb. Wrong thought.

The cleaning people weren't in evidence and I wondered what catching up would look like for Allison and Harry. Getting their stories straight, burying bodies, some kind of exchange in which whatever it was, Harry got the better deal. No matter what they were doing, I thought Allison would want to meet in her office and he'd go along because, after all, he got tenure. I might have ten minutes. There was no light under Harry's door, no rustling papers within. I stood in the hall for a moment, just listening to my own heavy breathing. When I was a baby, my mother said she could hear me breathing all the way down the hall. When I'm anxious, I sound like a runner on the last lap. And when I run, I sound like a freight train.

Panting away, I pushed on Harry's door. Locked, of course. A real detective would whip out a credit card and jimmy the little latch. I tried that and bent my Mastercard. I gave the door a discreet, ladylike shove and nothing happened. Finally, I took out the Swiss Army knife Theo got me when I was twelve and used the long, flat blade to push back the wobbly catch. It worked. I was amazed.

The sun was high and hot and outside the campus looked lovely, caught in a golden haze. The room was half in shadow but I could see enough. I shut the door behind me and looked around Harry's cubicle. With the promotion, he might move up to a 15 × 15 room, with a rug and maybe a nice armchair. But for now, he had a standard issue assistant professor's cubby: black-and-white speckled linoleum, black desk with fake-walnut trim, and matching fake-walnut chair with an orange cushion. The only nice touch was the large bay window and its window seat, desecrated by another fluorescent orange cushion. The university must have gotten a great deal on that fabric. It clashed with everything and was in every office I'd seen—except the president's. There were two photos of Hemingway, one with tuna, one with cat. The bookshelves were filled and the books looked thumbed-through and none of them looked like they contained those hidden safes you see on the infomercials. I flipped through a few. I knew that if I were the real thing, I'd open every book, shake the pages, watch clues come fluttering down like useful fall leaves. I shook out the five closest books.

I paid more attention to the stuff on his desk, looking through at his congratulatory letter on nice, thick paper, from Liz Cutty (her formal title crossed out and *Congratulations! Liz* written in a big blue scrawl). He didn't have a paper calendar but he did have a card for Salon Di in New Haven stuck into his blotter, showing an appointment next week. He had the card of the bank manager at Cromwell Savings. I took a picture of those cards and every other piece of paper. I have been lazy and careless and I was over my head but I am attentive by nature.

I heard footsteps coming down the hall. Cleaning people? No clanking buckets, no swishing mops, no voices. Only one set of footsteps and they were heavy-ish, not clicking heels. There were five offices on the floor.

Standing beside the door wouldn't do me any good in such a small room unless I planned to knock him out the second he walked in. I wasn't sure I could, even if I wanted to. I needed to act like a visitor, not an intruder. I climbed onto the window seat and turned expectantly towards the door.

Harry came in and flicked on the light. I tried to smile warmly and not squint as his eyes adjusted. A splotchy red flush crept up from his collarbone, along the sides of his neck, straight to the tops of his ears. A map of anger, but his voice was pleasant, even flirtatious.

"You broke into my office? That's a nice surprise." His voice stayed smooth, his body language was rougher.

He stepped towards me, his right cheek muscle jumping, and I pretended not to notice. I kept watching his bright, wary eyes.

"I didn't have to. It was open. I figured you were coming back soon. I hoped. Nice chat with Allison?"

"She feels you're picking on her, just because she had such problems with Bullfinch."

"Gee, I didn't mean to pick on her. I find, well, I find she's a little sensitive. Maybe a little thin-skinned? You don't think so?" I sucked on my lower lip. "I don't want her to feel that I'm checking up on her when she tells me about Bullfinch, or about you, but, you know, I am investigating a murder."

His shoulders relaxed. No matter how good a person you are—and I was pretty sure Harry was not a good person—it's relaxing to watch other people parade their flaws. I tossed my hair, keeping things ambiguous. Maybe I don't think he's a killer. Maybe I'm just kind of needy. Maybe he hurt my feelings when he didn't call again. Any which way, it's okay. I kept thinking, *It's okay, Harry, it's okay*.

"Great."

He grinned and stretched his arms up, touched the ceiling, and dropped them to the walls on either side of the window seat. Maybe he was really buying it. Maybe he was pretending to buy it so he could get me out of his office and into a quiet place, just right for bashing my head in. He might have a bronze bust of Hemingway. I kept watching his hands, long, sunny, pink, and covered with pale yellow fur. Like a big, blond monkey. He bit his nails. Big, manly man, and he bites his nails? Harry lowered his face to mine, keeping his arms up. This was supposed to read as romantic. I was breathing like a locomotive now and hoped it would read as a sexual response. I tried to make it more convincing by shaking my hair back one more time and holding his gaze.

"Let's get out of here. A little walk and talk," he said, dropping his hands to my shoulders, running his fingers under my collar. "I'll tell you a little bit about Allison Shein, bad feminist."

"Sure. Great." Now I was even talking like him. Talk about identifying with the aggressor. "Let's go to The Safari for a drink."

His arms dropped to his sides.

Get up slowly. Keep smiling. Rub your neck with one hand. Walk towards the door.

Harry turned off the light behind us.

I wondered if we'd pass someone who'd recognize Harry or me, and by recognize I mean, recall after my demise. The campus was as deserted as an after-hours movie set. Harry led me on the back route through the campus, heading towards the maintenance sheds and garbage cans past the gym. I hoped someone would notice us, before I disappeared into a dumpster. Harry kept his hand gripped around my elbow, in a very unromantic way, making it clear that a sudden move would give me a useless right arm for life—if I was lucky.

"So, Harry," I said. "I love Hemingway." I don't.

He looked at me, curiously, and I couldn't blame him. I was prepared to vamp, while measuring the distance to the nearest shed. I took a deep breath for the kind of scream that might startle Harry into loosening his grip. And there, striding towards us, gym bag in hand, was an angel in navy slacks and a white crewneck sweater, blonde hair shimmering back at the sun.

Michelle smiled warmly at me, ducked her head at Harry, and then, suddenly seeing his hand on my arm, smiled. I pulled forward, like a dog on a leash, to meet her. Harry could hardly break my arm publicly and he let go. He wrapped his arm around my waist as we stood in front of Michelle.

"Well, how are you two?"

I hated to spoil her good mood.

"We're fine but we're in a hurry," Harry said, beginning to dig his fingers into my side.

"Harry, give it a rest. I have to talk to Michelle."

Michelle looked concerned and Harry continued to pull at me.

"Come on, Michelle, don't let her dump me. She's breakin' my heart."

Michelle was pleased by all these signs of Harry's devotion but she couldn't put it together with my frantic eyes and his grim smile. She sighed.

"We'll see you later, okay?" Harry said.

He'd spent too much of his life with women who'd rather die than cause a commotion. I'd rather do anything than die.

"No, Harry, really. I have to talk with Michelle now. It's girl talk and you're not invited."

Michelle was confused but even so, she wouldn't side with a guy she couldn't stand against me, teetering as we were on the edge of friendship. She put her arm through mine and for a moment I looked like a Christmas wishbone. Harry released me, trying to cover his fury with a light laugh.

"Well, all right. But next time, I'll get you all to myself. See you."

I knew he would.

We watched Harry walking away. We got to the gym doors and I apologized.

"I don't really need to tell you anything, I'm sorry. I just needed to get away from Harry."

"That's okay, sometimes you need a little space. He looks like the jealous type. I think he really likes you, Dell."

I owed her something, but I wasn't sure if it was happiness or honesty.

"No, he doesn't. I'm making him nervous, that's all. He doesn't like me turning up on campus and asking questions. It's truly not a romance."

"No? He was certainly hanging on to you."

"It's a person of interest thing. We had a moment and that was very weird."

I was very sure he had a thing for Leah, but she hadn't asked me that and she probably knew, so I didn't tell her.

"You ought to know. And yes, to his weirdness. I'm supposed to meet with the Rape Crisis Center kids in a few minutes. I'm showing them how to fight back. We could still get together for a beer, later on."

"That'd be great. The Safari, six o'clock? Thank you for saving my ass. I wouldn't wish him on anyone."

She sighed. "I hear Morse is working on a couple of suspects. There's nothing coming up roses for any of the faculty."

I sighed, too. Nine girls were charging Michelle, ready to start beating the shit out of rapists. Michelle sighed again and I wanted to apologize for not being much of a detective and for bringing Harry into her life.

My phone rang and I scampered to a bench with good reception. Mr. Ross, the University of Michigan's lawyer, called me back. He didn't know much but he was what I hoped for, a chatty guy. He told me his sister-in-law's cousin was the lawyer that lots of faculty used to use for their personal affairs—Morty Schneiderman—and if he was still alive, he might be able to shed some light on the wishes of the late Professor Bullfinch.

And Morty Schneiderman was alive. He was upset to hear that Oliver Bullfinch was dead.

"Ollie? Ollie Bullfinch is dead?"

It took only a minute for Mr. Schneiderman to get to the other side, speaking calmly about the wheel of life and how Ollie had had a pretty good run.

"He must have been what, seventy-eight? That's not old, I'm eighty-four. I'm still working, but seventy-eight's not young. No suggestion of foul play, if you know what I mean."

I explained that there was, unfortunately, every indication of foul play and we were back to sighing and muttering.

I told him about his law office's stationery that I'd found in the Inheritance file and asked if he had prepared Bullfinch's will. He said he had. I asked him where it was. He said he didn't know. But if he could remember if there were any prime recipients.

Mr. Schneiderman said he couldn't possibly share any information with me. I said that I was willing to fly to Ann Arbor and he snorted.

"Is Miranda dead?" he asked.

I said she was and he expressed not even the conventional that's-too-bad.

"I'm not sharing the details with you. I am not—I am saying that I cannot tell you if there is a person named Judah Meyerhoff, who was mentioned in this one will, and I also cannot confirm that this person is a resident of Ann Arbor. I understand that many young people find things out about other people by Googling them."

I said, "This one will? That suggests there might be other wills."

He sighed.

"Were you also the lawyer for Mrs. Bullfinch, as well?"

"I was the attorney for the Bullfinch family."

I said that I appreciated his integrity. He snorted again.

"Ollie and I used to have a beer together once in a while. He was a smart guy. We were both in terrible marriages. He stuck with Miranda. Rich or not, she was a nightmare. I fell in love with my physical therapist, I had terrible knees, Ollie told me to dump my wife, pay whatever it cost, and marry Yolanda as soon as I could. He said he wanted me to have the balls he didn't. I took his advice. Twenty-five happy years next week. Good luck."

Sad Song

I went over to Theo's, to ask if he'd ever heard of Judah Meyerhoff, to be with someone who liked me, and to try to get used to Daisy. I Googled as I walked. Judah Meyerhoff was a painter (pictures, not houses) and even had his own Wikipedia page. His address, and his wife's name, was, like so much on the Internet, right there in plain sight for the curious. The painters I knew (pictures, not houses) were desperate for money. I put Judah Meyerhoff at the top of my list and turned the corner, reminding myself to appreciate the happiness Daisy was giving Theo, to admire that they'd chosen to make a life together, where I had found that convenience and pride made solitude so much simpler. I was talking myself into a state of serene acceptance when I saw the red and white ambulance.

Daisy stood next to a pair of EMTs loading the stretcher, piled high with Theo's bulk. I put my arm around her waist and peered down at Theo. Someone had removed his sunglasses and his lids were only half-open over his milky eyes. Daisy leaned her head against my shoulder.

"What the hell is going on?" I said.

Theo was not unconscious, not even distracted by pain or fear.

"What's going on is stupidity and miscommunication, Dell, and I would be much obliged if you could do something about it."

Two stocky men, one black, one white, both in ill-fitting red jumpsuits, pushed us aside.

"Please step aside, miss. Ma'am, please step aside." Daisy didn't look more than five years older than me. Her grief had elevated her to the status of *ma'am*. Or maybe I'm fated to look like a weary ingenue right up until my middle-aged overdose.

"There was an attack on the house, Dell," Daisy spoke to me like I was her idiot stepchild. "No, do not shut that door, gentlemen, I'm coming with you. Yes, I am coming with you. We're going to Salmon-Reese, meet us there."

The rear doors of the ambulance swung shut and I was left staring back at the curious neighbors. Either Theo was, surprisingly, almost dead and they didn't have the heart to deprive Daisy of her last few minutes with him or there was nothing they planned to do to or for him, en route to the hospital.

I went back to the guesthouse, got the Smokemobile, and drove, uncertainly, to where I thought I had seen signs for Salmon-Reese Hospital. I followed a series of color-coded hallways to the emergency room. All bigger and chillier than my lovely little Urgent Care and the excellent Dr. Weiss. By the time I got there, Daisy was calmly sipping tea in a ceramic mug.

"It's all right. They're putting him in one of those flexible casts, so he won't lose too much muscle tone. Not that there's so terribly much for him to lose."

She smiled, lovingly.

Adrenaline was streaming from my feet to my fingertips. Anger would be coming soon.

"Could you tell me what happened? Why is he getting a cast? What's broken?"

I was already sputtering.

"Let's sit down, he'll be out in about a half an hour. There's no concussion, no shock, they said. They're going to observe him for a little while and then we can go. Theo's doctor, Dr. Punich, is here, thank heavens. Love Dr. Punich. His wife is my yoga teacher."

She smiled, remembering some exceptional Flying Crane pose, and cocked her head and I reminded myself that Theo was her lover, that she had had a terrible fright and that even though she carried her own chamomile tea and her own fucking mug around with her, screaming would not help.

"Daisy—"

"You must think I'm a complete nitwit. I'm just so relieved. When that rock came through the living room window, I was in the kitchen. I heard the glass, the noise, and then he cried out. It was so terrible to see him in pain, that's what frightened me."

After several go-rounds, I knew what Daisy knew, which wasn't much. Around four o'clock, Daisy was making a pot of tea and Theo was standing in front of the living room window, enjoying the feeling of the afternoon sun, before he sat down at the piano. A large rock came through the window; Theo reacted to the noise and lurched to one side, tripping over the couch and probably fracturing his forearm as he fell to the floor. I was glad for his sake that no one had witnessed his fall. I was surprised to hear that Daisy had been able to roust Dr. Punich from his tennis club after she called the police.

"He's wonderful," she said. "His wife is my yoga teacher. I told you. Never mind."

I hoped that Nat Baker would walk through the ER door. The cop was fat, white, and looked stupid, even from fifty feet away. Not Nat.

It took Officer Randall a few minutes to figure out who we were, since Daisy and Theo aren't married and I'm not related to either of them and I didn't look like Daisy's sister or daughter or mother. He didn't blink when I gave my name so I guessed that he was so low on the totem pole that even Hadley and Morse, whom I assumed favored fat, white, stupid cops, didn't talk to him. His expression indicated that this was the kind of perversion he expected from people "on the hill" and Daisy's flowing blonde hair, nearly sheer sea-green silk caftan, and cooing voice clearly reinforced his belief that we were a ménage à trois and that Theo had broken his arm in particularly rough sex play. He raised an eyebrow, asked predictable questions, said he'd like to talk to Theo tomorrow, "no rush," and that it might have been some teenagers in the area, "a coupla dirtbags" who had already vandalized two other houses. Daisy thanked him charmingly and said that they'd expect him in the morning. He shrugged. I guessed he'd send someone else, if he could.

I waited for Theo and Daisy in the waiting room, texted Mary Clark, who either did or did not text, napped, and three hours later, there we all were. I took them home in my car, driving slowly, while Theo complained of the cramped conditions. All cars were cramped to him and I said so. That ended all conversations in the front seat and Daisy hummed Mozart until we got to his house.

Daisy turned to Theo. "Why don't you lie down for a while and I'll make some tea. Please stay, Dell."

Theo and I grunted affirmatively and walked into the library. I'd examine the living room after I got him settled, whatever that involved. He had an extra pair of sunglasses on the bookshelf and I handed them to him. The blank vulnerability of his upper face made me want to cry. We both pretended, always, that his blindness was just a minor inconvenience; he pretended for me, but I had no excuse.

"Thank you. Daisy is quite shaken, I wonder if we shouldn't get out of town for a few days."

I gaped at him. "If you think so, sure. You could go to the Vineyard, you used to like that."

I was surprised that he would turn tail, but I didn't want to disapprove. Who was I to suggest to an old, blind man with a broken arm that he stand his ground?

"I could stay with you for a couple of days, if you like—"

"No. Close the door and sit down. I'm sorry, I didn't want to tell you and I have to. There was a phone call, about twenty minutes before the rock came through the window. I didn't answer but I listened to the message. The voice, it was muffled and distorted, a robotic voice, the voice said, 'Tell your bitch friend to mind her own fucking business.' Simple but eloquent. I did not want to tell you this. Please do not blame yourself."

"No, of course not. Who should I blame? I can't believe I brought this upon you. Fuck me. I am so sorry. Let me look in the living room and you call the police again and ask for Nat Baker or Michelle Blanchfleur."

"Surely it can wait."

"It can't wait. And you need a real cop. Someone's trying to intimidate me by threatening you and this can't wait. If anything ever happened to you, I would not be able to live with myself. Please, call the cops and ask for Nat Baker or Michelle Blanchfleur, use my name. It might get them over here a little sooner. It might get Michelle over here a little sooner, anyway."

Theodor sighed. "I erased it. The whole thing."

"What?"

"It frightened me. I thought it might be a problem for you. I thought I would have the guts not to tell you about it, but I didn't. I erased it."

I walked around the edge of the living room, avoiding glass and the rock itself. I couldn't imagine that they'd pick up any prints from the rock, I didn't even know if a rock would hold a fingerprint. There was no note, nothing painted on or taped to the rock. No note on the front or the back door and I didn't expect a follow-up call. Theo got the message, I got the message. The doorbell rang. Tall, white, balding, and square jawed. Still not Nat. Daisy introduced me to Detective Morse, at long last, and we squinted at each other. Theo told him the whole story, rock included. Daisy moved away from me. Morse's reputation as an investigator didn't make me long for his assistance. He probably felt the same way about me.

"Miss Chandler, at last. I'm sure if you have some thoughts on this, you'll share them with us. And since your friend's life is endangered, I'm sure you won't hold anything back."

"I'm not holding back any information. I'm glad we're meeting. Maybe if we'd met sooner, this wouldn't have happened."

"Ya think so?" he said. "We would have been happy to cooperate, of course, as much as we could. We've got our eye on a couple of guys. Violent, unstable. Bullfinch's death was a theft gone wrong, is what it looks like. I'm not sure Mrs. Cutty really needed to spend Cromwell's money on this, but, hey, I went to Central Connecticut, what do I know?"

Some junkie killed Bullfinch, stole his wallet, cut my brakes, and then threw a rock at Theo, to scare me off? Even Morse, even without knowing about my brakes, must see that that didn't make any sense. I tried.

"What about this? You think your man, your murderous thief, tried to scare me off? You could reinterview your three or four most likely suspects and see who doesn't have an alibi for 4:10 this afternoon? Also, why not interview all the neighbors on the street and see if they saw a car coming or going this afternoon? Or the kids getting off at the bus stop on the corner, there were two, might have noticed, or maybe someone paid one of them fifty bucks to throw the rock."

Morse smiled at me. He took out his phone and made a note.

I said, "A few days ago, my brakes were cut. That doesn't sound like a random act of violence by some local loser."

"No, it does not. I'm sorry you didn't report it at the time. It sounds to me like one of the people you've become involved with, on a personal level, if you know what I mean, it sounds like someone was pretty upset with you. The heart wants what the heart wants, I guess. But, we'll wrap this up pretty soon. Mr. Gurwitz, I want to examine this room and then I'll need to ask you some questions, privately."

I hugged Theo without a word and thought about hugging Daisy, who kept her arms down at her side. Morse took a step closer.

"You know, Miss Chandler, in the scary movies, there's always that girl who goes into the haunted house alone and right before she gets chainsawed in half, everyone said, 'Why didn't she call the police?' Don't be that girl."

"No, sir. I will not be. I will be at the Cromwell guesthouse, cooling my heels, in case you have any more questions. And I certainly look forward to hearing about some junkie loser I never even met who is after me in such an admirably organized way."

The bad news was, the police were barking up the wrong tree. The good news was, if word got out, the right tree might relax a little, and make a mistake. I needed to capitalize on that. My insouciance was starting to look like stupidity. I'd go bother people, more carefully. I'd left texts and emails and phone calls for Cam Binh, the woman who'd found Bullfinch's body at the end of her shift, made her statement, and disappeared for two weeks. I'd go find her and make the circuit, avoiding private moments with Harry. I'd left messages for Judah Meyerhoff. Tomorrow I'd call Judah Meyerhoff, of Ann Arbor, Michigan, again and all day long. And if I had to, and I would have been delighted to leave Centerville, I'd fly out there.

My Lover's Prayer

Saturday, August 24

It was embarrassingly easy to find Cam Binh. She was at work on the first floor of the English Department, emptying the office wastebaskets into black garbage bags nearly her size. She was wearing tiny blue sweatpants, a child-sized Cromwell U T-shirt, and she couldn't have been more than 4'10", maybe 80 pounds. I'd already dismissed her as a suspect when she turned around. Her eyes were black and flat, her skin was the color and texture of sand, and she had a short, corded neck above her square, thin shoulders. She looked neither interested nor afraid; she looked like a busy woman with a broken dishwasher; she was trying to figure out how to solve an annoying problem.

"Cam Binh?"

She dropped her chin slightly, not quite a nod.

I walked over to introduce myself and shake her hand but as I was moving towards her, she was backing away so I ended up cornering her against the filing cabinets. I didn't want to terrify her, I wanted to question her. I backed up to a cardboard box and sat down. Now we were about the same height.

"Mrs. Binh, I'm Dell Chandler. I'm not with the police, I'm a private investigator. I'm trying to find out about Professor Bullfinch's death. I know that you cleaned his office every day and that you found his body at 8:00 when you went in to clean, that Tuesday."

I would have thought that she was deaf, except for the widening of her eyes. Perhaps it wasn't just the sight of big, bulky American me that froze her.

I tried to get a little conversational flow going.

"So, you've been a little hard to find. Were you on vacation?"

She looked right into my eyes.

"The police tell me, Mrs. Binh, that you found Professor Bullfinch's body and you notified your supervisor and you and Mrs. Jones, the supervisor, found a campus security guard and then you waited for the police, with the guard. Is that correct?"

A nod. Maybe I should order in dinner; we would be here until morning.

"Okay, good. I know you must have gone over this all many times with the police. And I know it's very, very hard to talk about such a terrible thing. And very hard to have seen such a thing, a dead man, lying on his desk."

I hoped my sympathy would make her expansive, make her want to repeat to me the details of the terrible thing she saw.

She shrugged. "I have seen many dead men. Five years old when we leave Saigon in 1975. My father, my brothers, my uncles. A dead man is nothing new."

"Not everyone liked Professor Bullfinch, I know. But . . ."

"Good man."

"I'm sure he was. I'm sure he was a fine man and I want to find his murderer. I don't think he deserved to be beaten and killed."

Smacked in the head with a giant paperweight is not exactly beaten and maimed but I wanted Mrs. Binh to know that if she thought Oliver Bullfinch was a good guy, then so did I. We were on the same team.

"Not easy to know. Not easy . . ." She gestured vaguely.

"Formal? Sort of stiff?"

Mrs. Binh nodded.

"Yes. Like my father. Cold outside, but kind inside."

"It sounds like he was very kind to you."

The yellow of the puckered skin intensified and pink broke out along her cheeks.

"Mrs. Binh, let's go get a cup of tea."

I would say nice things about Oliver Bullfinch all afternoon, if that's what she wanted to hear, and it was. The policeman interviewing her assumed that she felt about Bullfinch the way a lot of people had and started from there. Mrs. Binh kept her mouth shut, in anger and embarrassment. Now, she could tell someone how it really was.

In the faculty lounge, she described an Oliver Bullfinch I didn't recognize. Gentle, generous, affectionate, considerate, polite, and if, on occasion, he got a little overexcited, he always apologized afterwards and made it up to her.

This would have been a much more touching story if we were talking about dinners at a small restaurant, long walks, other pictures of autumnal love. What Mrs. Binh was telling me in her polite, elliptical way, was that she gave him either a hand job or a blow job every Tuesday and Thursday on her dinner break, and he gave her $100 a week, and when winter came, he gave her a credit card as well and told her to charge her gas and car repairs from Bill's Texaco on his card. Two years ago, she said, he started taking care of her rent, too, and bought her a nearly new car. He also told her she was beautiful, which was not true, and that she made him very happy, which probably was true. Her eyes filled up a few times when she was talking about him but she poked at them with a tissue and the tears didn't fall.

"He was generous. Yes, generous."

"Did you tell the police about your relationship with the professor?"

She blinked in disappointed surprise.

"And say? Bad things about him? Bad things about me? I answer everyone's questions. They say 'Did you see anyone leave his office, after you came to work?' I say 'No.' They say 'Did I hear anyone in his office, after I came to work?' I say 'No.' They say 'Did I steal his wallet?' I say 'No.'"

She shook her head, probably thinking about whatever else you could say about the murdering thugs her country had used for police in the old days, they'd known how to run a proper interrogation.

"I get it, Mrs. Binh. Let me try and do better. Did you see someone leave his office, before you were scheduled to be at work? Before five o'clock?"

She looked down and nodded. I didn't bother being delicate; this lady knew more about survival than I'd ever had to.

"Mrs. Binh, if I have to, we could do this question by question and it will take a very long time. It would be much easier for both of us, if you would just tell me who or what you saw, that you understandably did not tell the police about, and then I can go out and find the person who killed your friend."

"You find him and send him to jail?"

I nodded. I'd certainly do my best. I didn't see any point in discussing the vagaries of our criminal justice system.

"You said 'him.' You saw a man in his office? When was that?"

She kept her eyes down. "I went to the professor's office around four. He always said 'Come early, if you need help.' I had to fill out a form, for my son's school. Saint Ignatius. Oliver pays. I go to ask him how to do the form but I hear that someone is there already. A deep voice. I don't go in, so we are not embarrassed. I go down the hall, so I can go in when the man leaves. But, he walks out and then my supervisor gets off the elevator and asks me to start early. I never see Oliver after that." She corrected herself, angrily. "I never see him alive after that."

"So you had a good look at this man?"

She nodded, glancing up at me briefly.

"A big man?"

She nodded again.

I stood up and put my hand about six inches above my head, Harry's height. She looked up at me and shook her head.

"Not so big." She stood up as well and put her hand about a foot above her own head. Then put both hands up behind her head. I stared at her as she wiggled her hands and put her teeth into an overbite. A mouse.

"Professor Fiske?"

She nodded and lit a cigarette. I said good-bye and thanked her and did not point to the large No Smoking sign in the lounge. Fuck them.

I tried to organize my thoughts as I hustled over to Dan Fiske's office. It was dark and locked, which slowed me down and made me think. Did I think Fiske had lied to me? I did, but I thought that everyone lied to me. They lied because they resented the intrusion into their privacy, because they were screwing someone they were not supposed to, because they were breaking a law, usually concerning drugs or money, because they had authority issues, with which I sympathized, and, again, because they were screwing someone they weren't supposed to.

I had dismissed Harry's offering up Dan Fiske as a suspect as a crude attempt to get me off his own tail. But maybe not, maybe Harry had the goods on Fiske. Harry made such a good prime suspect, I'd failed to use common sense and pump Dan Fiske when he was willing to be pumped. Now, I'd have to go back and prime him all over again.

Tears of a Clown

Dan Fiske's house was one of the peeling gray clapboard houses maintained for faculty. It was a nice street of shabby colonials and reminded me of interminable visits to the houses of my father's colleagues, fending off their brats.

Dan Fiske seemed to be at home. Manchester Orchestra was singing about how things used to be. A bicycle, the seat still warm, leaned against the porch railing. I knocked. He opened. I had two inches and a good fifteen pounds on him. Whether he tried to run around me or over me, I could stop him. I shifted my weight from foot to foot, watching his eyes to see which way he'd jump. He didn't jump, he blushed.

"Hi, Dell."

"Hi, Dan. Can I come in?"

"Uh, sure. Let me turn this down. I was just going out but, sure. I mean I wasn't about to go out. But I had thought about going out."

The good news was that he seemed congenitally incapable of telling a convincing lie. What kind of college-educated murderer can't tell a lie?

"Dan, life is short. What were you doing in Bullfinch's office at four o'clock, the day he died? There's a witness so we can skip the protestations."

He sat down on the bottom of his staircase, holding his head in his hands. Maybe I was wrong, maybe his basic decency had caused him to kill Bullfinch. The sight of Mrs. Binh's little head in Bullfinch's nasty lap, and he lost it.

"Come on, Dan. If you killed him, I'm sure you had a good reason. No one liked the sonofabitch."

And, there's the bell. Mrs. Binh, I'm changing teams.

"I didn't kill him, for God's sake. Do I look like a killer? Really? I was angry with him and we had words, as I'm sure your witness told you. And yes, I threatened him, but it wasn't how it sounded. I meant he would be dead professionally, for God's sake, not really dead."

Maybe, maybe not. "What made you so angry with him, Dan? What made you so angry that you were forced to threaten him with professional death?"

He sighed. "I was angry about the way they were treating Allison. I wanted her to appeal the tenure decision and I wanted him to support her appeal."

"Even though he voted her down in the first place?"

"Well, no one's supposed to know how each of the tenured members of the department votes, are they? And, even so, he could reverse himself, he could say that upon reexamination of her book, upon reviewing her letters, blah blah. He could have solicited new letters. If he changed his vote, so would some of the others. And Mary voted for her in the first place, I think. He could have done it. He should have done it."

He went back to cradling his head in his hands.

"But since he wouldn't change his mind? Since he was going to block Allison's appeal? What did you do to him?"

"A student of mine, her roommate had complained that Bullfinch harassed her. I threatened him . . ."

He fell silent, again. I got impatient.

"That you'd support the girl pressing charges if he voted against Allison? And would shut the girl up, if he behaved himself?"

"I didn't offer to shut her up. Who would do that to a kid? The girl didn't want to go public with the thing. She's Iranian, for God's sake. It was a threat, Dell. A stupid threat. I never even spoke to the girl. I wanted to push him to do the right thing. I didn't want to ruin anyone's life."

"You don't seem to have given this your usual careful thought."

It was certainly not how I would have blackmailed someone.

"I wasn't thinking. Allison's going to Paris, anyway. She and Harry will probably be there, together. Eating Brie."

"Did she ask you to go to bat for her with Bullfinch?"

Fiske had blushed more in the last five minutes than I had in the last fifteen years.

"I offered. We were all sitting around and Harry was doing his gee-whiz-I-would-if-I-could thing and I said that I would go talk to Bullfinch and see what I could do. Harry tried to put me down, you know, 'What can you do?' but I knew that it meant something to Allison. Bullfinch was cruel to her. I heard he planned to block her time in Paris."

"I guess he failed. You're really crazy about her."

"Yeah, I am. It doesn't matter, I'm going to Iowa and she thinks Harry is God."

"Well, that makes two of them."

He shrugged a little.

"Too old to cry and it hurts too much to laugh, right? How'd you leave Bullfinch?"

"Apoplectic. Alive. He said that my charges were scurrilous and outrageous and he said that he'd speak to me about Allison tomorrow, that was the next day. Wednesday."

"Do you think he was going to roll over?"

Fiske thought for a minute.

"I doubt it. I think he needed some time to marshal his thoughts. He wouldn't vote against his principles."

"So, why'd you threaten him if you knew he wouldn't go for it, anyway? It certainly didn't do your reputation much good."

"I told Allison I'd try and I did try. Pointing out the merits of her case wasn't working, so I tried . . ."

Being in love had lowered his IQ substantially. As it does.

"Did you see anyone when you were leaving the office? Or anyone near his office later that day?"

"On my way out I saw that cleaning lady that he's having the affair with, she was at the end of the hall. That's it. I saw Harry coming out of Allison's office at around 5:00. We just nodded. Her office is about three doors down from Bullfinch's, you know."

I did know and I also knew that at the supposed time of death, Allison Shein and Harry Markham were each other's alibi.

"Do you know who Judah Meyerhoff is? Or this woman?"

I took out the photo. He shook his head.

I wondered what his thinking was. Support Allison's alibi and get Harry off the hook? Cast doubt on her alibi for Harry and clear the field for himself? Except that she'd be so angry with him for endangering Harry, there'd be no romance happening.

"Okay. Any ideas about anything?"

I could see him wrestling.

"No. Well, no, I don't think so. I do think Harry could've done it."

"Yeah, but why?"

Fiske looked down at his bony fingers and started cracking his knuckles. Nightmare.

"Because he's evil."

"What?"

"Well, you don't have to call him evil," Dan said. "You can say he's just a bad man. He's not psychotic, he has a sense of right and wrong. He just doesn't give a damn. He is a blight on this earth. Pull the screen door tight when you go out."

Dan Fiske got on his bicycle and left me in his front hall.

Cry to Me

I was too tired to work and too wired to rest. Thank God it was time for the beer with Michelle.

The Safari was the kind of bar I thought I'd be working in until I was fifty. I bartended everywhere I went, all the way through grad school, and I could make a dirty martini that'd peel paint and I knew the difference between a New York City Boilermaker (Bud and bourbon or Bud and rye) and one in Buffalo (in Buffalo, you drop a shot of peppermint schnapps into your beer and it's disgusting). The Safari had clippings from its glory days on the wall and over the bar: Mac Williams in his dashiki and his eye-catching, three-foot-across Afro and tiny, hot-pantsed Mrs. Mac, stretched out over their Caddy convertible, kicking up her shapely legs in tall, black patent leather boots and a halter top made of kente cloth. Mrs. Mac was now a large lady with a shaved head and complicated dangling earrings and she had not lost a drop of confidence since her days as a beauty queen. I'd been in The Safari more than a few times in my life, when heading north or south on I-95, and there was never a sign of Mac, except on the wall.

The place was almost empty, which I hoped would make Michelle's presence less troublesome. I assumed that in a mostly Black bar in the north end of Centerville, a tall, very white woman cop would be noticed and possibly not appreciated. On the other hand, on a slow Tuesday evening, I believed that Mrs. Mac would be happy to see anyone except the KKK. I took a table in the corner and Mrs. Mac nodded to me. I ordered V8 juice (not cheap) and the lunch basket of wings and fries, to show that I'd be a good customer. Michelle came in, did the cop 360 check for miscreants, and she and Mrs. Mac nodded pleasantly to each other. Michelle ordered an expensive bourbon and jalapeño poppers, reinforcing our good customer status.

"I bet you've been busy," she said. "I hear you've been sighted, in and out of Bullfinch's house, like it's your second home."

"I have. I don't think your partner was happy to see me."

She smiled. "Hard to tell, with Nat. Did he arrest you for trespassing?"

I told her he did not, and I didn't tell her the rest of the sad story.

She peered at me, over her bourbon. "Then he likes you."

We drank and ate, and ate out of each other's fried-food baskets, which is the beginning of intimacy, I think, and I told her about all the people I'd been rousting to very little effect, except to strengthen my suspicions of Harry Markham. I told her about the Allison-Dan-Harry triangle and her face darkened at the mention of his name. I said that Dan suspected Harry and Allison defended him. I said that Harry seemed remarkably unconcerned when my brakes had been cut. She shook her head over that and asked if I'd had the garage write up what they found. I told her that Danny Gallitto had written down *Brakes Cut* on a piece of ABC Garage stationery. I also told her of my plans for the Gallitto boys.

"Love them," she said.

We clinked glasses.

I told her about the rock through the window and she said she'd heard.

Weak-ass approach, she said. Not someone who's about to kill you.

I asked her if that was supposed to be reassuring and she shrugged. She told me about a woman who shoplifted an expensive coat, from the one fancy store in town, then posted a selfie in the mink. She said, "I'm not blaming her. I mean I blame her for the stupidity but not the coat. I love nice things. I didn't have any growing up so now . . ."

We clinked glasses again. I noticed that she wore beautiful rings. I said so.

"I told you, nice things. And Leah does, too. Thank God she's, she's sort of an heiress."

"Well, good."

I told her about Mrs. Binh and she laughed out loud. She told me about a bank robber who called Uber for his getaway car and then, two drinks in, we talked about our mothers.

"My mother died when I was fourteen," she said. "My father was a cop. My mother was a schoolteacher. Very strict. Her own mother, my grandmother, who I never knew was . . . she was a prostitute. My father met my mother in a whorehouse in Boston. She was cleaning the kitchen and he was busting a john. He took her home to live with his family—which must have been some kind of special Irish torture chamber. They were together from the time she was sixteen and he was twenty-two until she died, when she was thirty-one. Too much for him. Getting the whorehouse out of her life and keeping it out of mine, that was her goal in life."

"She succeeded," I said.

"Big time."

Michelle signaled for another bourbon and I thought I could probably drive her home, if I had to. She saw me thinking.

"I got a hollow leg," she said. "Irish and French Canadian, are you kidding me."

I said that losing my mother at thirty and feeling so devastated by it, made me feel like an idiot.

"I'm a grown woman," I said, shaking my head at my own weakness.

"I'm pretty sure that unless there's something really wrong with you, or with her, you miss your dead mother every day until you die and that's how it's supposed to be. And me, every woman I've ever had, crazy or stupid or just no good for me, I can never let them go."

We sighed and ate our cooling fries. She swallowed her drink and stood up.

"This was nice," she said.

"It was nice," I said. "We could do this more often."

We left a big tip and walked out together. She didn't stumble or miss a step.

Can't Quit You, Baby

I relaxed in my car, wishing I could drink like Michelle, thinking how great it would be if Judah Meyerhoff confessed.

Google Earth showed me a shabby, slightly listing farmhouse and Zillow told me that he'd owned it for five years. It didn't tell me why Oliver Bullfinch, whose taste seemed to run to Winslow Homer, would leave any money to an abstract painter. He no doubt left money to Mrs. Binh too, but I still didn't think she'd done it.

Judah Meyerhoff was upset to hear from me again. He thought I was crazy. He'd never heard of Oliver Bullfinch and if he was acting, the man was wasted as a painter.

"Your name is listed in Oliver Bullfinch's will, Mr. Meyerhoff. You'll be getting a call from his lawyer very soon. It's reasonable to think he knew you."

"It is reasonable but I've never heard of him. Do I get the money even if I don't know who he is?"

"You get it unless you murdered him."

Silence.

"Is that a joke?" he asked.

"Not to him and not to the police. If you can just tell me where you were on Tuesday, August 6, I can help you move this inheritance along."

"Who the fuck are *you*? I'm not going to talk to you."

He hung up the phone. Very few people just hang up; they announce hanging up.

I called him back and went to voicemail.

"Mr. Meyerhoff. This is Dell Chandler. I'm investigating the death of a professor here in Connecticut. I'm not your enemy. Just tell me where you were, and your relationship to Oliver Bullfinch, and I'll support your getting your money as quickly as possible."

I didn't add that nothing I said would make any difference to any judge or lawyer, anywhere.

My phone rang.

"Who are you?"

Once more about Oliver Bullfinch's death (not saying murder) and some obfuscation about my role and he cut me off.

"I was visiting my old college buddies on August 6. How long does it take for the, you know, the money, to go through?"

"Okay, please give me their names, just for August 6."

I heard the completely familiar silence of a liar gearing up.

"I was visiting a lot of people. I visited some friends, and I visited my mother. She's in your neck of the woods, Millbridge, Connecticut."

"Were you with your mother on August 6?"

Silence. Throat clearing. Cajoling, coming through.

"Look, how discreet are you?"

"I am the fucking soul of discretion. I am the crypt, but if you don't tell me where you were and with whom, when I pass this along to the cops, which I will, they will see you as our star suspect, since you have a ton of motive and no alibi."

None of this was untrue.

"I visited my mother for two days, the fourth and fifth, then I met with my friends in the Berkshires."

"Yes, indeed. Your mother's contact info and that of your friends, please."

"It's not really *friends* plural."

"I'm getting that. It's okay. Name, please, and contact info."

"Pierce. Pierce Feldman. I'll text you her details. Her husband was in Boston, all of August, teaching summer school. I just don't want Maya to know. Maya's my wife."

I understand that this is the way of the world, and I have been in the world for a long time, but listening to this stuff is like living in the sausage factory.

"Did anyone see you together?"

"Yeah, we were in a little B&B in the Berkshires. Dobby Inn. I'm sure the owner will remember us. I mean, it wasn't under my name, I paid cash. Also, we went to dinner with some of her friends. You see—"

Oh, I did see. Pierce Feldman, c'est moi. For that matter, same with Judah Meyerhoff. For that matter, same with his wife, Maya.

"Look, I'm texting you a photo of Oliver Bullfinch right now. I can't imagine you didn't know this guy."

"I'm looking. I'm sorry, I don't know this man."

"Send me a selfie," I said.

Oh, bingo, bingo, bingo. The same big blue eyes, the same ruddy, pockmarked cheeks, the same balding pattern. I didn't say this. I just asked him for his mother's contact info, thanked him, and told him that he'd probably be hearing from a Mr. Schneiderman within a week.

Ask Any Girl

Sunday, August 25

Sydelle Meyerhoff laughed when I mentioned Morty Schneiderman. She told me to come on up to Millbridge in the morning.

She had poured us both coffee and put out homemade vegan cookies,. which were not disgusting. She curled up comfortably on her ratty old couch.

"Oh, that Morty. He made me sign all sorts of forms to protect Ollie. Well, who can blame him? You see what a gold digger I am. I'm glad Judah's getting more than just this."

She gestured around her airy, artsy three-bedroom apartment at Millbridge Cove, a very nice assisted-living facility that made me think I should bring my father up for a visit as soon as I found Bullfinch's killer.

I showed her a photo of Bullfinch and she waved it away.

"I know what he looked like, sweetheart. I slept with him for a few years. I don't think I'd confuse him with someone else. Or, what? You think I had a string of lovers and maybe Judah is not Ollie's son?"

She grinned and sipped her coffee.

I apologized.

"No harm done. I'm old school. I think women have a right to do what they want with their bodies, without a lot of bullshit. Men, too, but I don't worry about them. I see it on the Internet, now. Slut-shaming?"

She gave the Internet her middle finger.

"You know what? I'll put it like this. I think Ollie was Judah's father and Ollie thought that, too. The thought gave him great happiness. It was the late '70s, when we started. I was a hippie chick. Look at my feet."

I looked at her eighty-year-old feet, which were still pink, still bare, and still a little dirty.

"I had a studio. I was starting to do some interesting work, in Ann Arbor. People dropped by and Friday night, I had an open studio. Wine, weed, a gathering. This professor started coming by. He wasn't always an old man, you know. Nice blue eyes. We hung out together. After a couple of years, we got careless and I got pregnant and I thought, now's a good time to have a baby. He disappeared, scared shitless, back with his rich, mean wife. I moved in with two other girls who had little kids. We called our house Calamity Jane but it worked. It's what I expected. A year later, Ollie found me and was full of remorse. And presents. He brought a high chair, a little rocking horse. He paid for a diaper service, and I tell you, that was amazing. I didn't love him and he didn't love me, but we did, really, like each other. And the sex was good. Judah had nice toys and the best preschool. Ollie told me he was moving to Connecticut, a really good job. I said I wouldn't interfere and we had ourselves a big cry. But I stayed out of his life."

"When was the last time Judah visited?"

She picked up her phone. "August 4 and 5. Right before his affair of the heart with Polly Feldman. Sorry, Pierce Feldman. Christ. Anyway, I have the Feldman girl's number if you need it. Judah can't keep a secret to save his life."

I stood up. I didn't think I needed to bother this nice woman any further. I thought that maybe I could bring my father up to Millbridge and maybe he and Sydelle would hit it off.

She put up her hand.

"I was born in Connecticut. West Hartford. Two years ago, one of the girls from Calamity Jane, she was also from Connecticut, told me she was moving here. I got a three-bedroom. She got a two-bedroom. She loves it here. I set up my potter's wheel in one extra bedroom and the other's for guests. I called Ollie. I figured, if his wife was dead, or they'd divorced, fine. If she was alive, we'd have lunch once and no harm done. I knew he'd want to know about Judah."

"How long since he saw you or Judah?"

"Twenty-five years, almost thirty. What's your point?"

I didn't have one. There was, apparently, no statute of limitations here. Lust was guaranteed to fade but not love and not longing.

"We met halfway a few times. Maybe every two months, but not when there was snow on the roads. It was nice. I didn't want him seeing me here. There's a status thing in these places, like who drives and who doesn't, who's walking on their own, who needs a scooter. I didn't want him thinking of me with these old ladies. We found a nice motel. The last time was May."

Mrs. Binh and this old lady. Oliver Bullfinch, you wild, Viagra-popping surprise.

"You weren't angry, Judah wasn't angry, that Bullfinch hadn't been more of a father to Judah?"

"Ah, well, fathers. Mine was an asshole. Sorry. I had two very nice guy friends who stepped up. My friend Steve, gay as a fruit basket, he was all state at Michigan. A running back. He taught Judah to throw the ball, shoot a basket, wrestle, all that kind of stuff. Bob was straight and divorced, no kids and wanted one. He taught Judah to drive, deal with girls. Ollie wouldn't have been a good father. I didn't think he'd even be great at the every-other-weekend-with-gifts thing. He didn't like kids. He loved his work, he liked sex. He wasn't a giver, for the most part. I ought to take that back, now with Judah's inheritance."

"Is there anything you can tell me about him that might help me understand more about his death? Any new problems he mentioned?"

"There was this girl, Allison, driving him crazy. Sorry, woman. I don't know what it was. She and this other guy, I forget his name, they drove Ollie nuts. They were the Antichrist for him, the two of them. Her, even worse than him, I think. But, the good thing, the year before, Miranda died, left him a fuckton of money. It did make all the bullshit easier to bear, I think."

"How much," I said.

"How much is a fuckton? He didn't exactly say. I'll tell you something you already know. He loved me, in his way, or at least he liked me a lot. But women who want something, even if they're entitled to it, women who think they deserve things, made Ollie uncomfortable. He grew up with women give, men take, women cook, men eat. I happen to make a great lasagna and I never wanted a thing from him. Plus, he got to choose to be generous and I appreciated it and when he stopped, I didn't pester him. Pretty much, I was fucking perfect."

She yawned and I apologized.

"It's not you, it's me. They have cocktails at five-thirty and dinner at six. I'm programmed." She sighed. "I guess I should have told Judah about Ollie. I'm afraid if I tell him now, he'll be mad at both of us. What do you think?"

I said that I was in no position to have an opinion at all about that as I was mad at both my parents, for no good reason, and missed them both terribly. She patted my cheek.

"I know. We all do a terrible job," she said.

I did not think that Sydelle or Judah had killed Oliver Bullfinch. I'd check with the Dobby Inn and I would go upset Pierce Feldman and I was sure I'd be no further along than I was right now.

Mary Clark texted me that she was in Salmon-Reese, room 401, and happy to see me during visiting hours. She sent me emojis of a crying face and a martini glass. I called Mary's cell and it went straight to voicemail. I called Liz Cutty's office and got the little stockbroker. She said that her boss was too busy to see me right now.

I said, "You know what I wonder about? I wonder about those two-hour blocks of unaccounted for time on Mondays and Wednesdays. And a three hour one, too. You know the ones I mean, in the calendar?"

She said she didn't. She did.

She said, "If you look at President Cutty's appointment book, which you clearly have, you'll see that she has meetings every Monday and Wednesday—and also Tuesday, Thursday, and Friday. She has meetings all the time, and most of them, of course, are in her phone and mine, not in the notebook. I don't think you understand the job. She doesn't punch a clock, you know. She's certainly not accountable to me. She said that she looks forward to meeting with you but that she's in a meeting with trustees until eight o'clock this evening and would like to meet with you, at your convenience, anytime tomorrow morning."

"You bet," I said.

Tomorrow, I'd ask her who she used to meet Monday and Wednesday, who it was that she didn't meet anymore, ever since Harry met Leah. I'd roust Michelle with some interesting Michigander info about Bullfinch, courtesy of my friend Morty Schneiderman, and some Go-Badgers info about Harry, courtesy of my actual friend, Junie, who told me that the word on Harry was that he was a liar, a plagiarizer, and hell on women.

This is what passed for a plan.

You Put the Spell On Me

I ducked into the tiny pharmacy around the corner, for my second tube of Dermablend, before I chased Michelle. My face was still a variegated bouquet of texture and color. Wally's Drugstore struggled along with lottery tickets, high-priced milk, and a dazzling array of over-the-counter contraceptives and K-Y Jelly. That was the only section of the store that wasn't dusty.

As I walked over to the cash register for my gum, skimming another encouraging email from Junie ("Nail Markham's ass. He took that poor guy's thesis, from intro to end."), I saw a gleaming blond head duck down below eye level.

"Hey, Harry."

I hadn't seen him since I'd escaped from his clutches on the steps of Cromwell. Since then, Theo had had his bay window and his arm broken and Mary Clark had had more to say. Now, and in public, was a good time to talk to Harry. Certainly not a *bad* time.

He wasn't alone. I saw Leah in the shoplifter's mirror, before I got to their aisle. Her hand was gripping around his bicep, one of her opal rings glinting in the fluorescent light. Ivory blouse, embroidered with brown and red flowers, tucked into a wide brown belt, encircling that tiny waist and linen pants. On her dusty feet she wore tan gladiator sandals, scattered with red stones. She looked very Santa Fe and very sexy, if she hadn't been frowning and tearful. As soon as she saw me coming towards them, from across the store, she shook it off, whatever it was, and began to walk towards the door. Good thinking. She could pretend not to remember me, she could even pretend that she and Harry were not together, that she'd just run into him while picking up a tube of toothpaste. The planning and details of an affair overwhelm even intelligent and careful people; the rest of us get caught just thinking about it.

"Hey, Leah."

She stared at me, trying to decide whether to intimidate or charm me into keeping my mouth shut. She went with charm, sensibly, and gave me a dim smile.

"Why, Dell. Hi. I thought I recognized you. I just dropped off Michelle. This is like old home week here. I just ran into your friend Harry Markham, in the toothpaste aisle."

Nice touch, using his last name, to indicate friendly but not intimate.

"Uh huh. Don't lose your good thing, Leah."

"Oh, you, I never know what you're talking about. I've got to go. Bye."

She walked out quickly, careful not to run, not careful enough to make the purchase she said she'd come for. All the way to Wally's Drugstore for nothing? She would do the smart thing; she would tell Michelle that she had run into Harry and me at the drugstore and she would imply that Harry and I were together. That would play well and her evening would be improved, even if I had ruined her afternoon.

Careful, clever Harry bought a package of dental floss and sauntered over to me.

"Long time, no see, my favorite investigator."

Each time he smiled, I was astonished. Everything I knew about reading people was turned upside down by that smile; it was warm, joyful, even sincere.

"Let's talk, Harry."

"I can't do it right now. Sorry."

"Now."

"Not now, Dell. I've got an important meeting in a few minutes. Very important."

He grinned. I guessed that Leah would head right over to his house and wait for him there. She'd park her car a few blocks away and if God smiled upon them, Michelle would not come 'round the corner as Leah was walking onto the front porch.

"Well, now or later. I've been talking to some folks from Wisconsin. Go Badgers. Maybe we'll also touch on my brakes and my friend Theo's broken window. I think we will."

I wanted to see his heavenly smile shrivel. I thought of Milton: "Yet beauty, though injurious, hath strange power, after offense returning, to regain love possessed." They would not stop loving him, none of these women. I looked as deeply as I could into his pretty eyes, deep into the dark tunnel of his iris.

He shrugged, pleasantly. "Gosh, you are a very busy lady. Come for breakfast tomorrow. French toast and we can review all my crimes and misdemeanors. You think I broke someone's window? I wouldn't but, hey, it *is* a message."

"All right, your house tomorrow morning. Eight?"

"Eight it is," he said, chuckling. "Sweetheart, Centerville cops can't solve a hit-and-run. You think they can catch a real killer?"

He walked out of the store. I followed, not even attempting to conceal my moves. He jumped into his silly little car and took off, in the direction of his house. Of course, it was also the direction of the college, the hospital, and Big Betty's Extension Shoppe. I bet on his house. He parked, I parked a block behind, and Leah's car showed up a few minutes later. I saw her get out of the car, slamming her car door, stumbling a little. Anxious and angry.

I had to go back to Wally's for my Dermablend and worried the whole time about how cheerful Harry Markham was for a man with an angry lover.

Clean Up Woman

I was not cheerful. I was in the Centerville Y, located right across from the police station, with two full basketball courts, a sauna, and a weight room and filled with off-duty cops. Michelle's name was in the middle of the sign-in sheet. I was grateful. I planned to fill in a few information gaps, drive by Harry's house once more, just to see that he and Leah were keeping busy, and then make a quick trip to President Cutty's office and a longer one to Chief DiCenzo, to share my limited findings. I was not feeling lucky, but I wasn't dead and all three Gallitto boys sent me morning texts with hearts and flowers and beer mugs.

Michelle was bench-pressing in a corner, heat darkening her arms and face. She pressed slowly and steadily, her arms trembling slightly, her big legs steadying her. I didn't want to startle her; I didn't want her to drop anything on me. She sat up, wiped her bright pink face, and pulled her ponytail a little tighter.

"Do you press your own weight? That's the only intelligent question I can ask about weight lifting."

She smiled, breathing heavily. "More. And you're supposed to be impressed. Why're you here?"

"I wanted to talk with you. Are you almost done?"

"Yeah. I have to go stretch and shower. I've got to do the grocery shopping, dry cleaners, all that stuff. And the natural food store."

"A day in the life. I heard you're a really good cook. Gourmet. Oat milk?"

She looked embarrassed. "Well, they do have some very nice breads, a sourdough baguette, and a cheddar-broccoli loaf. Leah likes food that's sustainable and organic. We steam vegetables a lot, she makes a really good yogurt cheese, but she's thinking we should go off dairy. Vegan is how it's looking."

That is fucking it, I thought. Dump her. Let's go find you a big, good-looking girl, with a nice smile, just like yours, who likes to run a few miles in the morning before sitting down to flapjacks running with butter and clover honey and a glass of fresh-squeezed tangerine juice.

Oh, I am hungry *and* lonely.

"That's too bad. I'm not sure that people who eat to live and people who live to eat can ever understand each other."

Michelle looked at me sharply, mopping her face one more time.

"Leah and I understand each other. We've been together for three years. I realize that you and Leah didn't hit it off. She's really very shy and sometimes she seems, a little, aloof, I guess. She's a very sweet person and . . ."

She squeezed her damp towel tightly and we both noticed it.

"Wait in the lobby," she said.

In less than ten minutes, she was damp but presentable in her khakis and peach T-shirt. She carried a peach gym bag about four feet long and the guys near her ducked when she swung it over her shoulder. They called out their good-byes to her and eyed me. I didn't know if it was that they knew I was the PI on the Bullfinch case or if they thought I was Michelle's date. I thought I was a big improvement over Leah, in personality, if not in appearance.

"What's up?"

"It's about Harry Markham. Two things: Was there anything useful in that wallet that was found?"

Michelle looked at me. "You do understand that you have no right to ask these questions and you're not entitled to the information?"

"I do," I said. "Certainly. But I found some correspondence of Bullfinch's—"

"Where?"

"Lying around. Don't worry about it. I found it, just by happenstance. The long arm of coincidence. Anyway, in an email eighteen months ago, Bullfinch thanks a Professor Richard Warren of the University of Wisconsin's English Department, for sending him the interesting work of Mr. Aaron Adib, a graduate student of Warren's from Cairo by way of England. He, Bullfinch, said he hopes Professor Warren will offer the young man his, Bullfinch's, best wishes to the young man for his, Adib's, upcoming orals, and Bullfinch further wrote that

Adib's ideas regarding Hemingway and Melville were elegant and persuasive."

"I'm sorry. Who cares?"

"I talked to Junie Brown-Mainor, a friend of mine who went to Wisconsin, around the same time as Harry. She was in psychology, but she did . . . anyway, she took seminars in English, too. Harry was a year behind her, two years behind Adib. Adib left the United States, very abruptly, two months before his orals. He never defended his dissertation. He basically disappeared. Six months after that, Professor Warren retired, also very abruptly. Dead a year and a half ago."

Michelle raised an eyebrow.

"Aneurysm, while on the treadmill—no one's fault. And soon after that, Harry finishes his thesis, having moved along at a very respectable pace—which is unusual, since all of his previous written work was turned in late, dripping blood and tears—and Harry does a brilliant defense of his thesis. That dissertation is praised, published, lickety-split, as a book, and it's on Hemingway and Melville. Nice reviews. Tenure follows. Get it?"

"Harry plagiarized it and Bullfinch found out?"

"Maybe. Looks like. And Bullfinch started speculating, out loud and up and down the hall—and then maybe Harry killed him, premeditatedly or in a struggle. Plagiarism would be the end of Harry's career and if we're not going to call him a sociopath, let's just say he doesn't seem to be troubled by a conscience. The wallet's an obvious misdirect, right? No one thinks the wallet is a thing?"

"That's a lot of hypothesis, Dell, just on motive alone. Opportunity?"

I held up the *to be a* scrap, which I'd been carrying for a couple of days, wrapped in plastic wrap. I showed her the three typed words. She rolled her eyes.

"Well, this really, no one cares," she said. "Could have come from anyone, from any paper, anywhere. You think we're going to put the paper under a special light and it'll turn out that it's from a rare batch of papyrus that only Harry Markham had access to? It's from Staples, or someplace like Staples, and the ink is, too, and everyone in the world, except people without transportation, money, strip malls, or Amazon, have access to the paper and the ink. And the three words are not *Harry killed Bullfinch*, are they? Lots of people had opportunity, lots of people have motive, from what I can see, and lots of people have good alibis."

"I think Allison Shein'll change her story, his alibi. Harry had more opportunity than most people. No one else was on the floor, at that time. So, Harry had as much opportunity as he needed, he was seen in a navy-blue T-shirt that evening at the Y and he was wearing a light blue one in the morning. I got that from the registration desk kid at Cromwell's pool. Harry swims for exercise. What about that?"

"What about what? I just changed my clothes. If you hear the chief is dead, will I be a suspect? Maybe Harry doesn't like to wear sweaty clothes."

"Maybe he doesn't like to wear blood-spattered clothes. Come on, a little support here."

Michelle stopped on the sidewalk. "It isn't the same for me as it is for you. I have to show cause, I have to persuade DiCo, I would have to make a case—and this isn't even my case—that the DA would want to go with. We can't just waltz in with a cute theory and a scrap of paper."

He was making a fool of her department and getting away with murder. I pinched my wrist to calm myself down.

"I understand that. I'm not asking you to do something right now. I'm asking you what you think. Could this be it?"

"Could be."

She looked up, at the sky.

"What's wrong? What am I not understanding?"

"Leah would never forgive me for arresting this guy or even letting him be arrested. Never. If he's arrested, she'll visit him in jail, not that we'd even be able to hold him very long. Then he'll jump bail and she'll go with him. For a while. She'll think that's romantic, for a while."

She spoke with the bitterness of the less loved. I couldn't blame her.

"I'm telling you, he'll be the hero and I'll be the big bad cop. I know her. She's restless, she gets this way, every few years. She left Stephanie, her last lover, right before they were going to buy a house together. I met Leah when she took out a restraining order against Stephanie. We fell in love, boom. A few months later, she tells me she thinks I need a new car. And we should really get a new bed, that no one else ever slept in. And new bedroom furniture. A year later, she says a house would be a symbol of our commitment to each other. So, we have a very nice house. She's a trust fund baby. I can't complain but . . . now, I'm Stephanie."

Her eyes were brimming and she put on her cop glasses. Only her pink nose gave her away.

"You might be better off," I said. "Maybe she just isn't the right person for you."

"All of my friends say the same thing. Nat can't stand her. He never said so, but I can tell. We've partnered for four years and he never even mentions her name. They don't see what I see. You know what's really funny? She's the most jealous woman I know. I look at another woman, she's on fire. After we all had ice cream, I said I thought you were funny and pretty, which isn't so common. That's why she's off you. I said you were pretty. The kiss of death. She probably isn't the right person for me, but so what, you know? I love her. I can wait it out."

I didn't say, *You think I'm pretty.*

We'd come to the parking lot, I'd run out of encouraging remarks, and it looked like I would have to talk to Chief Smoothie DiCenzo myself. I should have run right over to his office then but I kept talking, making things worse. As one does.

"Easy does it. Leah will probably get over this little thing with Harry if you stay cool. Don't make too much of it."

Michelle stopped in the middle of the lot.

"What do you mean when you say 'This little thing'? What little thing?"

"Nothing. You just told me they were hot for each other; anyway, I could see that, you could see that, when we all had ice cream. I can't tell you how sorry I am that I introduced them."

"Me too. I'm sorry. Have you seen them together somewhere?"

I went with observation, not conclusion.

"Well, he, Leah and I were all in Wally's Drugstore at the same time today. She left first and Harry and I spoke for a few minutes."

"Okay. Thanks." Her voice was quiet and her face was blank.

"I gotta go," she said.

"Go slow, Michelle. You don't make anything better by losing your temper."

Unsolicited advice, worth every penny.

"I'm not going to lose anything. Not a fucking thing."

She got into her car and backed out at full speed. I couldn't tail her. I could drive by Harry's house, to make sure there'd be no mayhem. I didn't know what to do if there was. I put my plastic-wrapped, completely uninteresting scrap of paper back in my bag.

You Don't Miss Your Water . . .

It was quiet at Harry's house, no sign of Michelle's clean white Subaru or Leah's brown Tesla. Heiress.

Just Harry's little blue toy parked in the driveway. Curtains drawn, windows shut. One neighbor's house seemed dark, the other had kids screaming in the yard. I stepped out of my car, listening for the steady bang of a headboard against a wall. Nothing. I got back into my car. It didn't seem like a big convergence was about to happen. I sat there for a half hour and made myself stay awake long enough to drive back to my room.

No one had disturbed my hair-on-the-doorjamb in the last twenty-four hours, my bed was still unmade, and there was one Diet Coke on my windowsill. I drank it and took a nap. I didn't need as much Dermablend today but anxiety and the complete understanding that I was cocking this up knocked me out for an hour. I woke up, dreaming of Mary Clark, in a blood-spattered caftan. I texted her that if she needed a ride home, I could take her, and if she needed groceries, I could get them.

I drove over to Allison's half-a-house, an old duplex, with straggly boxwoods near the back of campus. Her car was in the driveway. Her light was on. I knocked. She didn't answer. I yelled.

"Come on, Allison, five minutes of your time. I haven't yet talked to anyone all day who wanted to see me. Either everyone really hated Bullfinch, *Murder on the Orient Express*–style, or everyone's in love with Harry Markham."

Door open.

"What about Harry?"

I sat down on her couch. Clothes were spread out on her couch and chairs and more clothes hung on the back of her kitchen door. She sat down across from me, bare arms wrapped around her muscular, bare legs. I hadn't noticed the strength in her arms before, either.

"You are in great shape. Yoga? Pilates?"

She couldn't be a dancer; no one could take years of dance class and walk through every room like a broken puppet.

"I do Krav Maga."

"Really?"

She jumped up and jabbed her right hand towards my face, then moved to my chest and another fist to my face, stopping short. I tried not to flinch when she whipped her right leg up and out and rested it on my sternum. She smiled a real and satisfied smile.

"It's all about threat neutralization. All women should take it. I love it. I go to class six days a week. My teacher said I've made great progress. I'm taking the test for my black belt in two weeks."

Maybe Harry had help. Maybe Allison didn't even need help.

"So," she said, "what about Harry? Oh, sit down."

I sat.

"Everyone tells me that he was in your office during the time of Bullfinch's death. I don't know how anyone could know this for a fact, since no one reports seeing him in your office, or even seeing him going into your office. You must have told everyone in the building that he was with you."

"He was. We were together."

"You're his alibi."

"You're jealous. I know you're jealous. Harry told me that you made a pass at him, practically right after the Freedmans' dinner. We see each other a lot, we talk frankly."

Was Allison rewrapped around Harry's little finger, ready to swear he'd been inside her at the moment Bullfinch was getting his?

Feminism and rationality weren't helping. I went for the awful female favorite: *You're great, I'm pathetic.*

"What can I say? You're right, I'm jealous. You two seem like you're really happy and I get it. I don't like it but I get it."

I smiled ruefully—who doesn't like rue?—and ran a finger along the edge of the couch. I could feel her eyes on me.

"I have to say, in my defense, I didn't exactly make a pass at him. You know how he is, Allison. You know him better than I do. We started talking and he told me about his work and he was so passionate—" I kept my eyes down, tracing the herringbone pattern over and over. "He didn't tell me everything but you know, he likes to share. Until it's over. One great week and then, boom, no more relationship. You get the great smile everyone gets, the story about Country Pie, and that's it. You know, there were some big question marks around Harry's thesis, which led to his book. Some questions of authorship."

"You slept with Harry?"

No interest on the thesis, no interest on Bullfinch's death.

"Well, yes. I mean, he said it would be all right with you, that you two had an open relationship, that even when . . . I am *so* sorry. Obviously, your relationship wasn't as open as he led me to think. I'm sorry."

I looked her right in her deep brown eyes and thought about how I would feel if what I was saying was true.

"I'm sorry. I don't sleep with other women's men, I really don't. Harry was very explicit about your relationship being nonmonogamous."

"He said our relationship was nonmonogamous?"

"Yeah. Several times."

I wanted her to picture the circumstances under which a man would say *nonmonogamous* several times.

She was caught now; wanting and needing to know, not wanting to hear but unable to stop listening. The essence of what I was saying was true, even if the story I was telling wasn't. I knew he fucked around; everyone in Centerville knew it, except Allison. That's denial. What I was doing was rationalization. Don't say I haven't grown as a person.

"I didn't know," she said.

"I'm sorry, I keep saying that. I know it doesn't help. I feel bad that he lied to me, and to you. He even told me earlier this month, when . . . Forget it, it doesn't matter now."

"What?"

"I didn't mean to say anything, and I know how annoying it is when someone starts and doesn't finish, but I feel like I'm betraying a confidence, even though he told me you knew. I can see you didn't know any of the things he told me. Because I was just a fling, so he could tell me."

My starts and stops, my hesitance and awkwardness, sealed the deal.

"I want to know what else he told you."

"Do you really? I don't see the point. You're back together, everything's okay now—"

"We're not back together. We were never really together. He was being nice to me because— He liked to make a good impression. He said people were always lying, to hurt him, to get him in trouble. I believed him. I've recovered."

Her lips curled in self-loathing. I almost liked her. If she had to choose between liking herself and loving him, she might choose herself. Especially, if Harry wasn't there to do all those things with his tongue and his fingers.

"Well, he did go somewhere. He said it had something to do with getting last-minute funding for his stay in Paris, he was, I don't know, very keen about money. Not that he even gave a damn about *my* grant for Paris or what— He didn't want the news leaking out before it was finalized.

"He said he had to go, around five, and I went and did some copying in the basement. I didn't see him until seven, after he'd gone swimming. When the police came around, he asked me not to mention the meeting, he didn't want it to look bad, lose his funding. Piece of shit," she said.

She sat down on the arm of the chair, talking to herself.

She squared her shoulders. "So, yeah, to be very clear, Harry was out of my office, for over an hour, while I was printing some stuff on the basement copier. Mrs. Groth did see me at one point, around five."

She began pulling at the threads on the chair, avoiding my eyes.

"I ought to go, Allison, I'm really sorry."

But very glad to have persuaded Allison to hand me a big piece of Harry: Opportunity.

Was I really so persuasive?

Who's the mongoose, who's the snake?

Heard It Through the Grapevine

Monday, August 26

Having never even imagined Leah Fields before the ice cream disaster, I was now seeing her all over the place. With Harry. I saw them three days ago, sidling towards each other the way secret lovers do, hoping to accidentally on purpose brush arms or touch thighs. I saw them two days ago at Jerry-San's Sushi, at the ass end of town, when I was driving to the Gallittos'. They looked happy. And I saw them just a few minutes ago, as I drove past Harry's house on the way to visit Mary Clark. They were on the porch and they did not look happy. Leah looked more than angry and more than heartbroken. She looked murderous. Harry looked calm, his chin set.

I was still seeing their faces and the marked lack of love and almost bumped into Albert Freedman walking out of the hospital as I was walking in. He brightened, stared at my chest, and gave me a thumbs-up, which was either about my chest or about Mary. When I got to her room, she didn't look good. She had four tubes running in and out and she was on oxygen. She patted the edge of her bed. Her voice was ragged, each sentence ending with a little gasp.

"Sit. You ran into Albert?"

I told her the story of the dinner party and she laughed and gasped and laughed some more.

"That's good," she said. "Well, he's made a life."

I asked her why Mrs. Freedman was such a wreck and what the hell pretending to be Irish meant.

"Lois was okay until their son died. Heroin. Then she just tossed over everyday life. No one could get her back on track. That's ten years of being a walking disaster but . . ."

She shrugged.

"And the Irish thing," I said. "What is that? The place was like the County Cork Gift Shop."

I laughed a little. I thought it was funny.

"His family came here from Rumania in 1932. He was born, I guess, 1936. His mother died and the father changed their name to Freedman. Lichtblau, now Freedman. There you go. The father couldn't do anything about his accent but Albert could and did and from what I understand, by the time he applied to Princeton, Albert had made himself Boston Irish, with very high test scores and vague Kennedy connections. It wasn't as good as being a Protestant football player but he had the ginger hair and white skin and it was better than being a Jew, if you're trying to get into Harvard and the man has made it work."

She did nothing but breathe for a full minute.

"You don't know," she said. "You've never had to be anybody but you. You're a good-looking white girl, with good genes, probably born to decent people. You grew up with books and people who spoke to you every day, made sure you went to school with clean clothes and a lunch, and put you in your own bed, which you did not share, every night. Aside from being a woman, no one has ever kept you out of anything."

I mumbled that aside from being a woman was not a small aside and she wagged a finger at me.

"Don't start," she said. "My particular point on this is not misogynoir, it is that some who don't have your luck, they make their own. Where are you with the murder of my friend?"

I said I didn't know much.

She wagged her whole hand furiously and the meaning was clear: Do not fuck with me.

I said, "I think Harry killed him. I don't know exactly how it happened but I think that Oliver Bullfinch slipped and cracked his head, someone finished him off, and the someone was Harry. You told me Oliver was angry with Harry. I think Harry plagiarized his whole damn thesis and Oliver found out. Allison's told me that Harry wasn't with her the whole time. She also told me she's off to Paris."

"She told you . . ."

I waited.

"Off to Paris? Ollie told me that he had made damn sure that Allison didn't get to Paris. He said, she wasn't going to get her way at Cromwell and she wasn't going to get her way with the folks at rue de Girasole—that's Omni's French office. I told him that he was being vindictive. He said he didn't care. He showed me some of the emails she sent him."

She gasped and went on.

"Her language was vile. I told him, don't lower yourself. He said if it was the last thing he did Allison Shein was not going to whoop it up in Paris, on Omni's dime."

"But she *is* going to Paris."

"You said that. But . . ." Mary said. "I am sure he said that he'd persuaded them not to."

She shook her head.

"I don't know. I'm useless from whatever they're giving me. But if she's going to Paris, Ollie must have given his okay. Sandrine Boulanger was his student. He helped her become Omni's director . . ."

She closed her eyes.

"I don't understand," she said. "Do something."

I emailed easy-to-find Sandrine Boulanger at the Omni Foundation in France, hoping she was an English-speaking early bird.

Tonight's the Night

Harry's house was still dark and quiet, but the noises of the night seemed very loud to me: Dogs barked, the wind rattled the branches, and a car drove by, top down, music blasting full force. It was end of summer, 1:00 A.M.

Harry didn't keep his porch light on at night and I tripped on the tip of an old wicker rocker. It didn't seem like the kind of thing he'd own—sentimental and old-fashioned and sagging in the seat. Hemingway's Florida rocker. Even Harry's nostalgia was for someone else's life. My stumbling didn't arouse Harry. I peered in through the windows. Nothing moved. A cheap wall clock hummed loudly. I could make out the outline of the furniture, couch, two armchairs, coffee table. Two wineglasses on the table. Maybe Harry and Leah having a good time, making love on the living room floor before Leah ran home to the high-fiber, low-fat dinner she'd make Michelle cook.

No pets snored or stalked or fluttered. I heard a door creak and I tightened up, flattening myself against the side of the house, hoping the moonlight didn't make too clear a silhouette. It was the kid across the street, struggling with his front door after getting high somewhere.

I drove back to Allison's house. Also dark. Her car was in the driveway. I peeked in the window and saw her suitcase still open but the house was empty. I could feel it. Harry and Allison?

Just for the hell of it, I drove past Michelle's house (dark) and Nat's (very dark).

No one to talk to. I called Michelle and, desperate times, desperate measures, I called Detective Morse. I said to their voicemails: "Just saying, Bullfinch told everyone he was making sure Allison got turned down for a big grant from the Omni Foundation and she didn't get turned down. I think that was more than just great networking on her part. I think you should consider her a suspect, as well, and make sure she doesn't fly the coop."

Not succinct but clear enough, I thought. I drove to the guesthouse and fell asleep, again.

The girl at the desk knocked on my door very early, the next morning.

"You gotta go," she said. "We need the room."

I hadn't seen a soul all week and I said so. She opened the door and folded her arms.

"It's a wedding. They're taking the whole place. We gotta clean and stuff."

I couldn't argue with that. I left twenty dollars under the lamp for the chambermaid (or the brat at the desk) and packed up. I sat on the porch, thinking about my next move. The couch in my office had some real appeal but there'd be commuting. I saw myself, eating a pulled pork sandwich, watching HBO with my father's password. I might have just one beer. Nat Baker drove up, honking like a high school boy. I waved at him, like I'd been waiting for the bus and had just gotten a better ride.

"Hop in," he said. "I took a chance. I made coffee. Put your bags in the back."

I was happy and afraid and found a new mantra: Keep your clothes on, stupid. More helpful than Om Namah Shivay ever was. I wasn't always who I am now.

This time, there was no rain. The sun was up and the pines were deep green and there were birches, behind the house, which I hadn't noticed before. Two great silvery stands of them, like guardians. The house I grew up in had birches all about; whenever I see them now, I feel better, not alone.

We walked slowly up to the house, not having to dash through the rain. I admired the wildflowers to myself. When I say those things aloud, most people react as though I'm Rebecca of Sunnybrook Farm on a tear. There was chicory and red yarrow and even tiny violets at the base of the stone wall. I was very happy.

"You sit here," he said, in the kitchen. "And, I'll cook and you'll kibitz. A little music?"

I nodded, curious about what he'd pick. He put on "Them There Eyes" and I listened to Billie Holiday and watched Nat Baker make breakfast.

"My parents live in Springfield," he said, keeping his eyes on the mixing bowl, sifting flour into the cornmeal. "You can pour us some coffee. My father's retired from the post office, my mother's a schoolteacher, first grade. My dad, he really loves gardening. You liked those flowers when we came in—my parents' backyard is a dime's worth of land and a dollar's worth of flowers and fruit. We were three boys, coming up. I'm the only one still around. My younger brother was a world-class fool, got shot in the head when he was twenty-one. Good looks, lots of style, shit for brains. He robbed a 7-Eleven that had been taken six times in two months. My brother said, 'Just hand it over and no one will get hurt, ma'am.' And ma'am said, 'No one but you, sonny.' And blew his fucking head off."

I shook my head and watched him stir the eggs and check the biscuits. Nothing was burning.

"I'm the middle boy. My brother—my older brother—was a hero. He got blown up, a mine, in 2002, in Afghanistan," he said.

He checked the biscuits.

It all got done on time, at the same time. He poured us more coffee.

"So, why don't you drink?" I asked.

Nat picked up the pepper grinder and began rocking it back and forth, running his fingers over the wooden grooves.

"Well, I guess, it's for health reasons. If I didn't stop drinking, I would have died. But I could have kept on for a long time before I lost my liver, before they took me to dry out on the company plan. The Soaks and Jokes Home for Recovering Police Officers."

He looked like he was going to throw the pepper grinder across the room, but he put it down firmly on the table.

"Let's eat," he said.

"Sure, I said. "I can listen, too."

"My brother and I, we were just normal, social drinkers. But when he died, it was just a house of grief. My father worked late. And he worked every night, not to hear my mother praying, I'd drink 'til I fell asleep. My mother, being the rock that she is, recovered, and I kept on drinking. Got A's, moved out, finished college, became a cop, kept on drinking, every night. Good cop, good record, pretty women. Only drinking on my days off. Only drinking after nine P.M. So, then, I met Adrienne West, pretty and quick, junior executive, and this girl loved to drink. So."

I don't know what my face was doing all this time. Sadness, concern, jealousy (where was Adrienne now?) kept pulling at my face. I tried just to sit still.

He got up to turn off the oven and when he was behind me, he bent down and kissed my neck and kept on.

"Adrienne got pregnant, cut back on her drinking, I give her credit, she cut back to nothing and was a total bitch the whole time. We got married, I kept drinking. The day our baby was born, I was face down in my father's garden. It rained. They left me there."

His face softened with shame. He started talking again, his voice very tight and fast.

"And, Adrienne switched over to cocaine. When Odette was one, Adrienne left. No note, no number, no Facebook. I went to my parents and my mother said 'We'll raise this child, for her, not for you. You don't deserve her. And if you can't pull yourself together to be a father to her, then you won't be.' And my father took Odette's clothes and her diapers from me . . ." Nat stopped for a second and cleared his throat. "And he shut the door in my face. It took me a week to stop drinking and a month to get sober. And five years of AA. So"—and he exhaled, like a slow train—"so, I don't drink now and I've been sober for five years and Odette is my everything. Today, she's with my parents."

He showed me her picture, a little girl version of Nat, big legs, tiny ears, and huge, watchful eyes. Someone had put her in a starched pink dress with four hundred pink ribbons in her cornrowed hair. She looked like she'd rather be playing ball. My kind of girl.

"Now, you know everything about me."

"She's adorable," I said.

I put down the picture of Odette and started to turn around in my chair, towards him. He wouldn't let me turn and came behind me, kissing the back of my neck, each kiss slow and emphatic. I felt like someone was tattooing me, very gently.

We poked at our food for a while, not doing justice to his eggs or his biscuits. Even though my stomach was twisting, I could tell he was a good cook. I could see him, a little bigger than Odette, under his mother's feet, with her shooing him away from the burners. I couldn't quit smiling. He took my hand.

"Let's start all over," he said, standing up.

I stood up, too, and we were eye level.

"Okay," I said. I stood still.

I didn't know who should be in charge; neither of us seemed trustworthy. Nat led me to his bedroom, which turned out to be taupe and white, not gray, as I had thought. He sat me on the bed, like a recovering shock victim, and he undressed for me. He pulled off his shirt first, which is the right way for a man to do it, I think. His chest was broad and smooth, with a cluster of crisp, little black curls in the center. His arms were round and hard, lifting weights, or boxing, I thought. He slipped off his slacks, and stepped out of the khaki puddle on the floor. He was wearing those little bikini briefs; I'd never seen them on an actual man before. When I saw them in the ads, on male models who'd never looked twice at a woman, it didn't do much for me. On Nat, I wanted to take them off with my teeth. He stood there, like a gift, at home in his body. There was so much pleasure in his eyes, even six feet away. Pleasure in what was coming.

I lay back as he moved over me, like a dream. This time, we did everything right. He seemed to have all the time in the world and then, even the world faded away between us. Our hands entwined, pressing hard against the wall. Whose hand, whose mouth, whose feet are these? I could see him and see him and never grow tired of the sight of him or the picture we made: our pink, pink tongues connecting mouths to breasts, the flowing of honey, the sipping and swallowing, lightning gripping us in blinding flashes.

When we woke up, it was dark outside and I had to feel for him. He lay on his back, breathing lightly. Perhaps he hadn't slept at all. I put my hand on him and tugged on a few chest hairs.

"I surrender," he said.

I laughed and ran my hand over his hard chest and softer waist. I don't like forty-year-old men with sheet metal stomachs. They take themselves and their fading youth too seriously. I want someone to have dinner with, not to do *Magic Mike* for me on the kitchen table.

"How about a biscuit?" Nat asked.

We went back downstairs, a settled old couple, and ate leftovers. The reheated chili was ugly but delicious, and the biscuits warmed up nicely, after I sprinkled them with water and sea salt and wrapped them in a tinfoil cocoon.

"Nice. I didn't think you knew how to warm things up. Investigating here and there, getting your PhD. When did Superwoman learn how to cook?"

It wasn't just a compliment and I tried to read his mind.

"That was not cooking," I said. "Even I know that. What's up?"

"Nothing."

His eyes were bright. I put my arms around him. He hugged me back and we polished off the biscuits and a significant amount of Heath Bar Crunch. Everything was copacetic. He washed the dishes while I cleared the table and then we went into the living room and listened to Jerry Butler's "Never Give You Up."

"I think I had it wrong, about Harry Markham," I said. "And about Allison."

"Could be," he said. "I love you."

"You don't."

I sat down at the kitchen table, to pull myself together.

"I do. I don't know what to do with this but I'm not interested in pretending we're friends with benefits and just sneaking up on ourselves, six months from now. You don't hear that freight train coming right past us?"

"I don't know what to say," I said.

I'd had friends, back in the day when I had a posse of girlfriends, who'd tell stories about the fabulous guy who won them and wooed them with fireworks, and vacations, declarations of love and intimations of marriage, and ghosted after two weeks of amazingness.

"We can come back to it," he said, lightly. "What's your next step? Chase down that Francophile girl? Interrogate Harry Markham? But you can't get very far because"—he drew a finger down my arm—"you are not a police officer. Really, let them do their job, assholes though they may be."

"It's cool," I said. "I'm going back to New Haven."

Nat gave me a long look and smiled, forgivingly.

"Cool. Don't. You're going to try to slip into that house tomorrow and keep trying to get the goods on Harry. You could let us do our job, but you're not."

I put out my hand and led him back to bed.

My phone chirped, incoming email. I read it and then, I turned off my phone. As one does.

Dear Dr. Chandler,

We appreciate your inquiry and your interest in hiring Dr. Shein for the spring semester at the estimable Smith College. The reason you did not see Dr. Shein's name on the original list of grant recipients is that her application was approved a bit later.

I can share with you, as you contemplate Dr. Shein, that we had an exceptionally strong letter in support of her application only recently from Professor Oliver Bullfinch, one of the most esteemed American literature scholars in the world.

We are delighted to host Dr. Shein this fall and we hope we have been able to help you.

Sincerely, blah blah, French name. The Omni Foundation

As many colleges do, Smith's email addresses for students, alumni, and faculty are all the same, making it easy for me to appear to be (since I wrote that I was) Dr. Dellarobbia Chandler on the faculty of Smith College. Smith College would no more have hired me than Judy the Chimp but it had given me a great education, total mastery of beer pong, and a chance to play rugby like nobody's business. And I appreciated their email address and would use it until I was one of those old Smith alums marching at the head of the Ivy Day parade, ninety-three and not bothering with the bullshit of a walker or a wheelchair.

"*Only recently.*" For example, August 6.

I could see it. I could see Allison, the last year spent facing the fact that she wouldn't get tenure, a year of bitter acceptance and endless hustle. She comes to terms with it. She hustles. She doesn't get mad at Harry, who has sway. She doesn't completely disappoint Dan Fiske. She puts herself forward for every committee and conference in North America. None of it comes to anything but there's still the Omni Foundation, which will add a little sparkle to her CV. She speaks French. She has a shot. She gets her rejection letter. She knows, like you know when the airline said delayed but meant cancelled, what's happening. Bullfinch has blocked her. She goes to his office and confronts him. He acknowledges it. Like the rest of us, he underestimated her. Loving Harry, and those god-awful clothes, made her look weak. She wasn't a weak person, in any sense. She whips out a few Krav Maga moves, startling him the way she did me. He smashes his head on the desk. So far, not murder. He sinks to the floor. He loses consciousness. Or he doesn't. He writhes and moans. The door is already closed behind her. She wrestles with her conscience, which she sees right now as a weakness, a hypocritical rag. She is not the kind of person who can easily bludgeon a man to death. But she does. She braces herself and bashes him in the side of the head one fierce, awkward time. He groans and lurches a little, away from her. She waits until he's quiet. There are places near his body, under his shirt, where the blood is so deep, she can't see the linoleum beneath it. She edges closer to his desk, avoiding the corner which shines with blood, like jam on a knife. So far, there is nothing in the room to indicate that Allison has been a part of anything except a chat with a colleague. She carefully sidles over to the window to let in some of the humid air. It feels good, warm and scented. He has stopped making noise and his hands are not clenching. She takes off her shoes, and climbs over the furniture, avoiding the red floor. She stands behind his desk. His computer is on. His screen is open. It's nothing to get into his email, which is set up just like hers. She writes to Sandrine Boulanger, as Oliver Bullfinch, saying what Oliver Bullfinch should have said in the first place. Hatred can be a form of understanding, and Allison knows just what he would say. The letter glows with praise for her, and for himself. He apologizes for his previous position (she doesn't know if he wrote or made a call, so she doesn't say) and blames it on ill health and a misunderstanding. It would kill him—she writes—if his bad temper had interfered with Dr. Allison Shein's well-deserved grant. He expresses regret that there was so much competition at Cromwell, in her field, they could not offer her tenure. It is a wonderful letter and if the miserable old fuck had written it in the first place, he wouldn't be where he is. She wipes the keyboard with his old cardigan, which is on the back of his chair. She wipes the window latches, too, and puts the cardigan back. She tiptoes back to the door and closes it behind her.

I could see it.

I said, "Maybe Allison Shein killed Oliver Bullfinch. Harry and Allison were apart when someone bludgeoned Bullfinch. I thought Harry. I'm beginning to think Allison."

Nat lay still beside me. "You gonna show me the email?"

I didn't move. "I will."

"Is Allison still in town?"

"I don't think she's going anywhere. I think she's a confident woman, these days. Let's worry about tomorrow, tomorrow."

And I kissed him hard enough to make him forget his name and the ridiculous idea of love.

Backfield in Motion

Wednesday, August 28

Nat kissed me and whispered that he'd see me after work. I didn't open my eyes. It was 6:00 A.M. I wrote up a summary of what I thought (hoped, imagined, intuited) had happened to Bullfinch and sent it to Morse and Hadley. I blind copied Nat and Michelle.

By eight, I'd walked, stretched, showered, and borrowed a fresh shirt from Nat's closet. I didn't want to leave the quiet kitchen or the lightly moving trees outside the windows. I didn't want to leave the possibilities in the small house. I straightened up the kitchen a little more and hoped that he'd notice that evening. It didn't seem likely that I'd be back here later, but maybe. Maybe I'd gotten luckier than I thought. There were three voicemails from my father.

I called him.

"What's wrong," he said.

"Nothing's wrong. You left me three voice messages but you didn't say anything."

"I read that's what young people do," he said. "No one listens to messages anymore, they just call you back. What's on your mind?"

"Pop," I said, "you called me. Is everything okay with you? With Bev?"

There was a pause and I could feel him taking an accounting of himself and of Bev.

"We're fine. Why did I call you? Ah. Ah. Bev is having a picnic at her house this weekend and she's bringing me a lot of leftovers on Monday. She suggested that you and I could have our own picnic."

I had no idea how to process this. I had met Bev when I hired her two months ago. She was a tall, stern dark woman with an imposing bouffant, glinting metal glasses, and the softest thing about her was her Antiguan accent. Now, this lady was suggesting to my father that he and I have a picnic dinner together, with her leftovers, and he was calling me to tell me so. I missed my mother so much my stomach hurt.

"All right," I said. "I don't know if it will be Monday. There's a lot of shit going on, but when I get back to New Haven, we will have a picnic."

"Bev'll bring her leftovers, you see."

I did see.

"Pop, is Bev there?"

"She's gone for the day, Dell. How many hours do you expect the poor woman to work?"

"Pop, have breakfast. It's morning. I will call you tomorrow and I will come see you Monday. Put it on the calendar, okay? Monday, Dell comes."

"Monday, Dell comes. I've got it. Your mother'll be thrilled to see you. Good talking to you."

I walked back to my car and drove past Allison's house, saw her car and a lone, female shadow rocking out in the kitchen. She'd gotten everything she wanted. She could take her time and she knew I had nothing to confront her with. If her sneaker had had a trace of blood on it, it had been burned in an incinerator in Massachusetts. Socks, too. That bronze bust was as clean as a wet plate and Mrs. Groth had seen Allison moping by the copier at five o'clock. If I were Allison Shein, I'd be dancing to Beyoncé while I packed for Paris, too.

I drove on to Harry's house. I made my telephonic rounds again and knocked on his door. It was almost eight-fifteen and I was ready for coffee. Possibly, he'd have one of those milk frothers and then we'd heat up a couple of muffins. I could see blueberry preserves. Possibly, eggs. Possibly, he'd apologize for having been weird in most of our encounters. He'd tell me that I was right, that he had cut my brakes and paid a kid to throw the rock but that was all behind us now. Even better, he'd tell me that he happened to have a taped confession from Allison Shein. Or someone.

I banged, rang, and texted. Nothing. Enough of nothing. I pushed in a soft, old screen and went into the dining room.

No shower running, no water boiling. I called his name. I went quietly up the stairs and looked down the dark hall, carpeted and windowless like all these old houses. All the doors were shut.

I opened the first door on my left and found a very small guest room, with a futon and a nightstand and a Peloton. I opened the door on my right and found his bedroom. The sheets were rumpled and it stank to high heaven of sex, but it was beautifully and peacefully empty. The second door on my right was his bathroom, toilet seat up. I pushed open the last door, probably his office, and hung back, in case.

Harry's bare-chested body was splayed over his desk, his blood-spattered arm on the desk, and the Colt revolver still in his hand. I made myself look closely at the hand for gunpowder residue, like they did on TV. I didn't know what gunpowder residue looked like and it was hard to see what was underneath the blood and bits on his hand. His head was all over the walls and ceiling, clumps of blood and hair jelling on book covers, tiny ribbons of skin sliding down to the floor. His blue-striped boxers were dotted with red and the narrow trails of blood snaked from his chest to his ankles.

The person was gone. All the different blues in his eyes, gone. That warm, surging cornflower blue when he looked at Leah. That chilly, November blue when he saw me pressing Allison. Whatever his blue eyes had looked like when he was at Amherst, being made to feel small and stupid, that boy was gone, too. His body was still but the strong breeze against the windows made a little noise. A fly landed on him and then on me and I almost screamed. His cell phone buzzed, on his desk. I went to the kitchen, wrapped my hand in Press'N Seal, which is so great for so many things, and opened his phone. I went through his Calenmob app as quick as I could, writing down every appointment I could find. *LC*, what a surprise. They met regularly then they stopped. His haircuts continued, every three weeks. Leah, he didn't have to put in his calendar. No one has ever had to type in *Raging desire, Th., 2:45*.

I dialed 911 and decided to wait, keeping the flies away, and browsed what I could on his phone, knowing that my presence would give rise to questions. I opened his file cabinet, found three files, one marked "Bank," one marked "Travel," one marked "Projects." I took the first one and closed the cabinet. I didn't have much energy on concealing my presence. Press'N Seal was as far as I could go. I felt weary and indifferent, which is when burnt toast, shaving cuts, and fatal accidents come your way. After I called it in, I left the study door as I had found it, knowing I'd trampled the scene, even as I tried not to. Then I vomited in the upstairs bathroom, probably destroying more evidence.

The two young cops arrived first, with the local ambulance service right behind them. They didn't need an ambulance but they'd find that out for themselves; as Morse had reminded me, cops do not appreciate unsolicited assistance. I stuffed the Press'N Seal into my pockets. The two young men looked like the Campbell's Soup Kids in blue. I was not in a good frame of mind and my thoughts kept returning to Harry's changeable eyes and the face he had had. The cops were nervous and excited by my presence. They politely asked a few questions about my discovery of the body, all while looking frantically for clues, while trampling the scene. Then the real detectives came. To my pleasure, I saw Michelle Blanchfleur trudging up the steps. She seemed less bouncy than usual and her face was more white than pink. She barely focused on me, told the young cops to try and avoid tracking blood all over the floor, which they had indeed done, and, rather curtly, dismissed them by sending them out to "cover the grounds."

As Michelle looked at me, speculatively, Nat came up behind her. Nat leaned in to kiss me on the cheek and thought better of it. Michelle arched an eyebrow and went out to tell people what to do. He said that he'd heard the call for Michelle in the middle of working out and had run over, without his gear. There was a short silence, while we each gathered our thoughts. It felt as if I was seeing him for the first and last time. He was wearing a white T-shirt and black baggy shorts. His legs were like mahogany trunks, the enormous, wide calves and enormous thighs I loved, and had so recently been climbing on. We stood there in the living room, with the strong morning light pouring in through the windows, and sweat sluiced off him. The sun hit and warmed his shoulders and chest, steam began to rise, and he looked like photos I'd seen of the mist clearing off Mount Kilimanjaro. He cleared his throat and he put his hands in his pockets. I put my hand out towards him and he backed away, just a fraction of an inch.

"Why are you here?"

"Harry invited me for breakfast."

"You didn't tell me that."

"I forgot." I smiled. "I had other things on my mind. Plus, you left very early."

"Sure. It must be difficult for you. I'm sorry. Finding your friend like this."

"You don't think he was a friend, do you? It was just like you said last night. He was a suspect in a murder and I was trying to do my job, the one for which Liz Cutty hired me. You know, find the murderer, since the police didn't seem able to."

"Sure," Nat said, soothingly.

"Which is it? You think I popped up from your bed to his for an early morning tryst or you think I killed him last night—before we went off for fun at your house—and have now come back in the morning, to cover my tracks? Which?"

I was barely not yelling.

"Neither, of course. Just wondering when you last saw Harry."

"I saw him last about half an hour ago, when, after ringing and phoning and banging on the door, I got no answer. I then went upstairs, peered into his study, and noticed that his face was scattered around the room. So, I didn't actually see him, only what was left. You'll find my hand and footprints everywhere."

I was pissed.

"I'm sorry, this must be upsetting."

Not a dent on that tank.

"Yes."

And I, too, am taking no prisoners, you sonofabitch.

"But you were a friend of Harry's? I mean you did have this date for breakfast, at his home."

"I wouldn't say we were friends. I know you better than I know him."

His eyelids lowered and my spurt of triumph fizzled as we stepped away from each other.

Michelle came forward, putting a hand on my arm, asking me the same where and when questions that the Campbell's Soup Kids had. She thanked Nat and told him he could go home, since it was his day off. He nodded and walked out without another word. Michelle went through the routine, but her mind was elsewhere. I knew she knew she wasn't talking to a murderer.

"So, did you hear a shot or see anyone near the house?"

"No," I said, getting out of the way of the medical examiner on his way in, keeping the folder under my shirt and trying to avoid stepping on the crew. "I was at the house. Nothing. We were going to have breakfast, as I told you. All I can tell you is that it didn't happen at 8:15 this morning. I'm sure the ME can tell you when it happened."

"Yeah. It doesn't matter that much. Even those two clowns weren't able to lose the note he wrote."

"He wrote something?"

"Yeah, lots do, you know." She held up a large plastic bag, with a blood-spattered piece of paper in it. "Brief and to the point, I'll give him that. He knew you had him, and he knew we were coming for him. That conversation in the drugstore, you must have scared him good."

"He didn't seem that frightened. I'm not sure I had the goods on him. I think maybe Allison—"

"Oh, you scared him," she said firmly. She smiled, more warmly. "I got your message about Allison. We all did. Don't worry about her. I want to wrap this up, but I won't overlook anything, I promise. I'll talk to every neighbor, I'll run down every print, I'll even consult the department shrink about the note. Anyway, I know how you feel."

"Tell me."

"You feel cheated. You were going to put him away and he weaseled out of it. He robbed you."

Two days ago, she would have been right. After I stopped being sick to my stomach, I would have felt ripped off. Now, I felt that I had set into motion every bad thing that had happened since Allison killed Bullfinch, the one thing for which I was not holding myself responsible.

"Look, you got him, you just didn't get him the way you planned. It's all right. He was scum, Dell, and he knew it."

Her eyes were as cool and matte as turquoise stones.

"Michelle, please, listen. I heard from the people in Paris. It's pretty clear that Allison—"

"We have a suicide here. And a confession. It's a good day for us. We can follow up on Allison, and her Paris adventure, a little later, okay?"

She patted my arm. Cops pushed past me. I walked out of the house and looked around, without much hope, for Nat.

You'll Never Get to Heaven If You Break My Heart

Theo had left me a voicemail: *We just heard about Harry Markham. We're not leaving town and, as always, my house is your house.* His house, which I had indeed thought of as my house, when I wanted to, was changing. Clean, muslin curtains open and revealing. A nice teak bench had appeared in the backyard and the first few yellow leaves had fallen on it. I knocked and entered and was thrilled to find no one home. My sneakers had blood on them. I put them in the shower and turned it on. I lay down in Theo's very spare guest room. Bed, unsteady nightstand, small oval mirror nailed to wall, gooseneck lamp from a 1963 Yale dormitory. Daisy hadn't fluffed it up, yet.

Bullfinch's death was receding for me. It shouldn't have. The fact that he was old and awful and ill shouldn't have made a difference. In the Harry Bosch novels, Michael Connelly has his hero say, often, "Everyone matters or no one matters." I don't quite understand that (does Hitler's well-being have to matter?) but I appreciated the tone. I felt bad, meaning furious and stupid, that Allison was getting away with killing Bullfinch. Her getting away with it was more upsetting than the snuffing out of Oliver Bullfinch's candle. And if someone was getting away with killing Harry, that was even more upsetting. I don't think that's the way I was supposed to feel.

I dressed in Theo's spare room. I also toured his bedroom, just to spy on him and Daisy and see exactly how many fucking silk caftans she owned. Six, that she kept at his house. Therefore, probably dozens. There were also some very expensive sandals on the floor of the closet. I drove to Allison's, in a dazed, slo-mo frame of mind.

Back to school. Students were arriving and moving in, up and down her street. Boxes, bags, books. Parents and siblings and friends in little parades from the street to the door, up the stairs. The ones with experience did a bucket brigade and let their parents take them out to lunch. One father and son had beers on the front lawn and the other families looked at the two of them, twenty and fifty, both long-legged and a little bored with how easy it was. The eighteen-year-olds clung to every object as if only they knew where it should go and how it should be handled. In twenty-four hours, I had slept with Nat Baker, discovered that I loved him, lied about it, found Harry's corpse, and been dumped (I think) by said Nat Baker and definitively hip checked off the case by Michelle. And here I was, unarmed and unofficial, ready to chat up Allison, phone in hand, so we could both read the email from the Omni Foundation and see what conclusions we came to. I didn't think I could stop her if she decided to Krav Maga me, but I thought my gun could. There's no martial art better than a gun you know how to use, which is why I don't study karate. I had put my gun in my bag, Michelle-style.

I stumbled up the stairs and Allison opened the door before I could knock. She didn't do her usual hunch-and-sulk. Her clothing was as I remembered it: black-and-white gingham blouse, one button missing, baggy olive green corduroys, but her hair was piled on her head in one of those Brooklyn ballerina updos and she'd managed to get a little tan.

"Come on in," she said energetically. "Poor Harry."

Her face was different. She was pretty and pink and those rheumy, half-closed eyes were open and bright. Something very becoming.

"I have to move these papers. I'm sorry, I'm in the middle of going to Paris and now I do have an offer, associate professor, at Iowa, starting in January. Barbara Hill's moving to Emory, she got one of those Coca-Cola chairs and she decided, last minute, to take it. I get to go to Paris for the fall and then take her place in Iowa, if I want. What a lucky break. And poor Harry. Is it true you found him?"

She almost winked.

"Word travels fast," I said. "Iowa. Isn't that where Dan Fiske is going?"

He shot Harry for her and the payoff is they get married and move to Iowa? She shot Harry for him, just because Harry was so handsome and annoying, and the payoff is he helps her get a tenured position at Iowa, when the time comes. They always loved each other since they were kids way back when and they shot Harry together because once she'd killed Bullfinch, why not rid the world of another asshole? Okay, that would be more like me.

Allison looked down, coyly. "Yes, it is, as a matter of fact. It's very nice that I might end up there. Also, I FedExed my manuscript to the department chair at Iowa. That helped. I was just so blocked until . . . really, last week."

She said all this with a chuckle in her voice, while Amy Winehouse filled the room.

"Allison, look, you're out of here. What do you think about Harry's suicide? Do you really think he killed Bullfinch and then killed himself?"

"I think so." Her voice was low and sure. "It seems clear that's what happened. Harry was, in his own way, a person with a sense of honor and so he killed himself."

"For killing Bullfinch?"

"Well, the facts are what they are. Harry didn't always behave well and his motives were not beyond reproach and neither, maybe what we have to face is, neither were his methods. I mean, that rock through your friend's window. Just pure impulsive Harry, right? Charming, unscrupulous, and just a little more violent than we thought. Well, we loved him, didn't we?"

She gave a small sigh and smiled, in a worldly way. Apparently, murder and Paris was a cure for every single thing that had ailed her.

"Where were you two nights ago?"

"What difference does that make? Poor, guilty Harry killed himself, which is perfectly understandable."

"Were you alone?"

"Not at all. I was with Dan. Oh, for heaven's sake, Dell. With Dan and with Marilyn Kozlowitz from History and Dick Price from Astronomy. Dan made a late dinner for us all and we played bridge until midnight."

She was so much more attractive now.

"And from midnight on?"

"I wasn't alone." She smirked. "Life goes on."

"Well, for you, yeah. Congratulations."

She grinned a little at my tone, shifted her hips to "You Know I'm No Good," and asked if there was anything else on my mind.

"I see you're packing. It must be exciting going to Paris. Your first time?"

She smiled and answered in French, which I don't speak.

"What's that?"

"I said, you don't know anything about me. All you saw was Harry. I said, I've been to Paris more often than you've been to Pepe's Pizza. My mother's French."

She held up two passports.

"I was in touch with your French friends. Sandrine Boulanger. She wrote back. Shall we look at her email together?"

She didn't flinch.

"Absolument."

We stood close together, in the position of like-minded friends checking out a restaurant review or looking up an old friend on Facebook together. Her eyes slid over the text.

"I don't think it was right of you to lie to them. Smith *professor.* Really. But, you see what a lovely person she is. I can't wait to meet her," Allison said, brightly.

"You don't have anything to say about an email coming from Bullfinch within hours of the time he was murdered?"

"No, I don't." She sighed. "I wish I'd known. I would have thanked him. We had such a hard time with each other. That was very, very sweet of him."

"And odd," I insisted. "He told everyone that he was going to block you for that big grant."

"He did say that. I know. Maybe he changed his mind. Dan and Harry both lobbied for me. I guess one of them was effective, at the last moment." Her eyes widened, playfully. "Ohhh. You think it wasn't Bullfinch. I mean, the time of death can't be that exact, of course. You know that, right—even though you're an amateur. But maybe you think someone wrote a recommendation from Bullfinch—meaning it wasn't really from Bullfinch—after he died."

I pocketed my phone. On television, people crumble when you show them evidence or an email that could, conceivably, constitute evidence.

"I do think that," I said.

"Oh la la. It could be, but it seems unlikely. It seems so much more probable and logical to conclude that having been pressed by me, Harry, and Dan on this very subject, he decided to do the right thing—at what turned out to be the last minute." She sighed, prettily. "That's what I choose to remember. Or, it could have been Harry, crossing the line, more than once. We *were* very close. And, after he killed poor Oliver, in a rage, I assume, over Oliver telling everyone that Harry was a plagiarist and talking about bringing him up before Academic Affairs, maybe he did this last graceful thing for me. But I prefer the simplest answer. Oliver Bullfinch did the right thing before an unknown assailant ended his life. Very moving. We'll never know. That's what's so difficult about all this, right? We'll never know."

She stood a few inches away from me, lit up with her own cleverness. Glowing with success.

"So," I said. "France. Great food and no extradition treaty?"

"None at all," Allison said. "But why would I care*? Bonsoir, Dell. D'accord, vas-y alors.* That means do what you have to do. I'll be around for a while, if you have more questions about Paris, or Harry, or Iowa, or the vagaries of human existence. You know, questions about shit that bothers you."

She walked me to the door, kissed me on both cheeks, and pushed me out. She didn't tell me to look her up if I was ever in Paris, or Iowa.

I called Marilyn Kozlowitz and Dick Price and got them both. I feigned an interest in bridge and they each told me about their fun evening with Allison and Dan. Kozlowitz even volunteered that Allison said that Dan Fiske wouldn't let her lift a finger. She giggled. I asked if Allison had been in the living room the whole evening. Marilyn Kozlowitz said she thought so. She said, as people do, that she hadn't really noticed. I pressed her again and she said, with another goddamn giggle, that everyone had been drinking margaritas since 7:00 and she really truly couldn't say where Allison was. It didn't seem likely that Allison had dashed out of the room, biked over to Harry's, knocked him out, shot him, and biked back in time to play a rubber or whatever bridge people did, but it didn't seem impossible. But why would she? And if not her, who?

Walk On By

Elizabeth Cutty was blowing up my phone with texts. She'd left three voice messages first, telling me first to come back at my convenience, then, to come to her office as soon as possible, then she left a voicemail: *What the fuck?* The convenient moment was clearly upon us.

She must have suspected Harry, of something, from the beginning. Maybe she just suspected him of extreme sexiness, ambition, and a bright blue eye for the main chance. She was too smart not to suspect him, even if she was, especially if she was, the *LC* in his calendar. I know a lot of people who trust their partners only when they can see them, with both hands flat on the table. (See Nat. See me.) Harry was too desperate for success not to have tried to use their relationship. He got tenure, he got a grant, and when there didn't seem to be more in the pipeline, he ended it. Or she did. I like to think she ended it, making the smart move. Her other smart move, I'd come to see, was hiring me. I didn't see us as sisters under the skin, but I don't think that in the end she cared that much about Oliver Bullfinch, either. She cared about bad publicity and she cared about saving her own ass, which included getting Harry's hands off it. If I came up empty-handed, as she expected, the trustees would be satisfied by the effort and eventually people would forget. If I got something on Harry, she could use that to keep him on a short leash, professionally and personally. In the worst case, I might rattle him enough that he'd become Cutty's lieutenant or choose to disappear entirely. She couldn't lose, counting on me and my marked limitations.

Pearly was in place, her suit a little darker and her face a little paler than usual. There were tearstains on her blouse. She didn't have the heart to spar with me and just knocked on the president's door.

"You must have heard the bad news," I said conversationally.

She grabbed a Kleenex off her desk and racewalked down the hall. I put my hand on the doorknob and almost fell upon Liz Cutty as she was pulling the door open. Another pale, tired lady. The blue lenses accentuated the violet pouches beneath them. She laid a heavy vellum envelope on the top of her beautiful, hard-rubbed desk.

"Not yet," I said.

"No? Aside from not responding to a dozen phone calls from me yesterday afternoon and leaving me to get word of Harry Markham's suicide from the police this morning and from my provost and now, just five minutes ago from the *Cromwell Gazette*, and aside from not coming to me as soon as you had information that pointed to Professor Bullfinch's murderer, we could say you did what I asked. You found the murderer. You apparently even rid us of him, by hounding him to his suicide, which was truly beyond the call of duty."

"Sergeant Blanchfleur was here?"

"With Detective Morse. And Chief DiCenzo. You just missed them. They were quite informative. Your name was mentioned several times."

She was shaking and turned to look out the French doors, leading to the pretty patio. "You were supposed to come to me first."

I didn't think she'd appreciate my hand on her shoulder. I sat down on the edge of her desk and waited a few moments.

"Take your check. The case is solved."

I had already pocketed the check but I wasn't leaving until I'd filled in some of the gaps that kept winking at me, opening and closing with a mocking, unpredictable rhythm.

"I should have come to you first. But events . . . got away from me. I do understand that you want me to leave. We're almost there. You were sleeping with Harry."

"Good day, Dr. Chandler."

"Oh, God," I said. "I'm so sorry. I appreciate good manners and I think the world would be a better place if everyone had a set just like yours but it's not going to help. You call campus security and I go to the *Cromwell Gazette* with a great headline: *Sexy Prexy in Love Nest with Dead Murderer*. I don't want to blackmail you and I'm not trying to humiliate you. I just want to know what the hell has been going on."

I must have looked like I meant it.

"Harry and I had a relationship, of sorts, from sometime after New Year's until just six weeks ago."

"Good that you kept that to yourself. Please tell me now."

We talked in cool quiet tones, as if we were already at the funeral.

"We had a discreet relationship, for obvious reasons. I was aware that there might be certain . . . occasions of poor judgment in his past. He had asked for my help. I was able to give him some. Our relationship ended."

"Right. He fucked your brains out and asked you to fire Bullfinch, which you couldn't. Maybe wouldn't even if you could have. He asked you to help push Bullfinch out, through retirement, which you wouldn't, although you wished you had. He asked you to make sure he got tenure, which you actually did—and he dropped you like burnt toast."

I got off her desk as she came towards me, her long white hands clenched. She stopped herself. She took off her glasses and folded them into a pale blue suede case.

"So old-fashioned. He didn't drop me. We had run our course. I just stopped calling. The day Professor Bullfinch was killed, I was in a meeting with all of the deans from one in the afternoon, until we broke from cocktails at five-thirty. The police interrupted our cocktail hour to tell me about Professor Bullfinch's murder. And you know where I've been all this morning. I wouldn't kill for Harry Markham. I wouldn't kill a well-respected professor, sully my school's reputation and my own, just for a good-looking man."

"Me neither. But where were you late last night?"

"I was at home, watching *National Velvet*, with my daughter and two of her friends. Elizabeth Taylor was lovely. The service is in two days. He doesn't have any family coming. His parents died in a farming accident, you know. You needn't stay. Goodbye and thank you for your help."

"Well, I know this is a minority opinion but I think Allison Shein killed Bullfinch and I think Harry was murdered."

She sat down behind her desk and began reading some document, Montblanc pen in hand.

I put the fat envelope in my bag. As one does.

I went back to Theo's to brood. I read Harry's funeral announcement and there, right below it, a semi-update on the hit-and-run. Rural part of Centerville, noted. Victim, noted. (Older man, walking his dog. No family. Dog rehomed.) Two neighbors remarked that they'd heard the man cry out and the dog howl. No mention of a car heard zooming up or away. Daisy came by to ask if I had everything I needed. I said I did, whatever everything might be. She floated in the doorway.

"We might go out after all. They do opera at the movie theater, now."

"I hope I'm not driving you out."

Meaningful pause.

"I know how important you are to Theo. What matters to me is taking care of him and looking after him and if that includes looking after his daughter—"

"Goddaughter," I said. "Not daughter. I'm his goddaughter, I guess."

"Yes," Daisy said. "Of course. That's what I said. We're off to *La Bohème* and then, *Rigoletto*. It should be a blast."

She waved and was gone. Daisy had become my own personal White Rabbit. I drank myself to sleep on Theo's red wine, which was such a terrible idea, I had to wake up at 2:00 A.M., vomit, shower, and go for a walk.

I've Got Dreams

Friday, August 30

I put on my black dress and black heels and my big scarf so I wouldn't look like I thought I was the widow.

The funeral was brief, early, smallish, and self-conscious. Since everyone knew each other, there was no peaceful anonymity, no truly private grieving. Liz Cutty, brass balls clanging, was there on the arm of her perfectly presentable, well-dressed husband. The Freedmans, in all kinds of crazy disrepair, staggered into a pew. Professor Freedman gave me a little salute. Dan Fiske was there, looking like the nice man he was. He scanned the pews calmly and didn't look at me once. Wet-eyed, angry women glared at each other and wept alone. I assumed most of the men I didn't know were uncomfortable and dutiful colleagues. It was ninety degrees inside the chapel and I saw Liz Cutty indicate to the pinched young minister to speed things up. He gave a short eulogy that would have been appropriate for Saint Francis of Assisi. He overlooked everything that had led up to the suicide and even the suicide itself. He referred to "the candle snuffed out" and the "last falling leaf," implying that Harry was a golden, consumptive youth, cut down in his prime by a loving God. I didn't know if anyone else found this odd. No one spoke to me. Either I was paranoid or Michelle had taken out an ad in the paper announcing that I had driven Harry Markham to take his life. You know who wasn't there? Allison Shein. Leah Fields. I took my unlovable self back to my car and drove over to Allison's house, just to make sure that things had unfolded exactly as I expected. Her side of the duplex was quiet.

Her screen in her porch door was soft enough to push through to the real door and I had gotten the hang of the Swiss Army knife technique. It was the home of a woman who'd left in a hurry but not in a panic. Every room was a bit messy but empty, not compulsively tidy but fairly clean. Curling paperbacks on the bookcase, empty wire hangers in the closets. Every drawer was empty. In the backyard, she had a copper firepit and it had recently held a fire. All that was left were dry, thin ashes, not a speck of metal or plastic. She'd left a mug and a spoon in the drainer and a pair of keys on a placemat in the middle of her kitchen table, with a piece of paper underneath that said *Cromwell Housing Office*. Not an ideal tenant but a perfectly good one and with no one on the hunt for her, Cromwell's housing administrator would wander by in the next few days and no hue and cry would be raised, at all. There was a sealed envelope next to the keys.

> *Dear Visitor, I am so sorry to have missed you. You can reach me via email. Au revoir!*

Her name was scrawled beneath the type. Jaunty. Arresting and convicting Allison Shein would require some real international effort by highly motivated police officers. I didn't think Centerville had those.

I went by Theo's and left a thank-you note for Theo and Daisy, under a bouquet of supermarket stargazer lilies. I hope Daisy didn't care where flowers came from. My mother had once taken the supermarket flowers my father had bought as a hurried apology and burned them, plastic sheaf and all. I drove down the potholed two-lane away from Theo's house. I could not bring more trouble to his door. I was thinking about Harry and feeling about Nat.

Harry's note baffled me: *I cannot face what is ahead. Please forgive me for the terrible things I have done. I am sorry. H.* Beautiful Harry, in his pressed white shirts, swimming every day to keep his body perfect, getting his hair trimmed every month, so that it always looked tousled and golden, but never messy or uncared for. And this man, obsessed with his appearance, sat at his desk in a pair of boxers and stuck his father's revolver in his mouth, knowing what a disgusting mess he'd make, what a mess he'd become, for the whole world to see. For all the cops, all the colleagues, all the women to see?

A man who revised his own life constantly, who never missed a chance to present a newly polished facet of himself, who clipped every favorable mention of his name, who happily Googled himself, left a short, simple note and chose not to cover himself in glory or bravery for the last time.

The cops and their suicidologist, as Michelle referred to him, which I assume meant a guy with a diploma mill PhD who would look at suicide notes from people who had jumped off bridges or stuck their heads in ovens and announce that yes, indeed, Bob seemed to have jumped off this bridge, Susie seems to have done a Sylvia Plath. Everyone was happy with the note. Short, sincere, filled with guilt and panic at being cornered. The perfect note. How could he put a gun in his mouth and not refer to Hemingway, not cloak his death with allusions to his hero, who also could not face his life. Not that Harry would have looked at it like that. Or maybe he looked at it exactly like that.

I couldn't see it. Literally, I couldn't see it. Harry climbing the stairs, tears in his eyes, writing that heart-wrenching note, taking his father's revolver and blowing his head off. Even if he'd been the kind of man who faced things squarely and alone, which he surely wasn't, I didn't think he'd have the physical nerve to shoot himself. I felt more tired and worried than I had since my accident. Ends and means, ends and means. I kept running through the scene and the note, trying to focus on the process, not on the end. I had only had time to see a few appointments on his phone, swimming at the Y and Salon D, the haircut place in New Haven (not for Harry, the Italian barbers of Centerville). That appointment was for

August 28. And he must have made it not too long ago. I don't remember to call for a haircut three weeks ahead. Maybe he did. Maybe he had a standing appointment, every month. Do you care about your hair, when you're so depressed that you want to die? When I'm depressed, I don't care if I look like the dog's dinner. And if you're so pathologically vain that you want your hair to look gorgeous even when you're deeply depressed, do you then ruin a $180 haircut by spreading it all over the ceiling? And if you are Harry Markham of the etched abs and sculpted cheekbones, do you present yourself to the world in baggy white boxers horribly gaping, bleeding neck, and no head at all? I don't think so.

Who? Someone capable, strong enough, fast, someone he knew, someone comfortable with guns, someone he'd let in the door. Someone who knew that the police would swallow a suicide when it was spoon-fed to them. Someone who thought that Harry was a good suspect for Bullfinch's murder. Thanks to me, *everyone* knew Harry was a prime suspect. Maybe, like *Murder on the Orient Express*, it was *all* of Cromwell, getting rid of the blight upon their lives. I liked the idea, I would have applauded the action, but I couldn't see it. All I could see was Harry and someone else's hand on his gun. I had probably put that hand there, myself, with my big mouth. I turned the car around and headed back to Centerville.

I had been chasing and I should have been reading. My approach to problem-solving was usually chasing the squirrel, not studying their habits. I was trying to change that. I drove up to the Gallitto Garage and asked if the futon in the back was available. Stevie and Danny were delighted. More espresso, cleanish sheets (well, sheet), and a very tiny toilet. The door to my room didn't lock but it did close and I have rarely felt so safe.

I spread my folder out on the floor and the futon. I read the rest of Harry's folder and kicked myself for not looking harder and sooner. I could hear my Uncle Luis, *Antes que te cases, miro lo que haces,* which is basically "look before you leap," which should not be so hard to learn and do. The bank statements showed that ten days ago, Harry Markham received two bank transfers from two different bank accounts, one for $250,000, one for $125,000. Two different strings of numbers but no names on either account. At last, something. I texted Robbie Gallitto, who was out somewhere, and I offered to bring him a coffee and a few blueberry muffins and meet him in the bank parking lot as soon as possible. He sent back a heart emoji and a promise to meet me in half an hour.

I gave Robbie Gallitto his latte, his blueberry muffin, and my warmest smile. I brought out Harry's bank statements. He wet his thumb like a professional and flipped through the pages.

"These two," I said, looking over his shoulder. "These two little bank transfers. Could you find out what accounts the money was sent from?"

"Lotta money," Robbie said.

He sat down on a bench.

"Lotta money."

"Yes, it is," I said. "Could you possibly see who those accounts belong to? People or person?"

"Yeah. I could."

I gave him a hug, putting my arms more or less around his neck.

"It's not allowed," he said. "Ya know, you're not supposed to do this when you work for the bank."

"I know," I said, unhugging him, trying to figure out if a bribe or reassurance or some kind of threat was required.

He shrugged.

"I'm just saying. I take a lunch break. I get in a little walk. See you at the fountain."

At the fountain, after lunch, Robbie Gallitto said Michelle Blanchfleur is one and Leah Fields is the other. He said those accounts have been closed. Then he kissed me on the forehead and headed back to work.

I called Michelle, who said, pleasantly, "Dell? Where are you?"

"I had some stuff to do here in Centerville, so I'm in town this evening. Do you want to have dinner? I won't be up here that often, now that the case is closed so, I thought we could get together. If you're free."

"Okay. I mean, I'd like that. Why don't you come over here? I'm already cooking and there'll be plenty."

I could hear Leah snarling in the background but Michelle ignored her. "We'll expect you at 7:00, okay? We'll reset."

“That’s very nice. If you tell me what you’re making, I’ll bring an appropriate bottle of wine.”

“Rock Cornish game hens in Missouri barbecue sauce, wild rice, and grilled baby eggplant. Lime mousse for dessert. I’m on vacation this week.”

“I can tell. Thank God. All right, I’ll try to find something nice and I’ll see you at 7:00. Thank you.”

“You’re welcome. It’ll be nice to see you.”

She meant it, I meant it, but we both knew that things were already very different between us.

Next stop.

Theo was sitting in his study, waiting for me. I cleared my throat.

“How was the opera,” I said.

“It was fine. Operatic. I don’t like opera the way I used to. Going out again?”

“How’d you know?”

“You took a shower and you changed your clothes. Those others were getting pretty foxy.”

“You could have told me before I went and smelled up the whole town. Am I all right now?”

“Lovely. Purged with hyssop and whiter than snow. From *Miserere*, know your psalms.”

“I’ll try. Also, I think Allison Shein killed your friend Bullfinch and I don’t think anyone will be bringing her, you know, to justice.”

"Did you try?"

"I did. I failed."

"Well, you can't bring him back. He had pancreatic cancer, anyway. If you have the chance, some other time, do her harm. That's what I'd like."

I could try to do some harm, I thought. I could raise more questions about the timing and authenticity of Bullfinch's glowing email recommendation to Sandrine Boulanger. I could try to make things less comfortable for Allison but I didn't see me winning. I gave Theo a light kiss on the cheek and said I could be rude and send an email to a woman in France, right now. I said I was hoping to do harm. He nodded. I sent the email to Sandrine Boulanger, with as much information as I could fit, without sounding wild-hair crazy. I was informative.

"You're perky," Theo said.

"*You're* perky. I'm going out tonight and I need to bring some nice wine to go with grilled game hens. Where do I go?"

"Just go downstairs, Dell. There are some bottles against the wall. I'll never use them all and you'll get them then. There are some interesting California reds far to the right as you're facing the wall. The second row from the bottom, Château Meyney, that might be good for your game hens. Should I expect you back tonight?"

He didn't say *we*, which I hoped was revealing, rather than tactful.

"I hope so. I'm going to Michelle Blanchfleur's house around seven o'clock; she lives on Plumeria Drive. I'll give you her cell. I hate to say this, but if you haven't heard from me, after a day or two, you ought to call Nat Baker. I'll write it down."

"Nat Baker. A new man in your life. Blanchfleur, charming name. Plumeria Drive. Nice neighborhood. Not a social occasion?"

"Sort of, but not really. I'm sorry, Theo, I don't mean to worry you."

Which was stupid and self-deceiving since if I didn't mean to worry him, I should have gotten the bottle of wine and left without dropping ominous hints.

"Not at all. I'll hear you when you come in."

I smiled. "You're going to wait up?"

"Old people don't sleep, Dell, they doze a little here and there, they take longish naps. That's it. Have you spoken to your father lately?"

"A few days ago. He seems crabby. Plus his memory is just . . . in pieces."

"Yes. Call him before you go out tonight. Please."

In my whole life, Theo had never given me any directions or instructions about my relationship with my father.

"Pop," I said.

"I hear that Theo has a new friend," he said.

In keeping with startling things that had never happened before, my father remarked on Theo's personal life.

"Yes," I said. "She's very nice. He seems very happy."

My father snorted. "You think she holds a candle to your mother?"

"Well, no, but, why would she? What do you mean?"

"Well, I think you already know but Theo said you don't."

We listened to each other breathe.

"Pop, you stopped talking there. You were saying that Theo said I don't know something, but you think I do know. I mean, there is a lot I don't know but is there something in particular?"

There was a roar of noise from his end.

"The goddamn television. I tell Bev and I tell her, be careful with the remote but that goddamned woman. I have to go. This is unbearable."

"Pop?"

"You spoke to your father?"

"I did," I said. "Theo, please. What is it he thinks I know and you think I do not?"

I sat down close to him, so he could feel me.

"You should have been told. Your mother put it off. Shame on me, blaming her. We all put it off. Really, I'm the only one who wanted to tell you, and now, here we are, and I get my way. Your father is, of course, your father but I am, in the smallest, most narrowly biological sense, your father. My DNA and all of that. Your mother's looks, I hope."

I walked around the room.

"I realize this is a shock. Your mother and I loved each other. Your father and I were very good friends. We had a very unusual summer. Your father was in London for two weeks and then, your mother was pregnant. I didn't want children and I was almost blind. I couldn't drive, I couldn't go anywhere without a white cane. I begged her to get an abortion and we didn't speak for almost a year. I went to Florence for quite a while and by the time I came back, you were born and very beautiful, by all accounts, and she and your father seemed very happy. See, your father."

My parents had seemed very happy. My mother would run her hands over my father's long, lantern-jawed face and say, *My hero.* She went to his conferences with him, because he wanted her there. He adored her. When the Guggenheim took two of her paintings, he bought her a diamond bracelet, the kind of thing that had never appeared in their conversation, let alone in our house. When she was not invited to be part of a major exhibition, he threatened to burn the building down and raged about it until she begged him to calm down. But she was pleased. They ate dinner together most nights and if I called during dinner or their movie night, my mother would tell me to call back later.

"You haven't said a word."

"I don't know what to say. Thank you for telling me."

"We all loved you," he said. "We loved each other. We loved each other, although it was sometimes a little strained between your father and me. Naturally. I didn't want your father to feel that he'd lost anything. He didn't want to put me in an awkward position. Your mother said we should have told you when you were little, the way people do in the adoption books. We didn't. I'm sorry. Relationships. Complicated. You know what I always say—"

"Human beings are a mystery. I'm late," I said. "I have to go have dinner with possibly dangerous people."

"That was unkind," Theo said. "I deserve it."

I kissed him good-bye.

"All for love," he said. "Love and forgive."

"Remember those phone numbers," I said. "Also, it's okay. I guess I knew."

What a liar I am.

That's How Strong My Love Is

Leah and Michelle lived in a very nice development out of town, lined on both sides of a curving, curbed road with three- and four-bedroom houses, three-quarter acre lots, truly finished basements, the occasional basketball hoop, neat, deep-green lawns, and well-washed cars in smooth driveways lined with Belgian block. Some of the houses had elaborate wooden playsets in the backyard. Their house was the prettiest on the block, and the biggest. They had a three-car garage. I didn't feel at home and wondered how it was for them, no matter how pretty their lawn or sparkling their cars. I strolled past their very nice garage door, hoping for a peek, but the windows were tinted and there was just a discreet keypad. Michelle swung the front door open before I'd even gotten off the driveway.

I hoped, despite my wish to question her, that Leah was skipping our dinner. No. She sat in the beautiful living room, one leg tucked under her and no intention of getting up. I wasn't sure she even planned to speak to me but Michelle glared at her meaningfully and she waggled three sulky fingers in my direction. I think I was pleasant and I wasn't sure she was sulky. Anxious was more the vibe.

Michelle went into the kitchen and I followed her, expecting that Leah'd continue to sit, imperturbable as a cat, on her chaise. Instead, Leah got up and followed us, elbowing past me in order to be closer to Michelle.

"What a gorgeous kitchen," I said and I was not lying. I did not read a lot of house porn but even a bottom dweller like me knew the difference between Ikea and real furniture and between the dented GE stove that came with the apartment and a six-burner stove that was (1) bright blue and (2) fitted out with a dozen chrome handles. Michelle took a loaf of bread out of a small drawer *in* the stove.

"Is there anything else I can do? Everything smells wonderful. Delish, honey," Leah said.

The last time I heard Leah mention food, she was singing the praises of wheatgrass and staying as low on the food chain as possible.

Michelle looked at Leah with amusement and examined the bottle I handed her. She gave me a quick, appreciative smile and asked me to open it.

"Honey, everything's done. Why don't you get me a platter and I'll bring in the hens?" Michelle hadn't even looked at her; like royalty, she didn't need to check for a chair before she sat down. She put out her hand and the platter was put into it. I was speculating about the shift in their relationship as we sat down.

Michelle served and Leah murmured adoringly over every bite. I watched Michelle. She chewed steadily, filling her plate, pouring another glass of what turned out to be a smooth, cherry-tinged wine. I had a quarter glass and hoped no harm would befall me. Leah's admonitions about Michelle's weight obviously didn't matter anymore. Why not? Perhaps her knowing Leah's secret had caused the power to go from the beloved to the lover. Leah was afraid and Michelle was secure. Was that it? I would have been glad if it hadn't been for the shadows under Michelle's eyes and the speed at which she was working her way through the bottle. I was glad Leah was anxious, because I can be a petty bitch, and I needed to know exactly why.

Our dinner was quiet. I admired the pristine yard and the bluestone patio and the lap pool. And Michelle accepted all the compliments. Leah cleared silently, pausing only to put a hand on Michelle's shoulder. I saw a gold band on the fourth finger of her left hand and I said, "Wedding ring." And then I said it again, with enthusiasm.

Leah smiled. Michelle patted her hand absently, not unkindly. Her eyes were on me.

"Tell me about it," I said, like we were all girl squad.

"Nothing big," Michelle said. "Courthouse and private. We might take a little honeymoon soon."

Leah brought in coffee and the lime mousse and I mentioned again about Allison Shein, moving to Paris.

"Well, good for her," Michelle said mildly. "She was a favorite suspect for a while, mostly because she practically blacked out every time she saw you. I don't blame her."

"Me neither. So you don't think she killed Bullfinch and then killed Harry, faking Harry's suicide?"

Leah said, "That could be."

Two astonishing things: We agreed and Leah had a thought.

Michelle made her lips move in a smile, but unlike Harry, she couldn't make her eyes brighten on command.

"I know your feelings about Allison. Who doesn't? But you didn't come up with the kind of evidence that holds up in court. And, there wasn't anything fake about that suicide, Dell. I didn't think so, the ME didn't think so, even the psychologist we consult with thought it was open and shut. Let's go sit in the living room. Leah, leave the dishes. We can do them later, you're not the fucking maid."

Could have fooled me.

In the living room, Leah snuggled up to Michelle on the couch; I used to think they looked like a Siamese and a golden Lab. Now, with Michelle's hair loose and her casual show of strength, it was more deer and lion. No contest.

"I'm curious, Michelle. And I apologize. But you didn't think that there was some conflict of interest there? In the whole investigation? You know, given the relationship between Leah and Harry?"

I thought Leah was going to tear my throat out. Michelle's eyes narrowed a little bit but she managed another smile.

"What relationship? They hardly knew each other. The four of us had ice cream together."

"What?"

"You were there, Dell," Michelle said.

"That's right," Leah hissed. "I don't know where you get your information, Dell. I think Harry did like to . . . y'know, make himself sound like everyone was crazy about him. He used to talk about you, too. That could be a conflict of interest—if private investigators have ethics."

"Ah. So if someone asked what you were doing the night Harry was . . . the night Harry killed himself, you don't even need an alibi, because there's no motive."

"That's true," Michelle said.

Leah pulled herself together, snuggled Michelle some more, and looked away from me.

"But as it happened, we were both home. I took a long bath because I had pulled a muscle working out at the Y that day and we watched a little TV. Leah talked with her mother for a while. Then we went to bed."

I knew that there must have been witnesses at the Y and a record of the phone call to or from Leah's mother.

"You're close to your mother, Leah?"

She looked at me coldly, her eyes flat as coal. "Yes. We stay in touch."

"Where does she live?"

"In Butte. In Montana."

"I know where Butte is. So, you stay in touch. That's nice. I miss my mother."

No one cared.

"I'm sure. Sounds like you haven't really gotten over it. Yeah, I call her. We caught up. It was nice."

"Sounds like your evenings are pretty quiet."

Michelle spoke up. "Very quiet. We like them that way. We're homebodies. I know you don't mean it, but this sounds a lot like questioning a suspect."

"I'm sorry. Old habits. I do not, for a minute, think you killed anyone."

I stood up, Columbo-style.

"And you have a Tesla, right? I was thinking about getting one. Aspiring. Could I take a quick look at yours?"

Leah smiled again. "We like it but I can't show you. In the shop again. They don't tell you about that."

"Another time," I said.

Leah wrapped herself around Michelle, like a pretty vine.

"Sure," Leah said. "Another time."

"And congratulations," I said.

I texted Nat about coming by and he sent back a big brown thumbs-up.

I drove up to Nat's little house, hitting every bump and hole in the dirt road. There were no lights on and the forest was dark and still. I sat in the car, fiddling with the radio dial, hoping to find more help than I usually found in song lyrics. Nat would believe me and hate me or he would not believe me and I would be so frustrated and angry that I would hate him. I hadn't come up with anything else.

Some old-fashioned radio station was ending the day with an Otis Redding retrospective. I took a break and listened, eyes closed, to that rough, silky skein of a voice, tearing open his navy blue sharkskin jacket, falling to one knee, begging me to answer him, "What can the matter be? It can't be too serious, we can't talk it over . . ."

If God ever speaks to me, I expect it to be, I hope it will be, in the voice of Otis Redding.

I flicked off the ignition and walked up to the house, still hoping that someone else would be doing this for me. I made an enormous racket with the twigs and gravel and managed to scratch my arm on a wild rose bramble. No lights went on. I stood on the porch, feeling the August air on my face and the burning line on my arm.

"Nat," I called, too softly.

He'd only have heard me if he was lurking behind the front door, which didn't seem likely. I was breathing heavily, not quite able to catch my breath.

"Nat."

Almost loud enough. What if I startle him and he comes down and shoots me? What if I never get his attention and have to spend the night in my car, like a complete asshole?

"Nat, this is Dell Chandler. I want to talk to you and I'm on the front porch."

My father has a sister, Marjorie, a terrifyingly crisp criminal lawyer who lives in Westport and every Christmas she'd call and say, "Dellarobbia, this is your Aunt Marjorie, your father's sister, from Westport." My mother said that she thought Aunt Marjorie, my father's younger sister, was motivated by a lifelong fear of appearing needy. I was sympathetic now. I could envision, suddenly and vividly, a woman coming down the stairs to answer the door. She's wearing a white silk wrapper and she is exquisitely dark and small; she glows like a black pearl. Politely, she peers at me. Nat comes down behind her, pulling on his robe, covered with sweat; he goggles at me and hesitates before opening the door.

This vision was just infuriating and I shouted his name, causing a bird to squawk and two lights to come on. No woman floated down the stairs. He flew down, hitting every third step, shaking the house.

"Hey there."

And he hugged me so softly and sweetly that my chest got tight and my eyes itched. I wanted to float into him, slide around his big shoulders, and melt, like butter in the pan. I put my head against his neck and shut my eyes, ready to sleep right there, with my face deep in his spicy scent.

"Sorry for how I was—"

"Me too."

"Come on."

Nat pushed me ahead of him, up the stairs, and undressed me. I began crying and Nat stroked my hair, giving me little butterfly kisses. He held me and came inside of me and went on holding me. I think I fell asleep like that.

I woke up six hours later, like it was the classic morning after, from every fifties movie ever made. Birds warbled, sun splashed gold and yellow on the floor, and one white rose was on the pillow beside me. I was starting to get a headache, the small, right eyebrow one that afflicts me when I'm dreading something.

I put the rose in a glass in the bathroom, put on one of Nat's T-shirts and my underpants, and went downstairs, massaging my forehead.

"What's the matter?"

Nat handed me a cup of coffee and sat back in his chair. He didn't touch me.

I cleared my throat a few times and took a sip, scalding the roof of my mouth with coffee almost as good as Mrs. Martinelli's.

"I am so sorry but I think Michelle . . . I think Michelle is in trouble. Money trouble." I was doing a truly terrible job of this. "I'm sure it's because of Leah. But I think Michelle is being blackmailed. She and Leah put a lot—a lot—of money in Harry's account in the last week. And I don't know why. Also, I do not think Harry killed himself. These things might be connected."

The stone man returned. In the time it took him to put down his coffee cup, his face lost all expression. Have we been introduced?

"You know something I don't know?"

"I think I do. I do."

And I told him how I had gone back over Harry's bank statements, finally, and found two big bank transfers. I mentioned that Michelle herself told me she liked nice things and Leah had grown up with them. And the rings on their hands were not from Target. They weren't even from Zales. When I was young, Aunt Marjorie would let me play in her jewelry box ("Say *Cart-ee-A*, Dell. Say *Bool-gar-ee.*") and twist her diamond bracelets through my hair. I did know very nice ice when I saw it. I thought that these were people who could afford to pay a blackmailer. And one of these people might balk at that, if the blackmailer was pushy. One of these people might feel, after caving, *Oh no you don't, you slimy sonofabitch.* And I finished by telling Nat that Leah and Michelle had gotten married.

"Bullshit."

"Oh, no," I said. "Saw the wedding ring. Heard about a possible honeymoon."

"Uh huh," he said, like a cop taking a statement from an unreliable source. "I'm going for a little walk."

"Okay. I'll stay."

I tried not to make it a question. He didn't even nod. The screen door banged open and he was in the woods. That's it? Ten years ago, he would have come back to find a note pinned to the wall with a bowie knife. I was either growing up or getting soft. I looked around for a couple of aspirin and couldn't find any. He did have jars and jars of vitamin and melatonin gummies, which was informative, but useless. I made myself another cup of coffee, not nearly as good as the Gallittos', and went back to work.

I called Salon D, still looking for the ways and means of Harry Markham.

"Salon D, Linda speaking. If your hair isn't becoming to you, you should be coming to us."

Retro-snappy.

"Hi?" I said. "I, uh, just moved to Centerville? And my girlfriend, she lives in New Haven and her boyfriend, he lives in Centerville? But he gets his hair cut at your place and his hair is just, uh, outrageous?"

It turns out that upspeak is a great disguise.

"Sure, n.p." I can't allow myself to dwell on the fact that I will probably never hear *Thank you* again in my lifetime, that *No problem* is now archaically formal and the abbreviation is commonly preferred.

"Could I make an appointment with the same person who cuts his hair?"

"Sure," she said, perkily. "Who cut your friend's hair?"

"Oh." I sounded crestfallen. I was crestfallen. Things were going so well.

"I don't know. I thought maybe you had one of those big books, with people's names in it? Like who cuts whose hair?"

"All right," said the agreeable Linda. Maybe these places weren't so bad. The guy who trims my hair has a receptionist like Marjorie Taylor Greene. "What's the guy's name?"

"Um, Harry?" I was tempted to stop there, just to see how sweet-natured Linda really was. "He's tall and very blond, really cute. She's told me a million times . . . Markman, Markham. I'm sure it's Markham. He teaches at Cromwell?"

"Are you kidding? Have you spoken to your girlfriend lately?"

"No, she's been away for the last few weeks and I just got moved in. Why?"

"I don't know how to tell you . . ."

Linda's voice was a little shaky and I was sorry to be doing this to a perfectly nice girl.

"Anyway, the guy, your friend's boyfriend, is dead. He shot himself, just a few days ago."

"Oh, gross. How awful. I mean, my God." Then I counted to ten and sighed, a bewildered, not-wanting-to-be-inappropriate-but-sort-of-disappointed sound.

"I'm sorry you had to hear it from me. Anyway, CeeCee did his hair."

Good.

"Oh, thanks so much. I mean, God . . . I mean, shooting yourself. So violent."

"Yeah." Linda and I were taking it up a notch. "Cee really loved him. She was very upset and she didn't come to work yesterday."

I wondered if Cee was at the funeral. The wailing, waifish white girl with a pixie cut and a white kurta, who lay on the floor? The statuesque black woman, in the very small navy blue dress, who draped herself on the steps to the pulpit, wrapping her strong dancer's legs around the usher when he tried to get her back to her seat?

"If CeeCee's free some time, maybe I could come get my hair cut? Trimmed, really."

I was not prepared to have my hair cut off for this stupid case if it wasn't absolutely necessary. "Any day's okay for me, I haven't started work yet."

"How about later today? She's got an opening at three."

"Oh wow, that's perfect."

I was really getting into my new personality.

"What's your name?"

"My name? Toni."

Who is Toni and why have I suddenly given myself her name? Toni Baxter was my babysitter when I was nine and she was fifteen, until she got a real job at Applebee's, when she was a senior. She was blonde and bouncy and loved to watch Nickelodeon with me while we ate slightly burnt popcorn.

"Okay, Toni. I'll see you at three. CeeCee'll do you, then."

I sat back down at the kitchen table, running my finger through the little puddle of coffee surrounding my cup. I looked out the window. No Nat. Mr. Sunshine was probably deep in the woods now, scaring the squirrels, reviewing all the pieces, furious that I was questioning his partner's integrity, doubly furious that he hadn't seen it first and dealt with it.

I needed to call Mary Clark and check on her pneumonia. I needed to call my father and move into his house, for a little while, to get things straightened out, while there was still a path through the memories. I wanted to do the right, responsible thing, at every turn. I called them both and got voicemail and was grateful. Nat came in through the kitchen door and I put down my phone. His face was smooth and dark, all the feelings worn away. My headache, whose absence I hadn't noticed, returned full force.

"I'm glad you told me your theory," he said, quietly. "I'm going to pursue this on my own for a little, see what I can come up with."

He looked out at the woods. I tried to catch his eye, but he managed to look right past me.

"So, I think we ought to step back for a while, not step away"—he looked at me, for one second—"just step back, while we think things over, do what we have to do."

"Step back?"

What were we talking about, step back? Whatever he thought he was saying, I heard *good-bye*. I didn't want to wait around while he elaborated or prettied it up or reassured me that it was just temporary. This is why women put ice picks into men's hearts. It's not the other women or the forgetting of anniversaries. It's that they tear your heart out of your chest, kick it around a few times, and then refuse to acknowledge that anything unusual, let alone painful, is taking place.

"Okay, if that's what we need to do, that's what we should do."

I didn't even want to look him in the eye any longer. Coward. Bastard.

"Maybe we'll touch base later this week," I said.

Long pause.

"Well, maybe we should pursue independent investigations. I don't want to get in your way, make you feel like I'm looking over your shoulder."

That is good of you. "Fine."

I shrugged. I have been told that my shrugs are infuriating. I hoped so, hoped he would come towards me angrily, and I could smash the coffee cup across his cold, dead face.

"Well, I hope you find out that I'm mistaken about Michelle and I also hope you find who killed Harry, because Harry

Markham did not put a gun in his pretty mouth and pull the trigger. Also, although your colleagues don't seem to care, I have told them that I think Allison Shein killed Bullfinch. And, she's now in Paris, because it was easier for everyone to make it all Harry. Case closed."

And I hope you rot. I picked up my keys.

He walked towards me and touched my cheek with his forefinger. I didn't know what I was supposed to make of that, so I walked out to my car.

I sat there like a sack of groceries, leaning against the headrest. I looked towards the house and saw Nat watching me, so I turned on the ignition and backed out in a show of insouciance, hitting a rhododendron. If I lived with the Gallitto *cugini*, this kind of shit wouldn't happen.

Everybody Needs Somebody

I drove down to Salon D. Red neon lettering and hot pink lips made it easy to find. Next door was a junk shop, which called itself The Junk Shop. Pre-gentrification. The owner herself was a statement against gentrification: filling up a white vinyl recliner, on the sidewalk, fanning herself as sweat poured off her huge white form, marginally covered with a strapless terry cloth sarong, also white. The only spots of color were her deep red finger- and toenails and the onyx black of her eyes. She looked like a melting, jaded snowman.

"Hot enough for you?" she said.

I didn't think people really ever said that.

"Yeah. You've got front row seats there."

"Yep. Not much gets past me."

That was probably true. Nothing to do, not a lot of business, too hot in the store.

"You know, maybe you could help me. I'm trying to find a friend of mine, he moved down here a while ago. A long-lost thing."

"Why would this friend of yours come here?"

Maybe that wasn't intelligence I saw in those tiny black eyes, maybe it was just Sicilian heritage and a bad disposition.

"He told me he used to get his hair cut right here, next door. I don't know if he ever came into your shop or not. Tall guy, good-looking, blond, blue eyes, around 6'2", broad shoulders. If you saw him, you'd think athlete."

"If I saw him, I'd think, let's take a trip to paradise."

"Well, that, too. Did you ever notice him?"

"You mean Harry?"

"You met him? Yes, Harry."

No grass growing under my feet.

"Sure. He'd stop in, he liked old picture frames. I mean, he wouldn't have come if he wasn't getting his hair cut, this isn't the first place you'd go, looking for fancy picture frames, but I got a few. A few that are very nice," she said, a little more defensively than I had expected from the owner of The Junk Shop. "He was *magnifico*, eh? *Sensuale.* A man like that . . . Terrible thing, his death. Probably didn't kill himself, you know."

"No?"

Next, she could tell me how to get Allison arrested, entrap Michelle and or Leah without getting myself killed, and then we could start working on the situation with Nat.

"Nah. Come on, you look like a smart girl. Was he a special friend of yours? I shouldn't have put my foot in it like that."

I didn't want her sudden sensitivity to put an end to our conversation. I didn't want to let her know I was a private investigator. She wouldn't appreciate the competition.

"No, I wasn't one of his girlfriends. It wasn't like that between us. I already had a boyfriend. Harry was just a friend from work."

"Ha. You teach at that fancy-ass school, too, huh? See, I could tell you were smart. Harry, he was pretty smart. I mean, he thought with the little head, but whatta you gonna do? A man's a man, right?"

Tell me something useful, I thought.

"I saw him two Wednesdays in a row. A week before someone did the job on him. He was one excited guy. The way he'd get, every new girl was exciting. This one, even more than the others. He wanted sweetheart frames, ya know, the double hearts. Usually, he just got a single. The girls liked to have a picture of him, he said, so he put a nice picture of him in a nice little frame. Something special to show them that they were special." She shrugged, forgivingly. "Some were, some weren't, but he knew how to treat a girl. *Rispetto.*"

I wondered if there was a Mr. Junk Shop and if she forgave him the way she forgave Harry. She probably didn't get that honey-dripping sensation when Mr. Junk Shop stroked her chubby arm.

"Did Harry say who the picture frames were for this time?"

"No. Special girl, he said, and then last Wednesday, he came by again. He said he was decorating for a new office. Gonna be classy. I have some good things," she said. "Bookcases, walnut. Antique globe. Two leather club armchairs. And a little antique map, I had it fifty years. Wisconsin. He was gonna take it all, he said. He said he'd had some luck, he'd come into some money and he was buying a house. He asked me to hold on to the map and the chairs and the globe. He paid for them, y'know. Does that help?"

I glanced at my watch, not wanting to miss my next informant, not wanting to cut off my new friend, the oracle.

"Maybe. How much was the stuff he bought for the new office? The nice stuff?"

She shrugged. "Three grand. Does this help?"

"Yes, it does, but I have to go in for my appointment. Thanks, maybe I'll stop by again."

"Okay and tell your boss you do a nice job."

She showed a dimple now, her eyes dancing.

"Pardon me?"

"If you're not a cop, I wasn't married to one for thirty years, God rest his soul. And you're a lot nicer than the other broad, the big one tailing Harry. Her, I didn't talk to. I didn't like her attitude one bit."

She settled her jaw among her chins, remembering Michelle.

I didn't have to ask but I did. "What'd she look like?"

"Big blonde, could've been Harry's twin, practically. Very aggressive, very rude person. She came bulling in here about five minutes after Harry left."

"What'd she ask you?"

"Did he come here often, was he alone, did he mention any names. The usual stuff. And then she had the nerve to tell me he was a suspect in a homicide. *Tell it to the Marines, honey*, I wanted to say, but I just played stupid. Said I never saw him before this one time, and he was looking for a bookcase. Maybe she was a cop, she showed me the badge, but she wasn't here on a real beef, I could tell. Am I right?"

"Right."

"Next time, someone tells you he's dead, you gotta act surprised. You know, like this: *Hoo boy, dead? Madonna mia, no!* Like that. But, still, you did good."

She smiled encouragingly and wiped her face with a dingy white towel.

I ran into Salon D, afraid that at 3:20, my 3:00 appointment would have been cancelled. On the contrary, I was told that CeeCee would be ready for me shortly, meaning another 15 minutes. I was invited to have a Diet Coke and read *Xan*, a magazine without words but with lots of pictures of some very thin and some very large young people wearing expensive sweaters, sarongs, and gauzy things. CeeCee tapped me on the shoulder as I was studying a pictorial spread on the art of affixing beads, hemp, coins, and flowers directly onto your skin. She had a pale, heart-shaped face with bee-stung lips and dark brown eyes, ringed with kohl. Silver hoops ran from her earlobes to the edge of her hairline. Her very round head was covered with platinum blonde stubble, finished off with a wispy violet tail at the nape of her neck. She washed my hair with small, strong hands and squirted mint shampoo and coconut conditioner while I lay back, eyes closed and throat vulnerable, with my head in a basin.

"You have a lot of hair," she said, toweling it dry and combing out the knots. "Do you really want to cut it?"

"No."

She looked relieved and I began to feel better.

"Why don't you just trim off the split ends today and if I get up the nerve, I'll come back for a cut some other time."

She nodded cheerfully and began to trim my hair with impressive speed and concentration. I'd have about six minutes in which to get information from her. I thought about telling her that I was really a PI but since everyone who knew that lied to me, I stuck with being Toni, hoping to do better.

"Linda told me you knew my friend's boyfriend, Harry Markham."

CeeCee stopped cutting and met my eyes, in the mirror. "What was your friend's name?"

I hadn't expected that. "Laurel." Close to Leah, in case she'd heard a rumor, different in case she knew Leah. "It wasn't a big romance, but they had been seeing each other, you know, for a while."

CeeCee relaxed. "I know, I know how Harry was. He told me everything. You know, a hairdresser hears everything. I'm very discreet. I never even told my friends or my boyfriend." She smiled at me, hesitantly. "He never mentioned your friend by name. Is she the dancer?"

"Yeah."

"Oh. I'm sorry. I mean, I know it probably looked like he was being a real shit. I know it looked bad, just ghosting and everything. But really, he was such a sensitive guy, he felt so bad when he hurt someone, then he just couldn't see them again."

Low-life sonofabitch.

"Well, I know what you're saying. And Laurel didn't exactly let go gracefully. I guess she was really crazy about him."

"Well, he was a wonderful person, I know how she felt. He was just, you know, lovable. Such a little boy, really. I just can't believe what happened. I would never have thought Harry would kill himself. Never. You know, he made an appointment with me, for that day. The day he killed himself. Isn't that completely weird? I don't know what happened that night to make him take his life. Then I spoke to him at 3:00, he sounded fine. Better than fine. He said he'd come into some money and after the haircut, he was going to Nordstrom, to get some new clothes, and he was gonna get rid of his cute little car. He was looking at a Tesla. He was pretty stoked. He said, *Sky's the limit*, so I guess that meant things were really good 'cause he did have some money troubles, always. I mean, who doesn't? Always. That was Tuesday, when we talked and then *that*. Completely weird."

"Did the police come and question you? I mean, you were such a good friend."

"No," she said, with only a little surprise. "No one asked me. I couldn't go to the funeral, though. It was just too sad and Ozzie said if I was making myself sick, I shouldn't go."

This last said with some satisfaction.

"Of course not."

"Our baby's due in December."

"That's great. Congratulations." The floor was sprinkled with my quarter-inch red snippets. "Why do you think he did it? I know you said you couldn't imagine it, but . . ."

"I don't know. Maybe something from his past. He didn't talk about that much. His parents died when he was very young, you know. I don't think he ever got over that. They were like aristocrats, and they were on vacation in Europe, killed in a car accident, and he was raised by his aunt and uncle, until he went to boarding school. That's all I know."

"Wow. That is really sad. Thank you for the haircut. Good luck with the baby."

I stuck money in her hand, figuring $45 for the five-minute trim and a five-dollar tip. Linda at the desk, or someone just like her, smiled and handed me a bill for $80. Dr. Cutty settled up just in time.

I'm Your Man

Monday, September 2

I shut up and slept on the futon for ten hours. I woke up and called Nat at the police station, giving a fake name.

"Baker here."

"This is Willie Mae Thornton."

"This is Baker." I couldn't tell if he was keeping his sense of humor under wraps or if it had fled permanently.

"I'd rather not talk on the phone and I'd like us to meet later."

"The last place I saw you will be fine. I get off at 7:00 tonight."

"I'll be there."

The phone went dead and having almost forgotten it, I drove home again for the goddamned picnic with my father.

I found him napping in the recliner he'd occupied for twenty years. I sat until he woke up, which he did, startled and furious at being caught. He seemed to be himself again, which was good news, in terms of my near future, and bad news in terms of a fun picnic. He accused me of spying on him. Then, he complained that I was late. I agreed. And I apologized. That surprised us both. I put all of Bev's leftovers on a big tray and we sat on the broken patio furniture out back.

My father said, "This is nice."

I agreed.

"Why in Christ's name do we have all this food," he said.

"Bev brought her leftovers. It's great," I said. "Patties, mac and cheese, green beans, coconut cake."

My father wrinkled his nose. We had lived on takeout when I was growing up and to the best of my knowledge, my father had been eating Chinese American from Wah Fong down the street (they could deliver his two egg rolls, boneless ribs, steamed red bean paste bun, and egg drop soup before he cleared his throat) and bowls of Cap'n Crunch since my mother died. Neither of us really knew what to do with actual food together. He pushed away his plate and sighed.

"It was nice of Bev," I said.

My father stared at the backyard. The Japanese maple was starting to turn from burgundy to scarlet, just a few leaves.

"Your mother loved this tree."

I brought all the food back into the kitchen. I came back with two big bowls of Cap'n Crunch and a cold quart of milk.

"Cheers," I said. "The milk's not sour."

My father brightened.

"This is more like it." He waved a spoon at me. "*Semper tibi pendeat halec.*"

I responded as I'd been taught, "May there always be herring in your net."

We finished our cereal in silence and I made us both big mugs of coffee with a splash of brandy for him.

"Did you see Theo up there?"

"I did. I saw him a lot."

I hesitated to admit that I'd brought trouble on his old friend and I couldn't bear to broach the subject of my paternity.

"I'm sure that was gratifying for him. Conniving little bastard."

I stopped sipping.

"He never stopped chasing your mother, you know. And she loved it. All that 'we're both art lovers' bullshit. Did they think they were fooling me?"

My father knocked his coffee over and I mopped up around him and handed him a bunch of napkins and poured a new cup, silently.

"You were saying . . ."

My father stared at me and shrugged. "At my age, I'm lucky I remember my name. I usually watch the news around now," he said. "Throw out some of that food so Bev won't think we're unappreciative bumpkins."

I threw out the green beans and patties and put the garbage bag in the can in the garage, to hide the facts. I was thinking about nothing except whatever my father was saying about Theo and my mother.

"What were you saying about Theo and Mama," I began.

My father looked at me. He put both hands on my shoulders and kissed my forehead.

"Go forward," he said, with great kindness. "Love. Forgive. The past is a lesson, not a place to live."

I kissed my father, whom I knew to be my father, and asked if I could stay the night.

"Your room is your room," he said.

I drove back to Centerville very early the next morning, waving to the traffic cop behind the billboard and to the crazy cat lady, whose twenty cats stood on her roof and front porch, all watching the main road.

I called Nat again, on his cell.

I said, "Three hundred and seventy-five thousand dollars. All to Harry. From Michelle and Leah. Two different banks. And he bought some nice furniture and suddenly had the money to buy a house. And a Tesla."

"Seven tonight. I'll follow up," he said.

I heard the click and the nothing.

Nat had said seven o'clock and I showed up on time, in front of his house, as the sun was beginning to settle through the trees. We were both hurting and I wasn't pleased to find that I cared about his pain as much as my own. I didn't see it doing us much good. He crushed a few twigs and tore leaves off a sapling and I waited.

"We met," he said. "It was no good. I showed Michelle I didn't have a wire, I put my gun on the dashboard, for Christ's sake. She said that she was not dirty and that if I thought she was, I should go talk to DiCo. I don't think she committed a crime but . . . I'm gonna test that fucking Tesla, myself. I got a friend."

"What makes you think there's something, now?"

"She wasn't surprised. She didn't tell me to go fuck myself for suspecting her, for thinking there was something not right. I reminded her about that one time, a few years ago, when she fucked with the evidence. She's no actress," he said affectionately.

"What'd you tell her?" The woods were getting darker and his face blended with the trees and shadows. He pocketed his sunglasses, but his face was still masked.

"I told her it looked bad. I told her about the bank transfers. I said it would be easy to find an unsolved hit-and-run in Centerville this summer. I didn't say anything that tied you in to me."

"Why not?" I didn't want to get hopeful.

"So that you can call her and see what you can get. She won't confess to me. She knows I won't roust her without very solid evidence. Being gay hasn't helped her but no one's going to watch a good cop go down based on my guesses, even less on yours. You get it on tape, I'll take Leah in. We think it's Leah, right? I mean they both paid out but we think it's Leah's hit-and-run. Little weasel. She killed him. You don't get anything on tape we'll put all the scraps together and give it to DiCo. Let him worry about it."

His voice was as flat and frail as the bark he peeled off the tree.

"What happens then?"

"Who knows? Maybe he'll demote Michelle and she'll do traffic for the next twenty years. Maybe he'll suggest she resign. Maybe he'll investigate. No one is sorry Markham is dead. My ass'll be in a sling, anyway. Holding back all this stuff, giving Michelle time to get out of town."

"If she's not gone by tomorrow, Nat, I don't think she's going anywhere. Jesus, your partner said he thinks you're an accessory to a hit-and-run. And you or your wife killed your blackmailer. You either face down that partner or you get the hell out of town. Or maybe you shoot that partner."

"What's your guess?"

"I don't think she would kill you."

"'Cause I'm too fast or because she'd funk it?"

"How about because you're her partner and she loves you and because she's not a killer. Not really."

He sighed. "Loving me, if that's what she feels, is not going to stand tall when she's faced with losing her job, losing Leah, and doing time. Murder, even of your blackmailer, is murder. If someone got hurt in that hit-and-run, that's a felony, a big fine and maybe jail time for Leah, too. Where are you going to sleep tonight?"

It didn't sound like an invitation.

"Not in New Haven, not at my father's, and not at Theo's. I could stay with the Gallittos."

The woods were dark enough to hide my face, so I assume that he couldn't see my disappointment.

"Fine," he said. "You think Michelle's coming after you?"

"No. Not at all."

"Look, we could take a room at a motel, take a cab there and spend a few nights. It'll be safer, if we're guessing wrong about her. Safer for us. First of all, if she tries to shoot me, she's very likely to kill me. We don't shoot to wound, Dell. That's public relations bullshit, to keep the civilians and politicians happy. You don't plan to stop someone, there's no point in drawing your weapon. I don't think that's the way she's going to go. I think she's going to tough it out, lie like a rug, and arrange to transfer to another force. She doesn't think I'll drop the dime on her."

"Will you?"

"I don't want to. Aiding and abetting, that's not great. Murdering Harry, you can't get around that. I can't. If I can't get her to confess, I'll do what I have to do. We will find that hit-and-run and we will match it to Leah's car and its repair and those payments pretty much seal the deal. And that takes us to Harry. If you can't get her to talk, I'll take it to DiCo. I told you that."

He had faced what he had to face.

"All right, I'll call her," I said. "You want to get something to eat and go to the No-Tell Motel or wherever?"

"We sure could use one."

We took a long, quiet walk to downtown and ate at D and S Pizza, finishing off a Sicilian pizza with a pound of mozzarella and a pound of hot sausage balancing the two-ton crust. In a room full of tired, hungry people, no one gave us a glance. We gave off as much romantic spark as your socks. Nat called a Lyft to pick us up in front of the hardware store two blocks away from the pizza place and a cheerful woman dropped us off in front of the Cromwell Arms, which avoided true seediness as well as charm. It was clean, the carpet was cobalt blue, and the toilets were sealed with strips of germicidal paper. Here were Buicks and Plymouths and more than a few Lincolns and Volvos in the courtyard. A very nice green Jag was parked up by the dumpster. The Cromwell Arms didn't have to charm, it had no competition, as the robo–desk clerk made clear. We checked in and lay down on separate queen beds, staring at the ceiling. Nat clicked on the television and we watched shows that I thought had gone off the air twenty years ago.

"I'll call Michelle in the morning, okay?"

"Call her tonight," he said.

"Who the fuck are you? I don't have a boss, remember?"

"I understood you to be asking a question, so I was giving you an answer. I was not giving you a command or attempting to dictate to you."

I lay still for a few minutes. “I know I’m a little testy about these things. I’m sorry. I don’t want to make the phone call, so I wanted you to give me permission to put it off.”

He smiled grimly and clicked off the TV. I called Michelle. She wasn’t happy to hear from me.

“Michelle, I think we need to talk some more. Without Leah.”

“Why?”

“Well, there are some things going down that I think you ought to know about, things I’ve been hearing about that concern you. You know, we always got along, I wanted to pass the word.”

“What is it, Dell?”

She sounded tense but collected, probably reassuring Leah silently.

“Not over the phone. Meet me tomorrow, 11:00 A.M., at the Cromwell Arms. Just ask the desk clerk what room I’m in.”

I didn’t want any unexpectedly early visitors. Tomorrow, I’d rent a room in my real name; this one was in the name of Mr. and Mrs. Purple Rain.

“Okay. Anybody else going to be there?”

“No, of course not. I want this to be private. There’s no point to this if the whole world knows. And don’t tell Nat I called you. You don’t want him in on this.”

“No problem. I’ll see you tomorrow.”

She hung up and I could see her crossing to Leah and holding her, filling her eyes and hands one more time. I went and washed my face.

“So?” said Nat.

"So, tomorrow at 11:00, something should happen and this is the vaguest damn plan I've ever worked with."

"Do you have some suggestions?"

"No." Hard to believe that a week ago I thought we had a future. "I'm going to bed."

He got up and went into the bathroom and I threw my clothes on the floor and slid into my bed. Let him go out on a limb this time. He came out, bare chested, carrying his shirt and shoes. He turned out the room lights and sat down heavily on his bed.

"Good night, Dell. Be careful tomorrow."

"You too. Good night, Nathaniel."

I could hear him smile a little at the use of his full name.

"How do I do it?" I said.

"Do what?"

I got up and found my way to his bed. I felt him, warm, slightly damp, broad and smooth beside me.

"This is a surprise," he said, pulling me closer.

"To me, too," I said. "'Love alters not with his brief hours and weeks but it bears out even to the edge of doom.'"

"You love me?" he said.

"I do."

I could see my mother putting her hand over her heart, the way she did whenever I did what she wanted me to do that I had thought I couldn't.

"I love you."

We did what we did know how to do and fell asleep, hand in hand, a little less afraid.

Bring It On Home

Tuesday, September 3

In the morning, I woke up before Nat and ran slowly, hoping to find answers in the trees and cars and barking dogs. I checked back into the motel as myself this time and paid for a dinky room on the second floor. The clerk had only seen Nat the night before and a tired black man was not so unusual at this place. I knew the second floor limited my mobility but I was more concerned with limiting Michelle's. I was weaker but more agile and if we found ourselves outside the room, I thought I'd be able to get off the second floor without too much damage. I had, as usual, no actual idea what would happen and I hadn't seen a single *Law & Order* episode in which a woman my age jumped off a second floor and landed on the asphalt without breaking a leg or two.

Time crawled. Nat did sit-ups and push-ups until the cheesy carpet was damp and he finally took a shower.

I sat on the crappy balcony in the rusting lawn chair and called my father.

"Pop," I said. "Are you looking at your calendar, in the kitchen?"

Every time I visited, we updated the calendar, took off the old Post-its, and added a few new ones.

"I am," he said.

"Okay. Circle Thursday, September 5, with the red pen."

"There is no red pen."

"Pop, there is a red pen in the drawer at the far end of the counter. Where we keep the menus," I said, inspired.

I heard tons of rustling and some fancy Elizabethan swearing.

"Red pen," he said.

And I admired him more than I ever have. To be blind, unsure and map-less, in such hostile territory and trust me? I had to do better.

"That's great. You're doing great. Just circle Thursday, September 5, on the calendar and write *Dell comes*. So, if you do not see me on Thursday, call Theo, please."

I heard a sigh, which meant, *In a pig's eye*.

"Pop, it's just, it's just belt-and-suspenders." A favorite phrase of his. "Just write, *If No Dell, Call Theo*. Please."

I heard the pen.

"Pop, could you possibly read it back to me, just because. Just because I want to be clear. Sometimes, I think I'm being clear but I'm not."

My father chuckled, kindly.

"Human condition, my dear. Thursday, September 5. Dell comes. If not, call Theo. That bastard."

"Great," I said. "I love you, Pop."

"Ah, yes," he said.

And that would have to do.

I typed all my notes, my suppositions (many), my evidence (scant), high points of my interviews, and I reread it and deleted all the snark. I sent it to Joseph DiCenzo, to Nat, and to my aunt Marjorie.

I had thought, I had liked to imagine that what I thought was, I am ready to die. No bonds, no dependents, ready to rumble into the afterlife, and I was mistaken. I did not want to die. I wanted to take care of my fathers, and I wanted to find my way with Nat and meet his daughter and I wanted to finally become the woman my mother hoped I would be.

Nat and I moved up into the new room and drew the curtains.

"She'll be armed. I would be," I said. "Also, although I feel awkward saying this at all and especially now, I meant what I said."

"I know," he smiled. "I gotta concentrate. Does Michelle know you carry? She might have that little ankle job she likes. She doesn't really like wearing the holster."

He was embarrassed to be telling a civilian his partner's secrets.

"It's still a gun, right?"

"Right." He looked away, grimly.

"What if she finds you in the shower before she confesses?"

"I'll tell her I'm worried about you both. I say it fast."

"You think she'll come?"

"Yeah. I think I convinced her there was nothing anymore between you and me."

"Fantastic. What'd you say? That I was a lousy lay and stole your silver?"

"I lied. I didn't mention the silver . . ."

Again, there was that slight sliding towards contact and my chest ached. We put down the bath mat for him to stand on, for traction. He tried to make himself comfortable behind the shower curtain.

"You're not armed, are you?" he asked.

"Well, I am. I usually tell people I'm not. I don't like to use it."

I couldn't actually say I disliked using it, either. I'd only fired it at a practice range but hitting the paper target smack in the middle was gratifying.

He shook his head.

"Oh. Well, that's what makes us different from civilians, I guess. We love guns. Guns, violence, inflicting damage on the helpless. Hands up, can't breathe, don't shoot. Jesus Christ. Sorry."

I left the bathroom, turned out the light, and left the door just slightly ajar. I sat on one of the out-of-order vibrating beds and thought briefly about how I had gotten from my admittedly shitty office with two stained armchairs and a print by Edward Hopper to this pale green motel room, waiting for someone I liked to shoot me or Nat or maybe herself, pretty soon. As people around here did.

I put the revolver in my purse, then in the back of my waistband, concealed by my denim jacket. It was uncomfortable. Good for posture, terrible for speed. Speed was all I was going to have. I put it back in my purse. I admired Michelle's ankle holster enormously, but I couldn't very well stick my gun in my sweat sock, and if I did, I'd probably end up shooting off my toes. I didn't want to leave the safety catch on. "Please excuse me for a moment, while I fumble inconspicuously in my purse." I worried that if I left it off, if and when my purse hit the ground, I'd be in as much trouble as Michelle. Humiliation was temporary. Death was permanent. I got up to ask Nat's advice. Footsteps outside my door stopped me.

I left the catch on and put the goddamn purse on the nightstand next to the chair I planned to sit in, top unzipped and facing away from the other chair.

Michelle knocked sharply and I opened the door. We looked at each other, with equal parts affection, mistrust, and guilt. I wish we had just stopped there and I had told her that I knew all about it and she had apologized and moved away to Switzerland, goatherding as penance.

"Let's talk," she said.

I saw how tired she was; her pretty pink complexion was like an October evening and she had a cold sore on her upper lip. I nudged her towards the armchair and for a moment I couldn't tell if I was solicitous of her fatigue or trying to make sure my gun was out of her view. But I could tell. I knew. I didn't know what would happen but I planned to walk out of that room. My phone camera was recording.

"Leah doesn't deserve you."

I was surprised at how much I still wanted her to hear that.

"Yeah," she sighed. "She deserves better."

She waved a hand loosely, her diamond rings sparkling right next to the new gold band.

"No, for Christ's sake, that's not it. You are worth two, five of her. You deserve better."

She stared at me blankly and I could imagine what Nat thought of this tactic. Police interrogation techniques probably didn't include advising the perp on her choice of life companion.

"Forget it," she said. She had nothing to say to someone who didn't see Leah's perfection. "Is this about Leah?"

I could say yes right now and find out how fast Michelle's hand was.

"No. Not really. It's about . . . about money. And, other things."

I thought I heard a tiny, mechanical click. I tried to relax and listen beyond our breathing. She rubbed her forehead.

"Do you have a headache?" I asked.

"Yeah, since last week, I think."

"Want an aspirin?"

"No. All right. Thanks."

I hoped that Michelle mistook my hesitation for strategy, or at least caution. I kept hoping, even now, that something would happen to get this train off its tracks. My taste for confrontation had just about disappeared in the last twenty-four hours. I reached into my purse and thought, you *idiot,* now she's going to need water and you'll have to carry your purse with you to the bathroom.

"The aspirin's in my makeup kit. I'll get it." I took the purse with me and when she looked at me hard, I looked back and sighed, a little. "I also gotta change my Tampax, Michelle. I'll be right back."

I walked into the bathroom and didn't bother pulling back the curtain for a peek at Nat. I knew I was bungling, I didn't need to hear it in stereo. Nat glared at me while I got the aspirin, unwrapped one of the motel room glasses and filled it with lukewarm water. I left the light on and walked out.

"Thanks," she said. "What do you want? You want something."

Yes, I do. I want to let you go for murdering an acknowledged POS and I want to ride off into the sunset with that confusing, moody bastard presently hiding in the shower stall.

"Well, there seems to be a pile of evidence that no one else has noticed, indicating—I think that's too mild a word but—indicating that maybe Leah had an accident very recently, hit someone, I'm guessing killed them—in fact, him—out in the Glen Valley area and, probably scared to death, she confided in Harry Markham, and then she found herself blackmailed by that complete waste of human skin."

Michelle didn't blink.

"I don't know anything about that. I do know you seem to have a real bug up your ass about me. About Leah. Homophobia, maybe. Anti-cop sentiment. Can't stand to see a happy couple. All of that, any of that, makes sense."

My idea was get a confession, record it on the phone, and fade away. This did not look at all likely. The idea of me threatening her with a gun seemed even less likely.

"You tell me, you satisfy my curiosity and I tell you something the police don't know, which you do not want them to know and which, for $50,000, I'll make sure no one finds out."

She looked right into my eyes with her weary blues, so worn from watching and waiting they were almost translucent. She looked disbelieving and then disgusted and a little relieved.

"You're shaking me down? You're gonna blackmail me?"

"I'm interested in pooling our information."

I wasn't pleased that the voice of a blackmailer came so easily to me, but there you are.

"What do you know?"

"Come on, Michelle, life's short."

"Why do you care?"

"Because I have been wrong about so much and I am at least right about this. And I don't care. You give me the money, I keep this all to myself. You don't give me the money, the information—including the details of two bank transfers, one from you, one from Leah, the Tesla repairs, which I imagine you have arranged for in some remote garage, hundreds of miles away, and a thorough search of all missing persons and hospitals in Connecticut, and I think you will have a hard time explaining an appropriate relationship with Harry that includes those payments—goes from my lawyer to the police in forty-eight hours. I'm happy Harry's dead and I could use the money."

Michelle and I looked at each other and I rested my hand, casually, on the nightstand.

"Let's walk through it together. Leah was driving," I said. "Horrible, terrifying accident. She fled, understandably. She did not immediately tell you. During a brief encounter with Harry just a few hours later, she blurted it out. Understandably. He offered to help. Like a gentleman. He took her and her car to the garage. Did he take some photos? I bet he did. Then, she came home and then, she told you. And as you were figuring out what to do with your idiot girlfriend, I mean your wife, Harry had a better idea. And he shared that idea—blackmail—with Leah. And she shared it with you. And you played along. And then, he was just too much trouble. Which he was."

"You're wrong," she said.

I got up.

"Michelle."

"Wait," Michelle said, standing up.

"Leah killed him?"

"Yes," yelled Leah, running through the door, shoulder down, a tiny gun spitting out of her hand. She dropped the gun, fumbling it like a juggling act, and caught it. I heard the shot and saw Nat come out of the bathroom. Leah screamed through the room, arms shaking wildly as she tried to fire at me. Michelle whirled and reached for her ankle. I wasn't a good enough shot to get her wrist and I shot her in the arm. She kept on reaching and I shot her again. She fell backwards onto the bed, clutching the spread, blood blackening her clothes and the floor instantly. Her eyes were on the ceiling and she was gasping for air.

"No, no, no, no," said Nat, knocking Leah to the ground and taking her gun. He shoved her into the bathroom, and he went to hold Michelle.

"Do not let that bitch out," he said.

I opened my phone. "Do I call the ambulance?"

Nat pressed towels to Michelle's body and put his jacket over her, tucking it in around her. He grabbed my phone, dialed the ambulance, calmly gave them the address, said it was a wounded police officer, and threw the phone into a corner. He sat back down beside Michelle, stroking her hair, murmuring to her. The bedspread under her turned red and the blood dripped off the ball fringe, onto the flowered carpet. Nat sat beside her.

She never took her eyes off the ceiling. Nat wouldn't let Leah come near. He tossed me his zip ties. Just cuff her to the sink, he said, and I did. She cursed at me and lifted a hand and I pointed my gun right at her. Please, I said. I'm ready.

Nat had saved my life and I had saved his. I had also shot his partner and his friend and I had been right. I sat in the corner of the room, my arms wrapped around my knees, to minimize their shaking, and to keep down the acid surging in my throat. I was afraid to go near him.

We heard the sirens and Nat lifted his head. He got up and turned his face to the wall. I walked towards him when he squared off and slammed his fist into the wall. The whole room shuddered and the drywall crumpled like paper.

Leah was still mewling and cursing. Ambulance lights flashed red and white through the cheesy curtains. Nat beckoned to me. I backed away as the three paramedics came flying through the door to take care of a wounded cop. Nat walked alongside Michelle, her honor guard, as they carried her out.

Someone found Leah in the bathroom.

Nat paused beside me.

"I'm no good to you now. I can't hold you, I can't love you, I can't even thank you. We'll both have to talk to the chief, then you can probably go home. I don't think they'll arrest you. It was righteous. I'll tell them it was righteous."

I stepped into the parking lot and called my Aunt Marjorie, in Westport, to tell her that as she always expected, I needed a lawyer.

I called my father, to say I was okay.

Acknowledgments

I am grateful to my excellent, astute agent Claudia Ballard and to everyone (really, everyone) at Mysterious Press, especially the legendary Otto Penzler and his brilliant editor-in-chief Luisa Smith.

I also appreciate my early and insightful readers Julia Reidhead, Sarah Moon, Richard Mosier, Ellen Lubell and Lt. Kenneth Mainor (Ret.) of the LAPD, all of whom kept me from making more mistakes than I did.

I could not do this—or much—without my gifted, generous assistant (and devoted mystery fan), Jennifer Ferri.